THE ...
HE HAD TO MOVE.
FAST AND ACCURATELY.

Immediately Benton fell on the gun, clutched it and rolled away as rapidly as possible.

Three. Four times he rolled. Instinctively he knew that he must not allow Janssen leeway to maneuver.

He raised the gun in his left hand and, without thinking, fired blindly into Janssen's form.

Benton's arm jerked upward in recoil as a blotch spread rapidly from the middle of Janssen's chest.

"Who gives you orders?" Benton shouted. "Who?"

Blood bubbled from Janssen's mouth and he fell onto his side, a sardonic smile on his lips.

★

CROSS FIRE

RALPH YOUNG

W🌐RLDWIDE®

TORONTO · NEW YORK · LONDON · PARIS
AMSTERDAM · STOCKHOLM · HAMBURG
ATHENS · MILAN · TOKYO · SYDNEY

For Denise Proulx

CROSS FIRE

CROSS FIRE

CHAPTER ONE

Philadelphia

Christmas Day, 1700 hours

PHILADELPHIA HAD ROLLED up its streets and closed shop. The nineteenth-century statue of William Penn atop city hall complacently contemplated the frozen, nearly deserted city. W.C. Fields himself would have been the first to admit his good fortune at not being in Philadelphia.

A Canadian cold front had swept down unexpectedly on the Delaware Valley the day before. The temperature had dropped from an unseasonable sixty degrees Fahrenheit in the afternoon to a near-record low of eleven degrees by midnight. Then on Christmas Day strong winds set in. It had become numbingly cold, and if there was one thing David Marcus could not tolerate it was the cold. He hunched his shoulders as he drove his decaying 1975 Toyota along Lombard Street. Only another mile and he would be home.

Despite the frigid weather it had been a fine afternoon. Five games of chess and he had won three of them. It was usually impossible for him to beat George Tasco at chess, and the fact that he had done so, especially with his knight gambit in the fifth game, put him in a good mood. If only it were not so damn cold.

He turned right on Eighteenth Street.

VICTOR MARONE SMASHED the brandy snifter to the floor.

"Goddamn it, Mama!" he shouted, sliding his chair back

abruptly from the table. "Stop goin' on at me like that! I'm twenty-eight fuckin' years old. I'm not a child!"

"Listen to him! Listen to the language he uses at the Christmas table!" His mother, her hand held melodramatically over her heart, was close to tears.

Victor was on his feet. "If ya expect me to listen to lectures every time I'm here, then I won't bother to come home anymore!"

He went to the back hall, yanked his coat off the hook and headed for the door.

"He's drunk, Luisa, let him go." His father reached across the table, restraining the distraught woman. "Let him sleep it off."

The back door slammed and she broke into tears.

AT RITTENHOUSE SQUARE David looked at his watch. He would be home in five minutes. He was getting hungry. He thought about what he would have for supper.

VICTOR'S OLDSMOBILE careened down Market Street as he cursed loudly. He knew he was driving like a maniac, but he also knew that he would begin to calm down in a few minutes.

"Goddamn them!" he muttered, as he saw the light turn to amber at Eighteenth and Market.

He stepped on the gas. There was virtually no traffic on the road.

AS HE PROCEEDED across Market Street, David's mind was dwelling on that fifth chess game. He didn't see the Oldsmobile as it hurtled across the intersection.

The entire driver's side of the Toyota collapsed under the impact in a sickening shriek of metal and glass. The Oldsmobile pushed it for more than one hundred feet across the intersection and halfway toward Seventeenth Street. Victor saw the driver of the other car fly through the windshield and roll brokenly along the pavement as he suddenly, and soberly, jammed on the brakes.

The two cars stopped, locked together in deadly embrace, and Victor jumped out quickly. David Marcus's left arm was stretched out at an absurd angle, and his chest appeared strangely concave as Victor turned him over. As he looked at the faint, ineffable smile that was still on the other driver's face, Victor thought surely the man would open his eyes and laugh. It was an accident, after all. But with a sinking feeling in the pit of his stomach he knew immediately that the man was dead.

And he, Victor Marone, had killed him.

Midnight

THE PHONE WAS RINGING.

Brigadier General Thomas O. Forman awoke instantly, turned on the bedside lamp and picked up the receiver before it could ring a second time.

"Yes?" he said, looking at the digital clock on the night table and rubbing his hand across his face.

"Packer here. Sorry to wake you, General, but it's urgent."

"Go ahead."

"It's that scientist, Marcus, sir. He was killed in a car crash this evening."

"Was it an accident?"

"As far as our people can determine, sir. Some drunk ran a light and hit him. Dead instantly."

Forman thought for a moment. "Look, we better move up the meeting from Tuesday to tomorrow. Get hold of Thalberg and Matecki right away and have them at my suite at 1600 tomorrow."

"Right, sir. Good night."

Damn, he thought, as he replaced the receiver. Damned nuisance. This better be what it appears to be. But what if it isn't? What if Marcus inadvertently let something slip to the wrong people? How tight has our security been? What if it wasn't an accident?

26 December, 0930 hours

THERE WERE TWO squash courts on the roof of the Society Hill Club.

Christopher Benton was warming up on court 1. He had been up late partying, celebrating Christmas with some friends, and felt sluggish while taking swings with his racket. At age thirty-eight he had realized that the duties of an untenured assistant professor of English literature didn't give him enough opportunity for physical exercise, so he had taken up squash to improve his circulation and keep his muscles from atrophying.

He was tall and still had the mustache he had grown in 1968. In fact, much still remained in him from the sixties. Though the Society Hill Club was a bastion of yuppiedom, his economic position as well as his ideas tied him more closely to the sixties than to the eighties. He was, in some respects, an anachronism, and he knew it.

He looked at the clock on the wall outside the court. It was unlike David to be late. He went downstairs to the reception desk to see if David had left a message.

Cindy looked up from behind the *Philadelphia Inquirer* and a cup of coffee. She gave him an odd look. "Didn't you hear?" She hesitated.

He suddenly felt uneasy. "What? Hear what?" Foreboding.

She looked away. "He's dead.... It's in the paper."

"*What!* That can't be! I just spoke with him yesterday."

Wordlessly she handed him the newspaper. There was a brief notice on page three relating the drunk-driving accident.

Numbed, he sat down. He looked out over the balcony at the pool, up at the Plexiglas roof enclosing the pool and back to the newspaper.

Oh God! he thought. He put his left hand to his forehead and rubbed it, then gave the paper back to her and started for the locker room.

"I'm sorry, Chris," she said awkwardly. "Was he a good friend?"

He paused and turned to her. "I...don't know, really. A friend? Yes, I suppose so, but..." Words failed him.

He turned again, went into the locker room and changed into his street clothes.

1100 hours
"AERONAUTICAL ELECTRONIC SYSTEMS."

"Hello. This is Christopher Benton. I'm calling in regard to David Marcus."

"You *have* heard, haven't you?"

"Yes. It was a terrible blow. I was a friend of his."

"Oh, how awful. I'm sorry."

"I just wanted to ask if Colonel Thalberg is there. I know David had recently begun working with him."

"Yes. Please hold."

"Thank you."

Thirty seconds passed while the receptionist made the connection.

"Hello. Thalberg here."

"Hello. This is Christopher Benton. I was a friend of David's and I just heard about the accident."

"Yes, we're all very upset."

"Well, I'm sorry to disturb you, sir, but I have an unusual request."

"Oh?"

"I was quite unnerved when I heard of the accident, because he seemed to have had a premonition of his death. You see, he often talked with me about his work, and, well, these past two weeks he seemed to have changed. He had become very agitated, very distraught...."

"What did he tell you?"

"About a missile project he was now working on."

"*Missile* project? But you do know he is...was in the conductive coatings department?"

"Well, he never mentioned that, only that he worked on guidance systems. I was amazed at the sophistication of the terrain-matching system.... But what I'm really calling about is that only last week he told me that if anything ever happened to him he wanted me to fetch a briefcase from his office and send it to his sister in Florida."

"A briefcase!" Thalberg coughed and muttered under his breath.

"Excuse me?"

"Nothing...nothing... A briefcase, you say? Well, I'll look into it and have it done. What's his sister's address?"

"Well, sir, he was very explicit that *I* should do this. And I promised him I would, though I thought it was slightly absurd.... I laughed at him, in fact. But now...since his death...well, I'd like to make an appointment to stop by and pick it up."

"Don't worry, we'll see to it. I'm sure the company must have his sister's address."

"Please, sir, I don't want to be too insistent, but I *did* promise that I would do it."

"Okay, okay. Let me check into it and I'll get back to you. Give me your address and phone number."

Benton did so and said goodbye.

1545 hours

EXCEPT FOR THE SQUARE formed by city hall, Broad Street

cut a straight swath through Philadelphia; from Chelten-
ham Road in the north to Veterans Stadium in the south.
Just south of city hall the trees lining the street near the
Union League, the Fidelity Bank and the Academy of Music were lit with small white Christmas tree lights. The lights
graced the trees year-round, but for the holidays long
strands of larger red bulbs were strung back and forth across
the street between the office buildings.

A limousine proceeded slowly under the holiday decora-
tions and pulled up in front of the Hershey Hotel.

The uniformed doorman opened the door for Colonel
William Matecki. The colonel ignored the man as he strode
rapidly along the red carpet under the portico and up the
steps to the hotel lobby. Without hesitation he took the elevator to the twelfth floor.

Captain Edward Packer dropped the *U.S. News and
World Report* he had been reading on the table when he
heard the knock on the door. He walked past Colonel
Thalberg and General Forman, who were talking by the
drinks cart, and opened the door.

Matecki entered, took off his coat and sat in an armchair. He had been a career officer for twenty-nine of his
fifty-two years. He had not allowed himself to get soft or
complacent, as had so many of his fellow officers in the
NATO command. He neither smoked nor drank. He was
proud that he had no indulgences other than keeping himself fit. He was physically strong and trim and would probably remain so even after his retirement, which, he often
said, would be never.

Colonel Thalberg, who had just poured himself a Jack
Daniel's, knew better than to offer Matecki a drink. He
knew that at heart Matecki despised him. Despised his af-
fection for alcohol, his sense of humor, his disinterest in
physical prowess. Though Matecki was three years his sen-

ior, Thalberg looked fifteen years older than he. His barrel chest blended straight into his large stomach, and his gray hair was long on one side so it could be combed over the expanse of his bald pate. But his eyes were soft and smiling, and it was probably this more than anything else that Matecki loathed. It was Thalberg's fatal weakness, as far as Colonel Matecki was concerned.

Forman motioned Packer and Thalberg to the couch. He chose to sit in the armchair opposite Matecki. Despite the disparity between the other three, Forman knew they were professionals. Professionals who could be counted on.

"I'm sorry," he said, looking at Matecki, "that we had to bring you up from Virginia on such short notice, but as Captain Packer has no doubt told you the reason for this, I'm sure you realize the necessity."

Matecki made no reply. He looked over at Captain Packer. Packer, though he was twenty years his junior, had what it took. He was strong and eager and ambitious and devoted. He could be relied upon.

"First of all," Forman went on, "are we sure this unfortunate accident is what it appears to be? After all, it is damn suspicious that two weeks after Marcus is brought into our project he's killed. Is there any way that anyone else at AES could have found out about this?"

"No, sir," Packer responded, "the driver of the other vehicle had no connection with Marcus. Believe me, we've had the police check on this thoroughly. He had had some family squabble at home and had left drunk and angry. He was a menace on the roads. Poor Marcus was probably the only other driver out at the time."

Thalberg finished his whiskey and went over to the bar to pour another. "Someone called today. A Christopher Benton. He was upset. It seems Marcus had told him of our project. He even knew to ask for me by name."

Matecki raised his eyebrows. "Goddamn it! I need not remind you that I *did* say the less Marcus knew the better!"

"I know, I know. We should have listened to you. I've got a bad feeling that our security has been breached. No telling how much Marcus has revealed. But what's even more disturbing—" he paused, looking at their expressions, knowing full well the effect his words were having, feeling guilty about the breach in security "—is that Marcus left a briefcase in his office and insisted that this Benton character should send it to Marcus's sister in Florida should 'something happen to him.'"

"Good God!" General Forman leaned forward in his chair. He began rubbing his forehead with his left hand, a dark cloud taking shape on his face. "You, of course, located the briefcase and opened it," he stated icily.

"Yes. Yes. It had a combination lock, but it presented no obstacle."

The general waited for him to continue.

Colonel Matecki rose and walked over to the window trying to contain his anger.

"You guessed it," Colonel Thalberg went on. "The case contained transcriptions of every conversation he and I had. All the details of our plan that Marcus knew. Along with instructions for his sister to make sure that the files be made public in the event of his death."

The general's eyes narrowed. Colonel Thalberg shifted uncomfortably in his seat and took a gulp from his glass. Matecki glared at him from across the room.

"I'm supposed to contact Benton," Thalberg continued, "and set up a time for him to pick up the briefcase. Of course, that's out of the question."

"Of course," the general said. "Okay, it's quite clear what must be done. It's not just a question of stalling Benton, it's a question of finding out what, exactly, he knows. He knows something, that's certain, but maybe it's insignificant. But if he insists on claiming the briefcase, or if we discover that he knows anything incriminating, then he must be terminated. The fact that he knows Marcus was working on the missile's guidance system is already dangerous information. By the way, Sam—" his voice was calmer, almost soothing "—had Marcus finished going over the guidance system with you?"

"Just about. There were two minor details that hadn't yet been adequately explained, but I believe I can work them out based on what I already know."

"You *believe*?"

"Well, yes. Yes, I'm sure I can do it. I might need a few days."

"Then you'd better devote your full energy to that. After Packer called me last night with the news I already decided we have to hasten the preparations and return to NATO headquarters as soon as possible. We've come so far, and now the quicker we move into operation the less chance there'll be for something to go wrong. The Germans are ready and the test is to be scheduled for some time within the next two or three weeks. I spoke with Oster and he's nervous—thinks it's too soon. I don't want to give him too much time to think about security. And now . . . now that some other party has become involved . . . well . . ."

Matecki nodded, his lips pursed thoughtfully. Thalberg looked slightly anxious.

"Packer."

"Sir!"

"Get Janssen to Philadelphia on the next shuttle. We're going to need his services."

Thalberg turned to Forman. "Surely we're overreacting."

"No. We can't afford to take any chances. I don't like this at all. What do you know about this Benton?"

"Just his address. The receptionist said she recognized his voice. He used to call once or twice a week, Marcus's squash partner."

"All right," General Forman said, "Janssen will locate him and find out precisely what he knows. Perhaps he cultivated Marcus's friendship in order to infiltrate our operation. But more likely he is simply what he appears to be. In any case, he may already know too much. I don't think we have much choice in our course of action."

"Extreme prejudice," Colonel Matecki said emotionlessly and looked over at Colonel Thalberg.

General Forman glanced from Thalberg to Matecki to Packer, then he turned to the window and fell silent.

"Captain," Forman said an hour later after the two colonels had left, "give Janssen instructions to interview Benton as soon as he arrives in Philadelphia. Janssen is to find out what he knows. And then, of course, he must eliminate him."

"Yes, sir." Packer saluted and left the room.

The general poured himself a drink and looked out the window. It was already dark, but then the day had been cold and cloudy. He could see his reflection in the window looking back at him, the lights from Broad Street glistening moistly up to the twelfth floor. Over the years it had become progressively easier for him to look at himself after giving such orders. Once, ages ago, it had bothered him, even sickened him, but with the passage of time he had become inured to the consequences of wielding power.

He thought about Janssen. The man worried him. Janssen had been their top enforcer for many years, but he was losing it. He was no longer as sharp as he used to be, and Forman had recently been informed there were indications that he had begun using drugs again.

Hollywood, he thought, and sighed. For years they have made films that portrayed professionally trained CIA agents as invincible cold-blooded automatons. Unstoppable assassins who never made mistakes, who never gave up. He had known the best and none of them were like that. But reality and Hollywood never did mesh too well. He thought of Hunt and Liddy and the bungled Watergate break-in. He thought of the scores of elementary mistakes that had cost him some of his best agents. And he thought, again, of the troubled, all-too-human Janssen, who was, after all, one of "the best." It was probably time to retire him, but first Benton had to be dealt with, and Janssen was the only one he trusted enough to include in this project.

I'll talk to Janssen soon, he thought and looked at the light gray-blue of his eyes reflected in the window.

2125 hours

THE DELTA SHUTTLE from Washington touched down on the salted runway at Philadelphia International Airport.

A man with ash-blond hair and a thin, almost invisible mustache stepped out of the airplane. He carried one piece of luggage—a soft carry-on bag. He was wearing a Burberry trench coat and a pure cashmere scarf over his suit. Just another businessman returning from Washington.

Packer nodded to the man, who gave him a noncommittal glance in return. Without shaking hands or speaking, they walked quickly out of the terminal building and into the waiting car.

No words were exchanged during the drive into the city. Wulf Janssen looked out the window at the Philadelphia Navy Yard as they crossed the Girard Point Bridge. He could see several destroyers and an aircraft carrier in dry dock, then they were over the Schuylkill River and passing Veterans Stadium.

When the car stopped in front of the Holiday Inn on Fourth Street, Packer handed him an envelope and a small attaché case. Janssen put the envelope in his inside jacket pocket, took his bag and the attaché case, and stepped out of the car.

He checked in, entered room 463, examined it thoroughly for several minutes, then closed and locked the door. He opened the envelope. It contained a slip of paper with a single name and address neatly typed on it: Christopher Benton, 317 Pine Street.

He opened the attaché case Packer had given him, took out the Colt .45, attached the silencer and checked the action of the gun. After loading the Colt and removing the silencer, he placed the silencer in his pocket and slid the gun into his shoulder holster. Then he shut the case.

From another pocket of his jacket Janssen removed a small plastic bag. Sitting on the edge of the bed next to the night table, he carefully opened the bag and poured a portion of its contents into a mound on the glass-covered surface. He examined the white powder closely before adding more.

Quickly and expertly he used a credit card to sift and smooth the powder into two lines. Holding his left nostril closed with one finger, he inserted a thin silver tube in the right, and inhaled one of the lines. Then he reversed the process.

Closing his eyes he lay back on the bed, his feet still on the floor. Ahhhh, he thought, the real thing.

A few moments later, fortified, he straightened, slipped into his jacket and left the room.

2300 hours

GRAHAM MARSH WAS British. He and Christopher were sitting at the bar in the Copabanana. Loud music blared from speakers in each of the four corners of the room. A red neon sculpture of a Concorde jet hung suspended from the ceiling and was reflected many times in the mirrors behind the bar and on the side wall. Outside people could be seen walking briskly along South Street. Many had just come from the Theater of the Living Arts next door, others were heading for various bars and night spots along the street. South Street was always busy in the evenings. Nightclubs, bars, restaurants, fast-food joints, even a secondhand bookstore that was always packed with customers right up to 2:00 a.m., when the proprietor reluctantly closed for the night.

A group of teenage New-Wave types in pastel Mohican haircuts were lining up for the late movie at TLA, *Rock and Roll High School*. Graham vaguely wondered if their heads felt the chill. He turned back to Christopher.

"You know, Chris, in spite of all his gregarious social activities, I think David was really a lonely, miserable chap. I agree with you, it *is* a shock when someone you know dies unexpectedly, but I kept thinking all day, as harsh and callous as it may sound, it's almost as if he was put out of his misery."

Benton set his Dos Equis back on the counter. "Hmmm. He did seem such an unhappy character. I know he wasn't well liked at the club. There was an abrasiveness about him. Hell, when I first met him and we started playing squash I couldn't stand him. He was so aggressive. And the way he talked about women all the time! He always embarrassed me with his stupid sexist comments. But in spite of his personality flaws, I was beginning to appreciate him. He was honest, at least. It didn't matter to him what people thought of him and he never pretended to be anything other than what he was."

He took another hit on his beer. "Yes, he was truly unhappy. At least that's over with now, too."

"I was talking with George this morning. It seems the two of them played chess yesterday afternoon and David had beaten him. So he probably died happy. He always gloated so when he defeated George, seldom as it was. I can see it now—he was probably smugly reviewing the moves in the game with such intensity that he paid no attention to the traffic. If he'd been more alert the accident might never have occurred."

"That keeps going over and over in my mind. The indifference of Fate. Just think, if he had arrived at that intersection five seconds earlier or five seconds later, he'd still be alive and would never even know how close he came to dying. Probably wouldn't even have been a close call. It makes you think how tenuously all of us live. So often I've thought about the things I want to do and I keep postponing them and go on living the same way day after day. And then this realization today that at any moment Fate can step in and there's no time left at all and I've wasted all those moments in my life. I don't want that to happen."

Graham ordered another margarita. "When I last talked to him on Saturday I almost invited him to come over for a drink that night.... Sally and I had a few friends stop by Christmas Eve. But then I realized he wouldn't fit in with the others. Bloody hell. If only I had, he would have got up later the following day, and his whole schedule for the day would have changed. Then those five seconds... He wouldn't have been at that intersection at precisely that moment...."

They finished their drinks.

"I think I might head over to the Book Trader before going home," Benton remarked. "I want to pick up a map for the trip I'm taking at semester break. I've already written to British Travel and got the schedules for the RSC and the National Theatre."

"I envy you, Chris. It's going to be at least another year before Sally finishes her master's and we can move back to London. I really miss it."

They paid the bartender and walked the block to the bookstore. At the corner Christopher took leave of Graham and entered the shop. Despite the hour it was predictably full of browsers. Books were strewn all over the front desk, on the floor between the shelves and on the oak benches that the management had installed for the customers. Christopher couldn't remember ever sitting on either of the benches. But clutter did add to the atmosphere of searching for lost treasure. The place was a browser's paradise. Everywhere one turned there were books.

After half an hour of looking through the travel and drama sections, Christopher did not find what he wanted. But there were a few other books that caught his eye.

As he paid for the books he also paid homage to the store cat, Firbank, who seemed to be perpetually perched on top of the cash register. The cat, of course, ignored his attentions.

JANSSEN WALKED through the eighteenth-century marketplace at Head House Square. A couple hurried past him on their way to the bar at Dickens Inn.

It was the fourth time in an hour that he had drifted from the churchyard across from 317 Pine Street to New Market, through the square and back again. Still no light showing in the apartment windows. But it was late and he knew the mark would have to be returning soon. Unless, damn it, he was staying with a woman.

His plan was straightforward. Usually he found the most obvious approach was the most effective. He would simply enter the apartment. The silencer would be effective in not arousing unwanted notice. Of course he would first have to question the mark before dispatching him, but it was going to be easy.

He yawned and looked up again at the darkened window.

BENTON WALKED rapidly down Fourth Street and turned right on Pine. Years of living in the city had made him cautious and street-wise, and so he immediately noticed the shadowy figure enter St. Peter's churchyard. It almost seemed that the man had been staring at the building in which Benton lived. But he was not sure.

He hunched his shoulders and hastened his pace as he proceeded along the brick sidewalk toward his apartment. The facades of the predominantly Federal houses, many with Christmas wreaths on their doors and festive lights in the windows, gave a warmth to the street. The spire of St. Peter's Church was illuminated and cast a glow on the tombstones and trees around the structure. He crossed the street with one eye warily on the archway in the brick wall. But there was no longer any sign of the figure he had seen.

He unlocked the front door and closed it behind him, heaving a sigh of relief as he walked up the one flight. Before switching on the light, however, he carefully peered around the edge of the curtain and looked across the street. There was nothing to be seen in the graveyard; the only movement was the swaying of the tree branches in the December wind.

He dropped the books on the table and turned on the light.

FUCK! THOUGHT JANSSEN, stepping back through the gate. He spun left and leaned against the wall inside the churchyard. He was certain that the man walking along the street was Benton, and he was equally certain that he had been spotted. It was an amateurish mistake, his trying to keep warm by walking back and forth. He knew he should have remained motionless inside the churchyard until Benton returned. He prided himself that he seldom made mistakes. How else could he have survived all these years? And he realized it was his pride that had allowed him to be careless.

Still, Benton was not expecting anything, perhaps he had not been alarmed.

The light went on in Benton's apartment.

Hastily Janssen opened the packet of cocaine and dropped a small amount on the back of his hand. Without bothering to sort it into two lines, he took two awkward snorts. Possibly the drug slowed him down, he thought, and he really shouldn't do it while on the job, but, Christ, he reasoned, he was a professional and could outmatch any opponent. Besides, it enhanced his feeling of being in control; he felt surer of his powers.

He waited three minutes, then stepped through the gate and quickly crossed the street directly to the door of the building.

Taking four keys from his pocket, he examined the lock. He chose a key, inserted it in the lock and opened the door.

After stepping inside and softly closing the door behind him, he paused for a moment. He slipped out the .45, screwed on the silencer and released the safety. Then, keeping as close as possible to the wall, he started up the steps.

Damn these old houses, he thought, as each step creaked under his weight in spite of his care to stay alongside the wall. The muffled sound of a television in the ground floor apartment, he hoped, would mask the unavoidable groaning of the stairs.

Three minutes later he was standing in front of Benton's apartment. Holding the barrel of the gun an inch from the door he listened carefully. Then slowly he raised his left hand and tapped lightly on the door.

As his knuckles touched the wood, he heard the door to the ground floor apartment open.

A voice shouted, "Hey!"

As CHRISTOPHER HELD the kettle under the faucet he thought he detected the sound of footsteps on the stairs, but when he turned off the tap nothing was to be heard except for his landlord's television downstairs.

He grimaced. I hope old man Cohen turns it off soon and goes to bed.

There was a soft rapping on the door.

He started toward the door, the kettle still in his hand.

Odd, he thought, only Mr. Cohen would knock, but he seldom came upstairs, and then, never at night. Anyone else would have to ring the doorbell outside and wait to be buzzed in. Then he remembered the shadowy figure he had seen across the street, and the sounds on the stairs, and an uncomfortable prickly sensation on the back of his neck made him stop.

There was the sound of a voice downstairs.

"Yes?" he asked, and started to turn to his right to set the kettle on the table.

"I'm a friend of David Marcus," a scarcely audible whisper said.

Suddenly, the other voice, Mr. Cohen's voice, shouted shrilly up the stairs. "Who are you?"

Pfft!

Pfft!

Benton lunged farther to the right and under the oak table as the wood of the door erupted and splintered.

Pfft!

Pfft!

Four times. The sound. The splintering.

"What the hell's going on?" Mr. Cohen's voice shouted again. He took one step up the stairs.

My God! Benton's mind was racing. He was lying under the table, beginning to tremble uncontrollably. My God!

Footsteps running down the stairs.

"Hey!"

Pfft!

The outside door opened with a crash and the footsteps echoed up the street.

He lay deathly still, trying to control the trembling in his limbs. His chest felt wet. Then he realized water was spilling from the kettle he still clutched in his right hand.

Slowly he forced himself to set it upright on the floor, let go of the handle and crawled sideways out from under the table.

Four holes were spaced six inches apart in the form of a diamond in the center of the door. Chest high.

He put his ear to the door and listened, but all he could hear was the sound of his heart beating and the rasping of his heavy breathing.

In a daze he walked to the telephone, lifted the receiver and dialed 911.

"Police Emergency, Sixth District."

"Hello—" His voice broke. "Hello, please send someone to 317 Pine Street. There's been a shooting."

"Your name?"

"Benton. Christopher Benton. Please hurry. He may come back."

"We'll have a car there right away. Don't do anything."

The line went dead.

His intestines were churning. A rancid taste filled his mouth. Oh God, oh God.

He went to the door and turned the bolt. Very slowly he turned the knob and opened the door. A few splinters fell from around the edges of the bullet holes, making him jump. He peered out.

Not a sound.

He stepped into the hall and leaned over the banister. The outside door was open. A cold draft blew up the stairs. In the distance he could hear police sirens.

Lying half in and half out of the ground floor apartment was Mr. Cohen. One arm thrown over his head. His toothless mouth open. A mass of blood covering his chest.

Cramps racked Benton's body as he turned and ran back into his apartment to the bathroom. He barely had time to pull his pants down.

"YOU WHAT!" Packer exploded into the telephone.

"You heard me."

"Look, Janssen, we expect you to do your job, but killing a bystander was not part of it. It's going to raise too many awkward questions. Besides, you were supposed to interrogate Benton."

"I know, I know, but that sharp-eared old codger butted in and I had to make a spot decision. It was safest to shoot them both."

"Are you sure you got the primary?"

"Sure, I'm sure. There was no way he could have avoided those perfectly spaced shots. I know what I'm doing."

"Well, we'll verify soon enough. If you blew it . . ."

There was no reason to finish the sentence, Packer thought as he hung up and dialed the Hershey Hotel.

AS CHRISTOPHER SAT, leaning forward on the couch, he could see the flashing lights from the police cars in the street bouncing off the walls of his living room. He stared at the strobe effect, concentrating all of his energy on the flashing, the light, the shadows, the redness, the blueness. Cohen's body was being lifted out of the building into the ambulance while several policemen were examining the hallway and a police photographer took photographs. Only four or five curious people braved the cold outside, discussing what had happened.

A plainclothes detective was questioning Benton and jotting notes on a pad.

"And so, as far as you know, you can think of no reason why anyone would want to take a shot at you?"

Benton shook his head. His stomach was still rebelling. His legs felt weak. But the diarrhea had passed.

A second detective took the stairs two at a time and entered the room. "We've checked on this David Marcus. He was a research scientist at the Aeronautical Electronic Systems plant in Haddonfield. They're a subsidiary of Kline and Braun in Merced, California. It seems Marcus was the man killed in that drunk-driving accident yesterday on Market Street."

The first detective addressed Benton again. "You said this David Marcus was a friend of yours and that the perpetrator said that he was a friend of Marcus's?"

Benton nodded. "I don't understand it. Unless some nut thought I had something to do with it. But it's so absurd." His voice sounded alien to him. "Could there be any question," he continued, "that David's death wasn't accidental? Perhaps you should check into that."

The detective looked at him for a moment. "As far as we know, Marcus's death was an accident. But there does seem to be some kind of connection, even if we can't see it."

He rose. "Look," he said, stopping by the door, "whoever took these shots at you—" he fingered the bullet holes "—was a professional. If he knows he missed, then he might be back. But maybe it's another of these mistaken identity cases like the one over in Jersey last year. Just in case, we'll keep an eye on the house tonight. Maybe tomorrow you ought to see if you can stay with a friend for a few days. At least until we have some idea what's happening. Okay?"

"Yes. Thank you. I was going to ask you to leave an officer here. I appreciate it."

"Christ, we can't spare an officer. But we'll have a squad car patrol the street every few minutes. Don't worry."

The two detectives left, after telling him to keep them informed of his whereabouts.

Kline and Braun, Benton thought as he locked the door behind them. The name was familiar, but he couldn't place it. His entire body ached from tension. He took a bottle of Stolichnaya out of the freezer and half filled a glass, then took a sip as he went into the bedroom. He sat on the bed, leaning back against the pillows, sipped again and stared at the wall, feeling the syrupy fire slide down his throat.

27 December, 0600 hours

"GODDAMN IT, JANSSEN! I cannot tolerate your fucking this up!"

It was Forman on the line. Janssen was shocked. It was never Forman. Brigadier General Thomas Forman never dealt directly with him. This was serious.

"Get over there right away and finish the job. But for God's sake, be careful. The cops will be staked out. Get him out of Philadelphia and find out what he knows before you dispatch him. Make it look like he's going on a trip or something and do *not* let the body be found. Anything, as long as no one suspects foul play. We need two weeks. After that it no longer matters." He slammed the phone down before Janssen could reply.

0730 hours

CHRISTOPHER WAS LYING BACK in the tub. He hadn't slept all night and his mind was in a state of chaos, trying to piece everything together. Trying to decide what to do. Overnight his life had changed.

It all hinges on Marcus, he thought. David Marcus, the loner, who never seemed to be interested in anything except squash and chess. No personal involvements. But he had been involved in something. Perhaps it was no accident, after all. Perhaps someone had him killed. And whoever did so is now after me. They think Marcus told me something. But what? What the hell was David involved in? Was it connected with his job and the fact that he had begun working on some missile contract? It suddenly seemed to him that he really did not know very much about David after all.

He pulled the plug and stepped out of the tub. Whoever fired those shots, he reasoned, will probably try again, so I'd better do as the cops suggested and go where I can't be found until they catch him. But what if they don't find him? God, I can't live like a fugitive. Perhaps the answer lies with Kline and Braun. But surely the cops will investigate that.

An idea began to form. Alan Ruddick, a friend, a stock lawyer in New York, knew everything, it seemed, about American corporations. And going to New York would serve the purpose of getting safely away for a few days.

Christopher put on his terry-cloth robe and went to the telephone. Several seconds later he heard Alan's familiar voice on the line.

"Alan, hi, this is Chris. I wanted to catch you before you went to the office. I'm coming up to New York this afternoon. Will you be free this evening? I'd like to see you."

"Yes. Great! I keep telling you to come up any time. I'll make dinner reservations. Meet me at the Park Avenue office at four-thirty."

"Fine. See you then."

Benton packed a flight bag with a change of clothes. He reflected for a moment, then added his passport, checkbook and credit cards.

As he walked along Pine Street to Fifth he saw the blue patrol car parked around the corner. The police officer behind the wheel was drinking coffee from a Styrofoam cup and reading the *Philadelphia Daily News*. Neither of them noticed the man in the Burberry who was walking along the opposite side of the street less than a hundred yards behind

Benton. He followed Benton into the Society Hill Deli on Fifth Street and sat at the corner table nearest the window while Benton ordered breakfast at a booth in the back.

There was a brief, ambiguous article on page five of the metropolitan section of the *Inquirer* about an attempted robbery and the shooting of Benton's landlord. Nothing was mentioned about Benton himself.

Christopher took a sip of hot coffee and looked around. The aroma of bacon and eggs pervaded the crowded deli. Several tables were occupied by lone individuals grabbing a coffee on their way to work. As he looked around he wondered vaguely if he was being followed, either by the police, who would be protecting him, or by the people who had tried to kill him. No one seemed to be paying any attention to him.

When he had finished he left and headed for the subway stop at Fifth and Market. The crowded ride to Thirtieth Street Station took only seven minutes.

He was in luck. The train to New York was already waiting on the platform and would leave within ten minutes.

After purchasing a ticket and boarding, he found a window seat in a non-smoking car and took out the Penguin edition of *Tom Jones*. A few minutes later, as the train was pulling out of the station, a man in a trench coat carrying a slim attaché case walked briskly down the aisle past Benton, and entered the car in front. He looked vaguely familiar, but Benton couldn't identify the face. He looked out the window at the Schuylkill River and the Art Museum, as the train accelerated.

He began reading.

CHAPTER TWO

New York

1230 hours

"NEWARK! NEWARK!" The conductor walked down the aisle shouting gutturally. "Newark! Next stop Penn Station."

Benton awoke with a start. He had dozed off. He sighed, stretched and picked up the book, which had slipped off his lap onto the floor. He felt tired and stiff.

The train went under the Hudson, then finally came to a halt. Benton waited a few minutes until most of the passengers had hurried off, then drifted out and up into the waiting room.

There was plenty of time before he had to meet Alan. He thought he might as well walk to Fifth Avenue and look at the shops. It was strange to be in New York and not feel compelled to rush. He decided to get a sandwich, do a little shopping, then go to Park Avenue just before four-thirty.

He left the station and started slowly up Thirty-fourth Street.

Janssen had no difficulty keeping him in sight. He followed several yards behind, always keeping scores of people between himself and Benton. Occasionally, as Benton stopped to look in a shop window, he continued on past him, walking slowly so that Benton would eventually overtake him again. It was obvious that Benton didn't suspect anyone was following him, and this made Janssen's task an easy one. As he crossed the street and walked parallel to Benton he began thinking how he could get him alone.

If only he didn't have to worry about finding out if Benton was working for anyone and what he knew, before killing him, as well as having to find a way to dispose of the body! It would be so easy, he thought, to walk up behind him, shoot him in the back of the neck KGB-style and disappear instantly into the crowds. It happened all the time in New York. But Forman was insistent that now that the police knew of the first attempt on Benton's life they must not hear of another. Too coincidental. Too many questions. Too much curiosity. Janssen understood this very well. Benton must disappear. For good.

CHRISTOPHER SPENT the afternoon going through bookshops on Fifth Avenue and browsing at Dunhill's. He bought several blends of tobacco and, finally realizing it was almost time to meet Alan, he left and walked the few blocks to Fifty-fifth and Park Avenue. The traffic was moving at a crawl. Several panel trucks were double-parked in front of the building, forcing streams of cars to snake around them.

He had to wait for a few minutes in the outer office, a gray room with glass and tubular metal furniture. Alan came through the double glass sliding doors, smiling.

Christopher had often thought that Alan should have been a jockey. He was several inches shorter than Christopher and much smaller boned. Though Christopher was only six feet tall and 180 pounds, he always felt like a giant when he stood next to Alan. Alan was the archetypal yuppie. Very prep school, very successful, very good looking. All the women in his office considered him the most eligible bachelor in the firm. A view that was also, unfortunately as far as Alan was concerned, shared by many of his neighbors on Christopher Street.

"It's good to see you, Chris." They shook hands. "Let's go have a drink in the bar downstairs. Then we'll take a cab down to the Village. I've got reservations for us at six o'clock at Starthrower."

"Fine."

Several executives were sitting in the semicircular booths along the walls of the bar, participating in happy hour. A jazz pianist was playing an Art Tatum piece in the background. Two young women sat at the bar, one of them talking animatedly with exaggerated Barbra Streisand gestures, the other staring glumly at her drink—a pastel phosphorescent frothy thing. Christopher speculated that when they left they would change from their high heels into the Nike running shoes that were undoubtedly stowed in their shoulder bags.

As Benton and Ruddick talked, the bar slowly filled with more and more businessmen. Someone asked the piano player if he knew any George Winston pieces. The man smiled and shook his head.

After telling Ruddick of his planned trip to London between semesters, Benton filled him in on the critical events of the past two days.

"It's all so crazy," he summed up. "I can't believe that anyone would want to kill me or that it had anything to do with David's tragic death, but for it to be a case of mistaken identity seems equally ludicrous."

Ruddick sipped his bourbon.

"Anyway, could I stay with you for a few days until this all blows over? I brought my passport. I'm thinking of moving up my London trip and going from here."

"Of course. As long as you like. It won't cramp my style at all." Ruddick laughed. "In fact I have no style to speak of lately. Just work all the time. Several urgent corporate contracts have all landed on my desk at the same time, and I've got to devote all my energy to them."

"One thing I wanted to ask you is if you've ever heard of a company called Kline and Braun? They seem to be the parent company of Aeronautical Electronic Systems."

"Yes, of course. Why do you ask?"

"Marcus had just begun working on some sort of missile guidance system for AES and when I spoke to someone there he seemed, in hindsight, somehow wary. I thought maybe it tied in."

"Well, I can't imagine them killing one of their employees . . . unless—" he smiled and lowered his voice "—unless they thought he was a spy!"

"A spy!"

Ruddick laughed. "I'm only kidding. No, they're too clean, too reputable. They have the main government contract for developing the BGM-109 Tomahawk Cruise Missile."

"So it was the cruise missile?"

"Yeah, you know, the ones they've been deploying to NATO bases in Europe. Where have you been? Don't you read *Time* magazine?" He smiled. "I know you always crusaded against *Time*. Anyway a lot of crazy radicals are opposing the missiles, but the governments of the various countries want them."

"Crazy radicals? You're still a goddamn conservative, aren't you, Alan?"

"And you're still an idealist!" Alan laughed again.

Christopher stared at his drink for several seconds. "Not as many ideals as previously," he murmured. "Well, of course I know something about cruise missiles, but . . . anyway, maybe Marcus was working on some especially sensitive aspect of the project and had decided to sell some information to a Communist nation. Or maybe he was approached but refused to cooperate." Even as he spoke Benton realized the absurdity of the thought. Marcus was in no way a spy or a subversive. He was too damn ordinary. Benton was sure of it.

Alan lit a cigarette. "No. It couldn't be anything like that. The Russians have weapons that are at least as effective, if not better. No. If anyone was after any Kline and Braun research secrets it would be a competing company. That happens more often than you can possibly imagine in the megacompany world. You'd never guess how many 'spies' one company has in the employ of its chief competitors. Automotive. Construction. Electronic. Christ, probably even McDonald's has spies working at Burger King and Wendy's, lacing their beef with soybeans or photographing their secret recipes."

Benton smiled. He thought for a while as he filled his pipe, tamped down the tobacco, lit it, tamped it down again and relit it. Dunhill No. 10. A good tobacco, he mused, but not quite as satisfying as Balkan Sobranie. But Dunhill would never stoop to infiltrating the House of Sobranie, would they? It wouldn't be sporting. And the British were, if nothing else, always sporting.

"I've got an idea." He leaned forward, and Ruddick set down his drink. "Let's assume that Marcus was up to something. Kline and Braun found out about it and had him killed—made it look like an accident. Somehow I got tied into it. Obviously when I called about the briefcase they thought I must be in on whatever David was up to. Maybe he was an embezzler and the briefcase was loaded with money." He was beginning to get excited at his own conspiratorial thinking. He took a sip of his black Russian, his third. "And then they sent someone to kill me because I asked for the briefcase."

"You're joking," said Ruddick, "you're letting your imagination run wild. A company like Kline and Braun just wouldn't get involved with a small-fry like you. What the hell could *you* do?"

"Well, they don't know anything about me." Benton ordered another drink.

"It's probably those damn black Russians that are giving you such crazy ideas."

"No, they're not. I'm not drunk. But maybe I am getting carried away. After all, I was shot at last night and my landlord was killed because he saw the gunman."

Ruddick was quiet for a moment. "True. I'm sorry. I try to imagine how I would feel and react in the same circumstances. It's enough to make one paranoid."

"Anyway, my idea is this: Why don't I go out to California and snoop around? I have time before my trip and I don't need to return to my classes for another ten days anyway. Maybe I can uncover the solution to this mystery."

"God! Now I know you're nuts. You wouldn't find out a damn thing. They don't let anyone in there. Only authorized personnel!"

"At least I could find out if my theory is wrong. Look, I can let them know I'm there. If they take another shot at me, then we'll know they are behind it. So we go to the police with our theory—"

"Look at me!" Ruddick snapped. "This is a harebrained idea. You're telling me you want to set yourself up? And if they do want you dead, what makes you think they'll miss this time? Then what will you tell the police? 'Boo, I'm a ghost'?"

"*You* tell them then!" Even as he spoke he knew he wasn't serious. He had no intention of letting them make another attempt.

"Oh shit, I don't know. I just feel I have to do something. Sure, I'm paranoid, but you yourself said you would be, too, under the circumstances. But it's better to do something than nothing."

Ruddick smiled ruefully. "Yeah, you always said that. Every time you tried to drag me along to an antiwar demonstration back in college days." He signaled to the waitress and handed over his American Express Gold card.

After paying the bill, they left. Benton felt frustrated.

The streets were wet and the lights of the city were reflected from the glistening surfaces around them as they took a taxi to Greenwich Street.

Starthrower was a small restaurant located on a corner just off Seventh Avenue. Benton had often gone there with Ruddick when he was in New York. The place was a favorite of theirs.

They ordered immediately without having another drink. The ride in the cab had cast a clearer aspect of reality on Christopher's thinking. He realized that the alcohol had clouded his reasoning.

"You're probably right," he said after a while. "There's no point in going out there. But my curiosity is certainly not satisfied. I do want some answers. And I don't want to be afraid of every shadow."

"Let the police deal with it."

The meal was excellent. Ruddick had the trout and Benton the chicken en croûte. It was a tender boneless breast of chicken stuffed with Boursin and wrapped in puff pastry. They drank a bottle of Côte du Rhône blanc with the meal, but decided to have espresso at Caffè Reggio rather than at the restaurant.

They walked to Third and MacDougal Streets along Sixth Avenue. The café was only a few blocks from Ruddick's apartment and they sat there for another two hours, drinking espresso and talking about other things. Benton reminisced about his first visit to Caffè Reggio when he was in high school. It was in 1959, after a Harry Belafonte concert. The café was filled with Bohemian types with goatees and wearing horizontally striped boat-necked shirts and people playing bongos and reciting poetry at the oak and cast-iron tables. The beatniks were no longer there, but de-

spite the fact that the café had become something of a tourist attraction, it was still frequented by local artsy types, as
it always had been throughout its fifty-year history. The
ceiling was tin and the smoke-filled, dimly lit atmosphere
made it nearly impossible to see the subjects of the cracked,
gilt-framed oil paintings on the walls. Many people entered
as the two old friends sat there, and by the time they left
every table was full.

As they left neither of them took any notice of the man at
the table across from the door. Had they done so, Benton
might have recognized that he had already seen him twice
that day.

RUDDICK OPENED the sofa bed and brought out some sheets
and pillows.

"I'll have to get up early tomorrow. I have to be at the
office by seven-thirty. I won't wake you, though." He left
an extra key on the lamp table and retired to the bedroom.

Benton took a shower, got into bed and turned out the
light. He fell asleep almost immediately. It was a deep sleep,
for the first time in more than thirty-six hours.

28 December

LIGHT WAS STREAMING in around the edges of the curtains
when Christopher awoke. It was ten-thirty. He hadn't heard
Alan leave. He stretched contentedly. God, he thought, he
had slept well.

He got up and made a cup of coffee while he dressed.
After that, he felt thoroughly refreshed and anxious to go
out. He threw on his jacket and picked up the key. As he
opened the door the front doorbell rang.

At first he paused and decided not to answer it. But then
he thought it might be the mailman with a package for Alan.
He went downstairs.

He could see the outline of a man through the opaque glass of the inner door. He didn't seem to be wearing a uniform. Benton opened the door.

The man looked vaguely familiar.

And then he remembered.

A cloud. How could it be a cloud? It seemed to emanate from the man's hand. And then Christopher was sinking, sinking... Unconscious.

JANSSEN RELEASED his thumb from the clip on the "fountain pen" and shoved it in his pocket. Placing a mask over his nose and mouth with his left hand, he let the door almost close against his leg and waited for a full minute as the vapor dispersed. Then, swinging the door open again, he reached down, got his arm under Benton's shoulders, lifted him to his feet and pulled him through into the entryway.

The inside door swung shut and locked behind them. He adjusted Benton so it looked as if he was leaning for support on his shoulder, and opened the outside door. Without hesitation he walked unconcernedly down the steps supporting Benton. He opened the sliding door to the rented Ford van that was parked a few feet along the curb. He lifted Benton into the back and stepped in after him. After he slid the door shut he quickly snapped a pair of handcuffs on Benton's wrists and crawled over his unconscious form into the front seat. He started the engine and drove off.

It had taken less than three minutes.

Janssen smiled to himself.

HUMMING.

It was the humming sound that first filtered through to his consciousness. Cautiously Christopher opened his eyes.

Grayness. Metallic grayness.

His cheek was pressed into the gray floor of some sort of vehicle. He raised his eyelids, but not his head. That throbbed too much.

He could make out that he was lying awkwardly on the corrugated floor of a van or panel truck. The humming sound was the whir of tires against asphalt. His arms and legs were asleep and his wrists ached. He tried moving them slightly. He was handcuffed.

Everything slowly became clear. The man he had opened the door to. He had seen him before. On the train? Yes, that was it. Where else? He concentrated. Yes. In the deli. He was sitting in the corner. It didn't take much effort to surmise that he was probably his assailant from Philadelphia. This man had killed Cohen and probably Marcus, and had tried to kill him.

Now he was going to try again.

But why hadn't he killed him already? Since he hadn't done so, Benton reasoned, then he either wanted information from him or was taking him to an isolated spot where there would be no witnesses.

Escape.

He had to escape. He pulled on the handcuffs binding his wrists. They were solid.

He had to have a plan. Getting away was the top priority, but he had to reverse the situation with this killer. He would have to capture him. It was the only link with whoever or whatever was behind this. But how could he even escape much less overpower his captor? He tried to fight the sense of panic he felt rising within.

His eyes shifted around to see if there was anything in the vehicle that could be used as a weapon.

Nothing.

He looked toward his feet and beyond. He could see the driver. His shoulders and head. There was no passenger. Occasionally the man's eyes would shift to the rearview mirror. Shit! The man knew he was conscious. There was no point in feigning any longer.

He moaned.

The driver turned his head slightly. His profile was clearly outlined against the glare from the windshield.

Benton stirred and groaned again. He raised his head. "Where are we?"

"Nowhere." The driver smirked. This would be fun.

Benton slid himself forward and raised himself slightly so he could half lean against the back of the passenger seat.

"Where are you taking me? What have I done?"

"We're taking a little trip out to Long Island." He glanced down at Benton. "You know damn well what you've done. And you're going to tell me what you know. That is, if you want to get out of this alive."

He was lying about him getting out alive, and Benton knew it. But what the hell could this guy hope to learn from me? he thought.

"I really don't know what you're talking about. Look, I know it must tie in with Marcus somehow. I'm not stupid. But whatever Marcus was up to I knew nothing about it. He was only an acquaintance, hardly a friend."

"So you know nothing?" the driver asked.

"Nothing."

They fell silent. Several times Benton asked the driver more questions, but he received no replies. Finally, he gave up.

After some time they made a left turn off the main road that they had been on, and a few minutes later another series of turns brought them progressively onto smaller and bumpier side roads.

They must be far out on the island, Benton thought. He had no idea how long they had been traveling, but from what he could observe out the corner of the window he could tell they were in a remote spot.

Janssen made a tight U-turn and stopped the van. After pocketing the keys, he got out and stretched. He walked around to the side, slid open the door, unlocked the handcuffs and motioned Christopher to step out.

Benton swung over the edge of the floor and tried to stand, but his legs were too stiff to function properly. "Just a minute," he said.

"Take your time." Janssen took out a cigarette.

Benton's mind was racing. There was moisture on his hands. A mixture of sweat and blood from his chafed wrists. The man was going to kill him now. He knew it. He had to escape.

He looked around. He could smell and hear the sea in the distance. They were on a gravel road. Beyond Janssen shrubs and undergrowth crested up a level expanse of ground and seemed to come to an abrupt halt about a hundred feet away. No telling from here how far the ridge fell before reaching the sea. It was probably Long Island Sound, which meant there were rocks below the crest. It also seemed reasonable to assume they were far out on the northern fork. Christopher had been there several times as a child for summer vacations with his parents. The topography certainly had a familiar feel to it.

"Come on, surely you can walk now," Janssen chided.

Benton stood up.

"This way." Janssen pointed over his shoulder toward the cliff.

Christopher started walking, praying that his captor would believe him to be weaker and stiffer than he really was. His senses were sharply alert. Death was too close and it heightened all his sensations.

Janssen stayed slightly behind him and to the right as they headed up the slope. Benton shuffled his feet. Out of the corner of his eye he could see Janssen reach surreptitiously inside his jacket.

This was the moment. He had to move. Fast and accurately.

As Janssen's hand emerged from the jacket Benton hesitated for a fraction of a second. Then he lunged with all the power he could summon, and with both hands grabbed Janssen's wrist. Janssen had been swinging the gun out to the right from under his left arm. Benton had been slightly elevated in relation to the killer and his lunging movement forced Janssen's arm farther to the right as Benton's full weight took effect.

Pfft!

It was a familiar sound. The shot drilled into the sandy turf several feet away.

Janssen threw his left arm around Benton's neck as they tumbled over under the momentum of Benton's weight.

Ignoring as best he could the tearing at his neck and face as Janssen gouged at him, Christopher gripped the gun arm with both hands and repeatedly smashed the hand onto the ground. But the gun would not fall.

Adrenaline was surging through him. He was terrified. He smashed and smashed the hand against the gravel while struggling to bend back Janssen's thumb. Finally he got his fingers under the thumb and started pulling back with all his strength. It was a strength he never knew he possessed.

The fingers of Janssen's left hand were digging into Benton's eyes. He pulled his head down and tried to bite Janssen's hand, but it was beyond his reach. Finally, in desperation, he threw his head suddenly backward as hard as he could and heard a cracking sound as the back of his skull crunched sharply into Janssen's nose.

Janssen loosened his grip for only a second, but it was all that was needed to allow the gun to slip to the ground.

Immediately Benton released Janssen, fell on the gun, clutched it and rolled away as rapidly as possible.

Three. Four times he rolled. Instinctively he knew he must not allow Janssen leeway to maneuver.

He started to rise. Janssen was rushing at him. At the last possible instant Janssen lashed out at him with a karate kick. Christopher rolled again, but a glancing blow struck his right shoulder. He raised the gun in his left hand and, without thinking, fired blindly into Janssen's form as he was regaining his balance.

His arm jerked upward in recoil as a blotch of blood spread rapidly from the middle of Janssen's chest.

The man staggered and fell heavily onto one knee. "Christ!" he muttered. There was a strange gurgling sound in the syllable.

Benton was frantic. "Tell me! Tell me! What the fuck is this all about? What's going on?"

Janssen fell back abruptly onto his haunches, clutching at his chest. He had seen enough bullet wounds to know immediately that this one was mortal. There seemed to be an irony to it. He laughed. An odd croaking laugh. But there was no mirth in his eyes.

"Who gives you orders?" Benton shouted. "Who?"

Blood bubbled from Janssen's mouth and he fell onto his side, a sardonic smile on his lips.

Benton stood there numbed. He could feel the muscles in his arms and legs quivering. His right shoulder ached. His head felt as though it would split in two. He could feel blood, warm and sticky, on his face.

A wave of nausea came over him and he sat down on the grass and put his head between his knees. The acrid taste in his mouth remained but the nausea and dizziness gradually subsided.

Time passed. His breathing slowly returned to a normal rhythm.

He looked at the body before him lying grotesquely, like a broken manikin.

A flock of sea gulls were soaring and diving over the gray sea.

He rose and straightened out the body. He had to think. He had to act.

He went through the man's pockets, took out the keys, his wallet, a few papers, a plastic bag containing white powder.

A scrap of paper bore Benton's name and address. In the wallet, along with $430.00 cash, were credit cards issued to Wulf Janssen. The American Express was a company card issued to Kline and Braun. But the most curious item of all was a card identifying Captain Wulf Janssen of the NATO Security Division. The address was in Brussels.

It was getting colder.

Christopher walked back to the van and sat down out of the wind. He put the gun in the glove compartment. His entire body ached, but his mind ignored it. His emotions were drained. He analyzed his reaction for several minutes and felt only a mild curiosity over this apparent atrophying of his sense of emotional involvement.

For more than an hour he sat, looking at the papers, Janssen's body, the hill overlooking the sound. If it were less cloudy he would have been able to see the Connecticut coast on the horizon. He was vaguely aware of the beauty and solitude before him, but the incongruity of his presence and the nearness of death alienated him totally from it.

Slowly, pieces of the puzzle began coming into hazy focus. Marcus worked for a subsidiary of Kline and Braun. He was killed. Why? Someone thought Christopher knew what Marcus was doing and they wanted him dead, too. But why? Why would NATO kill someone who was working on missile development? And what did they think he had to do with Marcus's project? Janssen was sent to kill him, and it was only sheer luck and possibly Janssen's overconfidence that had allowed him to escape. Now Janssen was dead. Three people were dead.

And who was Marcus's new boss, Colonel Thalberg?

Nothing seemed to fit.

The sky was darkening. He got out of the van, trying to make a decision. He should probably go to the police, he thought, but what would they do? What a ludicrous story! Someone from NATO had tried to kill him. What would the cops say to that? If powerful people wanted him dead they would not have any difficulty in getting the police to hand him over to them. No. The police were out of the question until he could feel safe from those who sought him. Of course, the moment Janssen's body was found, then his bosses would send someone else to finish the job. He needed to buy time.

He went over to the body, grabbed both feet and dragged it across the grass to a line of nearby scrub. He pulled it a few yards into the bushes and broke off several branches to cover it. Sea gull sounds came up to him from the beach below. He went to the edge and looked over. It was a drop of about thirty feet, a small expanse of rocky beach, then the sound. A flock of sea gulls were sitting on the rocks. A few, now and then, flew out fifty or sixty feet from shore, diving for fish and returning.

Christopher turned back to look at the bushes. The body could not be seen from where he stood. He walked in a semicircle around the area, and still the body was hidden from view.

That will do for a while, he thought.

He returned to the van and started the engine. He looked in the mirror. He felt more of a wreck than he looked. A few scratches marred his face and his hair was clotted with blood. Apart from that, he was pretty much intact. He felt his scalp, but could find no wounds. Probably the clotting blood was Janssen's. He shivered involuntarily.

He shifted into first gear and headed back along the road away from the sound. He had little difficulty finding the way back. After about a mile of driving through an area of small pines and scrub he passed a house. It was shuttered. A summer residence.

The final two miles before he hit the main road was gradually flanked by summer cottages. He headed west on Route 25 and soon drove through the town of Cutchogue.

Now, he thought, no matter what he did, he was trapped. He had killed. Albeit in self-defense. But he had hidden the body in order to gain time and he was running. But where to? If he returned home, surely another attempt would be made. If he went to Alan's he might be found again. After all, Janssen had tracked him there. No telling whether the man had reported Christopher's whereabouts to his superiors.

Thalberg. Colonel Thalberg, he thought. Thalberg was the key. He had to find him.

He passed a gas station with a clock in the window. It was almost four-thirty. An idea struck him. There was still time.

He stopped the van at a public telephone booth, got the number from South Jersey information and made the call to AES.

"Colonel Thalberg, please," he said to the receptionist.

"I'm sorry, sir. He's not here. In fact, he won't be back for some time. He's returned to Brussels. May I take a message?"

"No, no. That's not necessary. Thank you anyway." He hung up.

Brussels!

Brussels. Yes. NATO headquarters. But he'd never be able to gain entry there, even if that was the last place he would be expected.

He thought of driving to Kennedy Airport and taking the next plane to Brussels. He patted his pocket to verify that he

still had his passport and credit cards. It was a crazy idea.
But then his world was slowly disintegrating.

At Riverhead he drove onto the Long Island Express-
way.

1900 hours
BENTON PARKED the van in the short-term lot at Kennedy,
left the keys under the driver's seat and locked the door.
Though he would have felt more secure keeping the gun, he
realized that the likelihood of getting it through customs was
small, even if it were possible for him to smuggle it past airport security onto the airplane in the first place. The gun,
too, was left in the van.

He entered the International Arrivals building and went
straight to the men's room. After washing his face and hair
as well as he could, he had a sandwich at a fast-food stand.

He got a cash advance with his Visa card from the Citi-
bank counter and added it to the money he had removed
from Janssen's wallet. Then he booked the evening Sabena
flight to Brussels.

Brussels, 29 December, 0700 hours
THE MORNING FOG was just lifting as Benton took the airport limousine into central Brussels.

He had a coffee and croissant in a café on the already
busy Boulevard Anspach and thought about his next move.

He waited until he thought the NATO offices had probably opened, then, after a good deal of frustration with the
telephone at the café, he finally spoke to the NATO switchboard.

Thalberg was not there, nor was he expected for several
days. He was either in England, they said, or was still state-
side. No one was really sure.

Christ! he said to himself, replacing the receiver. This bastard is elusive! Well, it looks like I'm going to take that vacation to England now after all.

He took the limousine back to the airport.

A look at the clock on one of the gray cathedral spires told him he had spent less than three hours in Brussels.

CHAPTER THREE

London

1535 hours

"HOW LONG DO YOU EXPECT to stay in England, sir?" The tired immigration official at Heathrow was the epitome of bureaucratic efficiency and politeness.

"No more than a week."

The bearded officer examined his passport minutely, looked up the number in a large loose-leaf book, then, reluctantly, or so it seemed to Benton, stamped it and handed it back.

"Enjoy your stay."

A few minutes later he was on the tube heading into central London. Stations flashed by as the train hurried toward the city. He passed green fields and cricket grounds. So remarkably green, he thought, even in December. Then the number of houses increased impressively. Thousands of them, and each one bore several chimney pots. Orange tile roofs and chimney pots stretching out into the middle-class distance. Then the train went underground.

Less than a quarter of an hour later he stepped onto the platform at Earl's Court. He remembered from the time he had spent in London in the early seventies that there were many students and foreigners living in the less expensive hotels and bedsitters of the Earl's Court district.

Within half an hour he had booked into a bed-and-breakfast on Hogarth Road. It was a run-down early Victorian–late Regency white-columned building desperately in

need of repainting. In fact, all the buildings on the street
were in the same state of disrepair.

After a hot bath he went to his room and got into the
creaky bed. Though it was not yet evening he was dead tired.
He piled on the covers and lay back. His mind was racing
and he wasn't able to sleep.

Tomorrow, he thought, he would buy some clothes and
spend the day recuperating. Then he would make some inquiries as to the location of American military bases in England. This, he knew, was not a secret and would not be
difficult to find out. He had read often enough in American newspapers about antimissile demonstrators who had
been camped outside one of the major bases for the past two
years. Surely any of the student residents of the area would
know where that was and show him how to get there. If not,
he would go to the London School of Economics. The antinuclear activists there would be able to direct him. He
would find out where Thalberg was and then he would confront him. But still, just what he would confront Thalberg
with, remained unclear. He trusted that he would know
when the time came.

30 December, 1000 hours
THE STREETS WERE DAMP and a light drizzle persisted
throughout the morning. From his window Christopher
could see the chimney pots on the rooftops of Earl's Court
and South Kensington stretching away to the east. In the
distance the tower of Westminster Cathedral and the government office buildings in Whitehall were visible through
the mist.

Christopher took a bus along Old Brompton Road
through Knightsbridge, past Harrods, to Hyde Park Corner. He decided to walk through Green Park along the
southern boundary of Mayfair. The air was damp and the
chill penetrated, but he felt comfortable enough. He never

could understand why people complained so predictably about London weather. The dampness, he considered, only accentuated the Dickensian atmosphere. And it was this that gave so much character and dimension to the city. It was the background, the canvas, on which London came to life.

He left the park near the Ritz and walked along Piccadilly. At Dunn & Co. he bought a Harris tweed off the rack, a pair of corduroy trousers and two shirts. He put on the new clothes and asked the clerk to wrap his old ones—and the extra new shirt—for him to pick up later. Then he walked through Piccadilly Circus and Leicester Square, disappointed to discover that his favorite bookstore, The Village Bookshop, had gone out of business.

He continued toward Trafalgar Square and entered the National Portrait Gallery, staying briefly to view and pay homage to the portraits of George Eliot, Charles Dickens, the Brontës and the Brownings.

After a pub lunch of shepherd's pie and a pint of bitter at the King's Head, he walked along the Strand to Aldwych and turned up Houghton Street and entered the main building of LSE.

The London School of Economics had always been notorious as a hotbed of radical politics, and he immediately found what he was looking for on the bulletin board. The Committee for Nuclear Disarmament was holding an all-night vigil into the New Year at Marble Arch the following night. Several students were nearby, handing out fliers. One of them saw him reading the announcement and approached him.

"Please do come to the vigil," a slightly accented soft voice said.

Benton turned.

A tall, striking woman handed him a flier.

"Thank you," he mumbled. He couldn't take his eyes away from hers. They were blue, but so dark as to appear almost brown. She had long, straight blond hair and full lips. Her nose was crooked and her cheekbones were a trifle too low for her to be considered beautiful in a fashionable sense. But her face had a quality of intelligence and depth to it. He was immediately attracted to her.

"Are you a student at LSE?" she asked.

"No. Just a tourist. And you?" She seemed too old to be a student. In her mid-thirties at least.

"I'm taking some graduate courses. Actually, I'm a teacher in Germany, but I've got a year off—a sabbatical you might say—so I came to London."

That explained the accent.

"Are you a member of the CND?" he asked.

"Yes. Can't you tell?" She laughed. "Yes, I'm quite active in it. It's the most important issue of our time." She paused. "You're an American, aren't you?"

He nodded. Curiously he felt almost a reluctance to admit it. "Yes. I suppose you would consider me the enemy, wouldn't you?"

She laughed again, a warm, deep, contagious laugh. "Oh yes, you Americans are horrible. Always fucking around with Europe and the Third World and expecting us to thank you for it. Actually, we are aware that it's the American government we're fighting and not the American people. Remember, we Germans cannot afford to be self-righteous. But, tell me, one thing I'm curious about, why isn't there a strong antinuclear movement in the U.S.? We know how concerned American students were about Vietnam, but we hear so little about the radical movement there now."

"Well—" he considered for a moment "—in Europe the movement is active and powerful because you are compelled to face the reality of all those American nuclear weapons being deployed here. If there's a war everyone assumes that Europe will bear the brunt of it. In America it all seems so far away and so unimportant to the average person. All he cares about is the economy and the Super Bowl."

"Super Bowl? I do not understand."

He laughed. "Oh, it's unimportant. It's something like the World Cup, but for American football."

"Ah." She nodded. "A brutal game."

"But in the sixties," he continued, "of course people were committed and active. Vietnam was an issue that affected everyone of draft age. When your ass is on the line you're going to try to do something about it."

"'Ass on the line'?" she repeated, puzzled.

He smiled again. "Pardon. An American idiom. But it pretty much means what it says."

She raised her eyebrows. "Ah...an American idiom. I hear so much about American idioms, but most of them are so farfetched, or so funny. I must make a note of that one so I can teach my class when I am back in Bremen."

The thought of her writing "ass on the line" on the blackboard in a German classroom made him smile. A warm feeling surged through him. After only five minutes he knew he liked her. And he was surprised at his responsiveness.

"Tell me, do you know a lot about the deployment and what bases have missiles?"

"Oh yes, we have a list of all the American bases in England, in Italy, in Germany, all over Europe. There are even statistics about how many missiles are there and how many are expected. Though we don't really trust the accuracy of any publicly released reports. In fact, we are quite certain that the American government has grossly misled its allies by releasing much lower figures."

"Are the missiles always at American bases, or are there NATO personnel involved?"

"Well, it's mostly under NATO command, but we know what that really means. Most of the military are Americans."

He thought of more questions but decided against posing them. He did not want her to think she was being cross-examined.

"I must go back to handing out my fliers." She motioned with her hand, her eyes sparkling. "It was nice talking to one of the enemy."

"Could you do me a favor?" he asked.

"What?"

"Could you get me a list of the bases?"

"Yes, that's easy. Why don't you come to the vigil? I'll be there. I'll have it for you."

"Great," he said, "it's a date."

"Date?"

"Oh...just another idiom." He felt foolish. "Yes, I'll be there and I'll look for you."

"Okay," she nodded. *"Tschüss."*

"Ciao."

As he was going down the steps to Houghton Street he realized that he had not even asked her name. She looked so very German, he thought, so he gave her the first German name that came to his mind.

"Gretchen," he mumbled under his breath.

IT WAS GOOD to be in London again.

Ever since Benton spent a year doing research on his dissertation at the British Museum he had felt London was a part of his blood. Much had changed, but the essential character of the city was still there, despite runaway inflation, the whims of artificially imposed fashion and the influx of American plastic fast-food eateries.

He walked along the Embankment to Charing Cross and then took the Hungerford pedestrian bridge to the South

Bank. He had tea at Royal Festival Hall overlooking the Thames and ambled about, feeling his spirits lift for the first time in days. It was a combination of being in London and the conversation with the German woman that brought about the sense of well-being. Not far below the surface, he knew, there were questions, and an inexplicable danger, but he forced these thoughts into the background. This moment was sufficient unto itself. He was almost happy. He felt free.

2345 hours
THE SATELLITE CONNECTION was crisp and clear.

"I can't think that Janssen failed a second time," said Thalberg, "but it's unlike him not to have reported in by now."

"Yes," General Forman answered, "I've got three men out looking for him. I have this bad feeling that he's back on drugs. I knew we should never have reinstated him even though the doctors had pronounced him no longer dependent. If we hear nothing within the next twenty-four hours we're going to have to assume he failed. If he did, he's a dead man. Anyway, how far along are you?"

"I'm driving down to Greenham Common on Monday. Matecki will come over from Brussels to meet me there. By Wednesday he'll be back at headquarters awaiting your arrival, and I'll be in Wetzen. Have you covered everything in Washington?"

"Yes. Monday I meet with the Joint Chiefs and we'll have the final timetable. The way it looks now, the exercise will be held next Friday night. Be ready though, in case I find it necessary, because of this Benton complication, to move it up a day. I'll call you at the base Monday night if there's anything new from this end."

"Right."

"Good night."

31 December

CHRISTOPHER SPENT another day walking through central
London. After he picked up the clothes he had left at
Dunn's, he went to Lee Ho Fook for dim sum. Then he
bought a pair of hiking boots on Charing Cross Road and
went to the British Museum for an hour.

He always felt a hush as he swung open the glass doors to
the Elgin Marbles, and this time was no exception. It seemed
as though he were entering another world, but not the uto-
pian world of the Olympian gods. It was a world destroyed
by jealousy and greed, by human pettiness and corruption.
He looked around at the fragments of frieze work that had
been "rescued" by Lord Elgin from the Turkish bombard-
ment, and he thought how someday, too, the British Museum itself would no doubt lay in ruins. Perhaps less of it
would survive than the Parthenon.

He sat for a while on one of the benches of the columned
portico and watched the tourists and scholars scurrying back
and forth through the courtyard, pigeons strutting, cars
crawling in and out of the car park, taxis hurrying by on
Great Russell Street, the billowing clouds above the row of
buildings facing the B.M., gabled roofs addressing the sky
in hushed whispers of empire.

London was his city.

He felt he belonged there.

He crossed the street to the Museum Tavern for a pint
before heading back to Earl's Court. People on the tube and
on Earl's Court Road where he exited were becoming in-
creasingly festive as the year waned. He went to his room to
take a nap before going to the vigil at Marble Arch.

2300 hours

COLONEL THALBERG, in civilian clothes, stepped out of the
taxi at Grosvenor Square. He glanced at the floodlit Amer-

ican Embassy as he passed it and walked briskly along North Audley Street. He turned left onto Green Street and approached Park Lane. There were already hundreds of people, mostly students and youths, gathered from Marble Arch to Speaker's Corner. Several buskers were playing their instruments and many people were handing out leaflets and buttons. Banners proclaimed the desire for a nuclear-free society and the end of nuclear weapons. There were individuals of every description on soapboxes addressing the small groups that clustered around them, and at the edge of Hyde Park, just across from the site of Tyburn gallows, a platform was set up with a podium and PA system.

Shortly after his arrival most of the isolated groups fell silent as an elderly, bearded tweedy gentleman approached the microphone. He spoke nervously for a few minutes about the reasons for their gathering and introduced, to a great deal of applause, the first speaker. A tall, striking, famous actress stepped up to the microphone and began at once denouncing the American government. Each of her sentences were received with enthusiastic cheers from the crowd.

"Fucking Communist," Thalberg muttered softly as he pushed his way to the left side of the platform.

Ulrich Sievers saw him first. He waited as Thalberg approached nearer then slipped beside him.

"Good evening, sir, so glad you could make it."

Thalberg grinned. "I wouldn't have missed this for the world." He paused. "I take it everything is in readiness. There are no hitches?"

"None at all. We have been most successful in our organization and planning. All we need is your signal and we'll be rolling."

"You have enough loyal people at the farm?"

"Yes, of course. Every aspect of the project has been rehearsed repeatedly. We'll be able to proceed blindfolded if necessary."

"I hope your confidence is well founded, but I have no reason to doubt your Teutonic efficiency."

Sievers paused. "I hope your efficiency matches ours," he said acidly.

"I was just joking." Thalberg laughed and slapped Sievers's shoulder.

The actress had left the podium to a resounding ovation. Thalberg and Sievers fell silent and waited until the next speaker began before concluding their conversation.

"I'll be in Greenham Common tomorrow," Thalberg continued. "Perhaps you could meet me at the usual place in case you want to discuss any last-minute ideas. When do you return to Wetzen?"

"I've got a flight for Tuesday morning. From that point on we'll be waiting for the signal. Of course you will be in Wetzen by then yourself."

"We'll probably be getting the code for Friday. But I've been instructed to expect it as early as Thursday. Be ready."

"Natürlich," Sievers replied.

CHRISTOPHER HAD BEEN standing at the foot of the stage during the actress's speech. When she finished he wandered back through the crowd, hoping to catch sight of Gretchen.

He arrived at the border of the crowd and began a systematic search, looking for a blond head as he circumnavigated the area. He had almost given up when he found her on Park Lane, handing out leaflets and urging passersby to join the vigil.

"Gretchen!" he called, as he approached her.

"What?" She turned toward him, her strawberry-blond hair streaking half-across her face as a light gust whipped at it. "Oh, hello," she said, brushing the hair back with one hand.

He smiled. "Excuse me calling you Gretchen. I made up the name after we met, because we never did exchange names. Mine, by the way, is Benton. Christopher Benton."

She took his hand in mock formality. "So pleased to meet you sirrr," she said, attempting, vainly, an American accent. "My name is Gabriele Witte." She pronounced it Gah-bray-eh-lah Vit-tah. "So, it's not so far off from Gretchen. But Gretchen's such an ordinary, common name." She grimaced.

"Well, I'm deeply sorry. I can already tell you are far from ordinary!"

They laughed.

"Here," she said, opening her shoulder bag, "try this. Happy New Year." She produced a half-liter bottle, took a sip and handed it to him.

"Happy New Year," he replied and took a cautious sip. "Whew...that's powerful stuff! What is it?"

"*Korn.* A Bremen specialty. I brought a bottle over for a special occasion."

"Is it schnapps or something?"

"Something like that."

He took another hit, then handed it back. "Did you bring the list?"

"Yes," she said, replacing the bottle and extracting several stapled sheets of paper from her bag. "This is as complete and up-to-date as possible."

"Thanks," he said, folding it and tucking it into his inside jacket pocket.

They walked back to the edge of the crowd. Another older man was speaking. Probably a local professor, Benton thought.

There was polite applause as he stepped down and a younger man replaced him. His hair was very thin and hung down in scraggly strands past his shoulders. His etiolated face was so pale that Christopher thought he could almost be an albino. He was wearing wire-frame glasses and a Ho Chi Minh wispy goatee.

"It is time for Europe to declare itself free from the diabolical influence of America!" he shouted, gesticulating with his fist.

Applause.

"Just as the American colonists broke from the yoke of British tyranny in the eighteenth century, the time has come when the common people of Britain, the common people of Germany, the common people of all of Europe, must and *will* break the yoke of American tyranny and imperialism!"

Shouts of affirmation and applause.

"We will not stand by as NATO, the right arm of the American government, converts Europe into the battleground for World War Three!"

Cheers.

"We will not allow Europe to become the stage for Armageddon!"

Gabriele was listening intently. Her gaze seemed transfixed on the speaker.

"Who is this guy?" Christopher asked her.

She glanced at him and then back at the podium. "Ulrich Sievers. He's a leader of the German Anti-Nuclear Proliferation Front. A very intelligent and respected man. We hope to elect him to the Bundestag this year."

"Well, he certainly has the politician's gift of rhetoric," Christopher said, and again listened to the speaker.

"America once was the hope of the world. Now she is its curse. America is the archenemy of the people, the mainstay of the oppressors. We must march! We must prevent any further deployment of missiles! We must be committed to the task of blocking and expelling the forces that would destroy two thousand years of civilization!''

He stepped back abruptly. For a moment the crowd didn't realize he had finished. But when they did, the cheering and applause were deafening.

Benton hoped no one would recognize that he was an American. The crowd would probably tar and feather him on the spot. He smiled to himself thinking of the Sons of Liberty and the Spirit of '76. Yes, this Sievers was right. American idealism, despite the peace movement of the sixties, was at an ebb. The dream had deserted the ideals of the founding fathers.

Another speaker had begun addressing the crowd. An Italian. Someone was translating for him.

The new year had commenced unnoticed.

After several more speakers, many of the demonstrators began opening sleeping bags and prepared to spend the night. He followed Gabriele over to a tree near a fence where she apparently had left a bundle. It was her sleeping bag.

"Are you staying out here all night, too?" he asked as the wind blew his hair across his forehead.

"That's what the vigil means. All night."

She spread out the sleeping bag. "You can stay too, if you wish."

"Oh no. But. Well, maybe I'll keep you company for a little while."

"Ah, you Americans lack commitment, don't you?"

"Perhaps." He looked across the silhouettes of trees in the park. "I do agree with your stand and with what the speakers were saying, but I fail to see how staying in Hyde Park all night in this weather is going to change anything. No one is convinced except those who need no convincing. The people who have the power don't give a damn if you freeze your ass off."

"But *I* do," Gabriele insisted. "And I know I must do what I believe is right. If no one cares, then eventually there'll be no asses left to freeze or burn. There will be no one...."

Christopher sat on the ground beside her as she huddled in her sleeping bag. For more than an hour they talked about being committed, even though there was no hope for changing the powers that be. They talked about the sixties and the nature of the commitment then, and about civil rights, and Martin Luther King, Jr., Eldridge Cleaver, Kent State, the Beatles, The Mothers of Invention, the Paris student uprising, Rudi Dutschke and Cohn Bendit, Germaine Greer and the rise of women's lib, the "American way" and the emphasis on superficiality that seemed to be the natural twin of concentrating on outward appearances—the apparent victory of form over content. "One thing that so disturbs me now," he said, "is that people don't seem to have learned the lessons of the past fifteen years. There's this revisionistic 'Ramboization'—this view that what was wrong in the Vietnam War was that we didn't send in Rambo to wipe out the Commies. We didn't win the war, but we're sure as hell going to win the movie!"

"You know," she concluded as he prepared to leave, "much of your viewpoint is quite sound. If only—" she smiled playfully "—if only you were a little more intelligent you would realize how imperative it is now, more than at any other time, to be committed."

He laughed. "I'll try to work on it!"

"I'd like to see you again," she said unexpectedly, "to check on your progress!" She smiled.

"How about tomorrow? I guess, tonight?"

"Oh, I doubt if your thinking will have progressed very far by then. Do you think so? Or are you a truly fast learner?"

"Do you like Indian food? I know a good and inexpensive Indian restaurant."

"Yes. Why not?"

"Good. I'll meet you at seven-thirty. Where do you live?"

She scribbled a Pimlico address on the back of one of her leaflets. He looked at it for a moment, then at her. And then he left.

SHE AWOKE about an hour before dawn, her breath hanging above her in a shroudy mist. She drew the string at the hood of the mummy bag tighter and looked at the sleeping form beside her. All around the area people were huddled together in their sleeping bags. Some sleeping, others still talking quietly among themselves.

Ulrich opened his eyes and looked at her. *"Schlaf gut, Gabriele,"* he said.

Her eyes had already closed again. *"Gute Nacht, Uli,"* she murmured almost imperceptibly as she rolled over and fell back to sleep.

1 January, 1930 hours

THE ROW HOUSES of Pimlico were smaller and more nondescript than those in many other areas of central London. It had always been a poorer district, and now it was favored by students and workers as a relatively inexpensive neighborhood.

Christopher walked southeast along Alderney Street and found the house. Gabriele smiled broadly when she opened the door and led him up the three flights to her small bed-sitter.

Despite the gas fire in the corner it felt damper in the room than it was outside. He kept his jacket on as he sat in the armchair she motioned him to. She sat on the bed.

"I'm glad you came," she told him.

"You didn't expect me to show up?"

"I don't know. Sometimes . . . Well, you're here and I'm glad. I wanted to tell you that I like you. You are refreshing. And even though you are somewhat naive and we don't see—how do you say the idiom—eye to eye—that's it, isn't it?—I think we do have much in common."

He was taken aback by her forthrightness.

"How about a cup of tea before we go?" she asked, sensing his uneasiness.

"Fine."

He looked around. There were several German political posters on the wall. He could make out that they were about past demonstrations in Bonn and Berlin and someplace called Brokdorf. There was a table in the middle of the room strewn with papers, books and an Olympia manual typewriter. A bricks-and-boards bookshelf was jammed to overflowing with both English and German books. The English titles were primarily literature, the German seemed to be mostly political and economic philosophy: Hegel, Marx, Engels, Lukács, Habermas, Adorno, Walter Benjamin. The single bed took up about a third of the room. On one side of the sink was a closet and on the other a small work space on which a hot plate stood. She filled the kettle and placed it on the hot plate.

He enjoyed watching her move. She glided softly and confidently. There seemed to be no self-consciousness or anxiety about her. Most people he had met who were as political as she, always seemed to be carrying the full weight of the world on their neurotic shoulders.

When the water had boiled she poured a cupful into the teapot, swished it around and emptied it into the sink. She threw three heaping tablespoons of Typhoo tea into the pot while the kettle again reached a boil. She poured the bubbling water on the tea, replaced the lid, turned off the gas and placed the pot and two cups on the table.

She saw him observing her. "When I first arrived in London I roomed with an Englishwoman, who after watching me make tea once insisted on teaching me the proper method." She smiled. "It's one thing the British really do well."

She put some milk into two cups, then poured the tea over the milk and sat down on the edge of the bed again.

"When did you arrive in London?" he asked.

"August. I'll be at LSE until June and then back to Bremen. And you," she asked, "how long have you been here?"

"Only two days. But I lived in London for more than a year once. Back in 1970." He sipped the tea. It was excellent. Strong and rich.

"I've looked through the list of missile sites," he continued, "and I've decided to go out and look at a couple of them. Have you visited any of the bases yourself? Which ones are the most important and strategic?"

"I've been to Greenham Common twice. That's where a group, primarily women, has set up a village. Members of the CND have been living in a campsite outside the gate for almost two years now. It's the major focus for the antideployment people."

"Two years. Does that really have any effect?"

"Well, at first I thought so—awakening of consciousness through press coverage and all that, but lately... lately I don't know. Certainly more people are aware of the issues now, and the group at Greenham Common has had an impact there, but what good that has done becomes more and more open to question. It did not prevent the missiles from being brought here. I think a lot of people are either losing heart or becoming desperate. We want the government to be responsive to us."

"What about in Germany? What were you doing there?"

"Demonstrations. Road blockages. But the cops, *die Bullen*, always just cleared us out. We thought that if we got thousands and thousands of people to come out we could halt deployment. Well, the people came out, but so, too, did the missiles."

They finished the tea, and a few minutes later they left the house and walked to Victoria Station. They took the tube, changed at the Embankment for the Northern Line and got off at Goodge Street. They walked a block north on Charlotte Street past various Greek, German and Indian restaurants while a light drizzle began to fall, and finally entered a small, unpromising and inconspicuous restaurant.

They were seated in the back room under a sitar that was hanging precariously on the wall. The wall itself was covered with a dingy burgundy velvet wallpaper in a paisley pattern.

"It doesn't look that great," said Christopher as they examined the menu, "but I think Natraj is one of the best Indian restaurants in London."

They ordered King Prawn masala, Rogan Jhosh, raita, paratha and Tandoori chicken. While waiting for the food, they each had a beer.

"Tell me something about yourself," she said after a while. "You're not married, are you." It was more a statement of fact than a question.

"I was. Once, back in graduate school. My wife helped put me through, but just as I was about to finish my dissertation, she ran off with the guidance counselor in the high school where she taught art. He was a poet. I wasn't."

"You got a divorce?"

"Eventually..." He looked somewhat distracted.

"Was it all very painful?"

"Huh? Well, yes. But that's more than ten years ago now. I don't think about it all that much anymore."

"Consciously."

"Consciously?"

"Yes. But you *do* think about it without being aware that you do. I can see that in you."

"You can? Well, then you see something I don't."

"I can tell you this. You've had affairs since then, but nothing long-lasting. Nothing deep. Am I right?"

He nodded.

"It's not terribly surprising, really. There seems to be a lack of commitment in your blood. Our talk yesterday about politics showed that—your typical American avoidance of commitment. And it plagues your relationships with women, too. You're afraid to lose. Commitment implies the possibility of loss. Even the inevitability."

The food arrived.

"My God, this is good," exclaimed Gabriele, sampling the prawn masala.

"Take up some of the raita on the paratha," he suggested, demonstrating the technique.

"Mmmm...superb." She began eating as though she hadn't eaten for a week.

He laughed.

"What are you laughing at?" she asked between mouthfuls, her eyes lively.

"You. You look as though you've never had Indian food before."

"Never. At least nothing this good."

They ate in silence for several minutes, now and then looking at each other. Contentment.

"You're divorced, too, I take it?" he asked after a while.

"Divorced? No. I was married. Still am, for that matter, but when we broke up it struck me that both marriage and divorce were meaningless. Irrelevant. We were too young to know what we were doing, so it ended. And it never seemed important enough to bother getting divorced."

She wiped up some sauce with paratha, then took a sip of beer.

"I've had three long-term relationships since I left my husband. *Zweierbeziehung*, as we say in Germany, or one-on-one relationship. But they didn't last, either. So you see, like you, I too have difficulty in commitment when it comes to people. But not with politics. I can find commitment there!"

"An escape?"

The waiter cleared the dishes and brought two more bottles of Kingfisher beer.

She poured beer into the glass expertly, using two hands, tilting both glass and bottle toward each other simultaneously and pouring slowly. She set them down and looked into his eyes. "Perhaps."

He felt attracted to her. Something about her directness, her unabashed comfortableness with her own personality. Her eyes seemed to shine, seemed to possess so much joy and playfulness, so much luminosity. Yet they were deeply serious without the overbearing solemnity he was used to seeing in intellectuals. There was a balance in her, and as he realized it he also saw that he lacked that quality.

He looked away, feeling suddenly unsure of himself.

She drank some beer. "You know," she said, looking at him, "you've got to let yourself go a little. Don't be afraid. Of women, of me, of getting involved with politics. You *have* to be involved with the world and being afraid is merely a waste of time."

He didn't know what to say. He was thoroughly aware that he liked her, he responded to her, he felt a longing for her, but he didn't want to rush. He didn't want to spoil it. But then, he thought, if he didn't spoil it... A vague uneasiness came over him. A premonition that she had the power to get through to him. That he was vulnerable. And it was this he feared more.

Take it easy, he said to himself.

"Do you want to go with me tomorrow to Greenham Common?" he asked, changing the subject.

She smiled. "No. But I'll give you a few names of people to contact. They'll be glad to show you around the camp."

He nodded. "Good."

They paid the bill, while the grinning and nodding waiter obsequiously fetched their coats.

The rain was no more than a light mist. It had the effect of making the streets and pavement appear softer. A haze surrounded street lamps and shop signs. They walked through Soho, finally entering a crowded Younger's pub on Wardour Street and were fortunate to find a single small table still unoccupied amidst the jocular drinkers. She sat down while he bought two pints of Tartan bitter.

"You mentioned you were in London once before. What brought you here?"

"Research for my dissertation. I spent several months in the reading room of the British Museum working on the 'regional novel.'"

"Oh, Hardy and Lawrence and all that?"

"Right."

"You finished it?"

"Yes. Now I teach at a small community college in Philadelphia. It's not much of a job. More bullshit in committee meetings, etc., than in actual teaching. But I consider myself very lucky to have got anything at all. In the U.S. it's nearly impossible at present for anyone to get a teaching job in the humanities."

"In Germany it's difficult, too. Even at the secondary level. There are more university graduates trying to teach in the high school than there are places." She opened her bag and began rolling a cigarette. "Do you smoke?" She offered him the papers and a pouch of Drum tobacco.

"A pipe only." He took out his Charatan and filled it with Sobranie.

"Do you remember that German who spoke yesterday at the vigil? Sievers?"

"Oh yes. I thought he did an impressive job. Do you know him?"

"Yes. We lived together for about six months. We were lovers. But it didn't work. There was too much competition between us. He felt insecure around me, always had to prove his intellectual superiority. It got very trying. So we split up a year ago. It's funny, we get along better now. Of course we hardly see each other. But even as friends I doubt if he and I could ever be close."

"Does he live in England?"

"No, but he visits here often. In fact he's been here four times since I've been in London. Gets in touch with me each time."

"Oh, I see." He relit his pipe.

"No. You don't. We're friends, that's all."

He felt silly at the pang he felt. "Do I sound jealous? Envious?"

She laughed. "Well, I don't think you need to be checking up on me." She paused. "Not yet, anyway."

Again an inexplicable pang went through him. This is dangerous! he thought. I'm reacting too much.

"So, your wife left you and you've never been able to trust another woman. A budding misogynist!" Her tone was almost mocking.

"Something like that." He paused. "It just seems I am incapable of opening to anyone. Last year, for example, I met a woman at a faculty party. She was my age, divorced, intelligent, attractive, I liked her. But she wanted commitment. Right from the beginning she was serious and it frightened me—so much so that I did everything I could to avoid her. Well, now when I see her she won't even talk to

me. I ruined it, and she hates me for it. Of course I can't
blame her."

"No one would." She finished rolling another cigarette.

"But this type of situation has repeated itself several times
in the past few years. I keep coming to the conclusion that I
just don't want or need a woman. But then . . . well, you
know, the old physical desires . . ." He felt reluctant to pur-
sue this any further.

She exhaled a cloud of smoke. "But on one level none of
this is your fault at all. You mustn't blame yourself. *You* will
know when you're ready for a serious relationship, and then
there won't be any problems."

His pipe had gone out. He relit it. "You aren't by any
chance a psychologist?" he asked, his eyes smiling.

"No, no." She laughed. "My *Schwerpunkt*, 'major,' I
think you Americans say, was sociology. And I studied a lot
of German literature."

They talked on about teaching, the differences between
the German and American educational systems, and literature. She patiently explained to him why his admiration for
the works of Hermann Hesse was politically naive. "You're
going to have to learn," she said in conclusion, "that you
can't go through life only concerned with your own problems. No matter how important the so-called 'inner revo-
lution' is, you're in relationship to the world around you.
You've got to make your life relevant to the world at large
even if you are successful in achieving a higher consciousness. Especially so then."

As they left the pub he thought how he had heard so
much of this before. Back in the sixties, back when he was
still in college, these issues had seemed so critical, so cru-
cial. He himself had argued for making one's life relevant,
for being committed to changing society, for achieving a
deeper awareness of one's self. Now he suddenly realized
that he seldom thought about any of these issues. His life

was too taken up with living every day and ignoring as far as possible the world at large. Gabriele looked on things the way he once had. Was she the naive one, or had he indeed lost something along the way? He looked at her and it was as though he was looking into the past, as well as the future.

Despite the cold they enjoyed walking through Green Park past Buckingham Palace and Victoria to Pimlico. They strolled in silence, chatting occasionally, but primarily content to remain silent observing the city, the night, the moment. In Green Park she took his arm and held it for the rest of the way.

When they arrived outside her door they hesitated. "Would you like to come in?" she asked.

He swung around to look at her, taking both her hands in his. For a moment he forgot what he wanted to say, as he looked into her eyes. The lines around the corners of them spoke of past joys and sorrows. A beauty shone through.

"Uhhh…" He was afraid he was about to stammer. "You know this evening has been wonderful. I haven't enjoyed myself so much for a long time. I feel I want to tell you everything about me. And that scares me a little."

She started to speak.

"No," he interrupted her, "let me continue. I know, you'll tell me to let myself go. And probably you're right. No doubt you're right."

Her eyes were quiet, smiling.

"But I've got to slow down a little right now. I've just gone through a terrible ordeal and…I…" He broke off, not knowing how to continue.

"I think I understand," she said.

"No. You can't possibly imagine, but, I'll tell you about it sometime. For now…for now let me say good-night. But I do want to see you again."

She squeezed his hands. "Come by tomorrow night. When you're back from Greenham Common." Then she reached up, put her left hand behind his neck and kissed him gently on the cheek.

"You're a fine man," she whispered, then turned gracefully and entered the house.

CHAPTER FOUR

Greenham Common

2 January

CHRISTOPHER AWOKE AT 8:00 A.M. feeling refreshed. After a quick breakfast he hired a car and by ten o'clock he was speeding along the A4 past Maidenhead.

Greenham Common was near the town of Newbury, between the Chilterns and Salisbury Plain. He had visited nearby Stonehenge once before, and anticipated that he would be able to see the base from a distance as he approached the eastern edge of Salisbury Plain. But the hedgerows on either side of the road, as he neared Greenham Common, blocked any view.

He drove through the center of the village of Aldermaston outside Newbury, past a few cottages and the obligatory pub and church, past Woolworth's and the blue shield of Boot's the Chemist. The way to the base was well marked by the protesters with signs and antimissile posters.

Suddenly the hedgerows disappeared as the road turned sharply. In the midst of the open field before him there was a small tent city. A few cars and vans were parked nearby. In the distance, on the far side of the camp, a double-wire electrified fence circled the nine-mile perimeter of the base. A few trees and shrubs behind the fence obscured much of the view, but several unidentifiable structures were visible from his vantage point. The road continued on right up to the gate, which was large and obviously well fortified. Dozens of military personnel were patrolling the area.

He looked again at the list of names that Gabriele had prepared for him and stepped out of the car. He approached a small group, mostly women, seated around a camp fire. They were dressed warmly; two of them wore shawls over their shoulders. One of the women read aloud from a book, while another held an infant to her breast, and three children, chattering happily, played nearby.

The scene reminded Christopher of protests and sit-ins he had attended back in 1968. There was that same intensely concerned look on people's faces, but the atmosphere wasn't charged with the sexual energy that had always added a festive aspect to the peace marches and demonstrations. These people seemed far more serious than the students of his day, perhaps because this was not a festival—they were actually living here, many of them had done so for more than a year.

He introduced himself and said he was a friend of Gabriele Witte's, that he was visiting from America, and she had told him to look them up.

He was warmly greeted. One of the two men in the group, a young man with a full beard and an intelligent face, volunteered to give him a tour of their camp. He was one of the people Gabriele had told him to talk to—Colin Robbins.

Benton liked him right away. He was thin and lanky, but he moved gracefully and compactly in a way that belied his height. His long hair fell over his shoulders and Christopher realized it was a long time since he had seen someone who looked so much like a sixties' activist. Thin lines like crows' feet creased his face around his gray-blue eyes, making them seem perpetually smiling.

Robbins answered his questions, described the founding of the camp by the women, and explained their strategy in trying to hinder deployment. But frustration had set in, and many of the original protesters had left after the missiles arrived. A few diehards like himself, he said, were determined to remain in protest, despite opposition from the people of Newbury, until all nuclear weapons had been removed from Britain.

He took Christopher on a tour of the site, relating anecdotes about some of the protesters. "Sarah—" he indicated a woman tuning a guitar in front of her tent "—has been here for at least two years. One of the first people I got to know when I arrived. Says she'll stay until the missiles leave, doesn't care if she gets married and raises a family and grows old and dies here, she's in for the duration. Every once in a while she gets arrested when the cops yield to community pressure and make a sweep of the compound. But within a few days she's right back here with her guitar."

They returned to the camp fire after inspecting several other small encampments scattered around the area. Robbins poured out two cups of tea. "Of course," he said wryly, "the only way the missiles will leave will probably be when they're launched!"

Benton laughed. "Do you know any of the men stationed on the base?" he asked, finishing his tea.

"A few. Of course, they're not exactly encouraged to fraternize with us, but every once in a while we corner a few soldiers in a pub in Newbury or Greenham Common and try to convert them. You'd be surprised at how many sympathize with us. But I doubt if we have any budding saboteurs working for us in there, though."

"Have you ever heard of a Colonel Thalberg?"

"Samuel Thalberg? Heard of him, yes, but not in connection with Greenham Common. He's probably been here, he's one of the NATO higher-echelon types. Quite an authority on the TELs. I've read about him."

"TELs?"

"Yes. Transporter-erector-launchers. Or mobile launchers, if you prefer. The significant thing about the cruise missile is that the launching is not confined to a stationary base. They have great flexibility. This means that they can be taken off base to any site the military choose. Confusing the enemy, as it were, so they won't know where to attack the missiles. We've learned there's going to be a test of the Transporter-erector-launcher in the near future. We intend to block the road so they can't take the launchers or missiles out. Got to confuse the enemy ourselves, don't we?"

"Is it possible to get on the base?"

"I take it you mean surreptitiously?"

Benton nodded. "I doubt if I could apply for a visitor's pass."

"But why do you want to see the base?"

"Because a friend of mine who had done some work on the cruise guidance system was killed. And then someone tried to kill me. There's a connection and I want answers."

"But how would it help to gain access to the base?"

"I don't know. Perhaps I'd see something and it would all make sense. Perhaps I'd learn nothing at all. I just don't know what else to do."

Robbins looked at Christopher thoughtfully for a moment, evaluating him. He looked into his eyes. He always could tell by the eyes if someone could be trusted. It was quite apparent that Christopher Benton was not a slogan-quoting theoretical revolutionary, nor did he seem to be the type to get involved in activism. He was somewhat bewildering, but maybe it was that infamous American naïveté showing through. He was nervous; like a hunted rabbit, but obviously sincere. Robbins nodded, deciding to trust him.

"There have been several times in the past months that we've got people in. Actually, it's not as difficult as that fence makes it seem. We know the guards' schedules and we figured out a way to get through the fence without tripping the alarms. But last month three demonstrators were caught and arrested. Now a general order has been made public that the guards are instructed to shoot first and ask questions later. They're really getting paranoid. We don't know how serious their threat is, but now that the missiles are here we have to assume they *are* serious."

He unfolded a large piece of poster paper while he was talking. It was a remarkably detailed hand-drawn map of the base, complete with notations showing the locations of the barracks, central administrative building, missile and warhead assembly and maintenance building and six "massively hardened" missile shelters.

"Each of the shelters," Robbins explained, "can house four TELs and two launch-control vehicles along with sixteen cruise missiles."

"My God!" Benton exclaimed. "How do you get such information? Isn't all this classified?"

"I told you, we've been on the base."

"You? You personally?"

He looked around in mock conspiracy, held his finger to his lips and winked. "What do you think? Actually," he continued, folding the map, "it's really no problem. If you want, I'll take you over tonight. That is, if you really are serious about getting on the base. Then you can see for yourself the awesome nature of our adversary."

"It's hard to believe that both the United States military and the local English constabulary can't prevent your access to this base. Surely they must consider it a question of national security?"

"They do. But what are we? Harmless crackpots. There's no way in hell they would ever consider us a serious threat. But as I said, they *are* showing signs of increasing paranoia."

As they spoke, a chauffeur-driven car approached the gate. Though it was more than a hundred feet away Benton could quite clearly see the profiles of both the uniformed driver and the civilian passenger in the rear seat. The guard at the gate stepped up to the driver's window. He examined the papers the driver proffered, and looked at the passenger. Immediately he stood at attention, saluted, then waved the car through.

Must be a bigwig, thought Benton.

The gate swung metallically shut and the guards on both the inside and the outside resumed their posts.

"Sure. Why not?" Benton said. "When do we go in?"

"After dark. Perhaps around seven."

"Will it be worthwhile? I mean, if it's dark is there anything we can see?"

"Everything is well lit. There are spotlights on all the facilities. What we have to worry about is not getting caught in the spotlight, or tripping any alarms. There hasn't been the problem of alarms before, except for the fence, but I half suspect they may have installed some after the arrest last month." He looked at his watch. "Why don't you go into the village and look around? You have all afternoon before we leave. Besides, I have some chores to do. Meet me here at six-thirty."

"Okay."

CHRISTOPHER SPENT several hours in Newbury, and then after a late lunch, went to the small village near the base and visited the church. He sat silently in a pew thinking for a while and then wandered around examining the medieval brasses and effigies of the knights and ladies entombed in the church. By five o'clock he had had enough, and as soon as the pub opened, he crossed the street and stepped in for a drink.

He ordered a pint of Whitbread Tankard and a package of peanuts and sat at a corner table by the window. The dusk view of the church across the road and the cemetery beyond certainly gave no indication of the excitement generated by the missile base nearby. If the street had not been paved the passerby would have thought he had slipped back in time several hundred years. The idea of automation, much less flight, was incomprehensible.

A man walked up to the door of the pub and stepped inside. He took off his parka and greeted the barman. Benton immediately recognized him as Ulrich Sievers, the speaker at Marble Arch. He must visit the encampment often, thought Christopher. Sievers took his beer and sat at a nearby table. He seemed to be waiting for someone.

Several minutes later three youths raucously entered the pub. In heavily accented voices they spoke animatedly with the barman about a job they had been doing at the Grubb farm. They moved over to the dart board with their drinks and began a game of three-oh-one. It was not long before two young women came in and joined them. Occasionally they glanced over at Benton and Sievers. Apart from that the two strangers were ignored by the locals.

Slowly the pub began filling up. Benton ordered another beer. He was surprised at the large number of people in the pub in this relatively small village. Apparently it was the principal social center. Men with tweed caps and rough-hewn faces drinking beer or whiskey. Women with new uninspired hairdos drinking cider or lager and lime. He looked at his watch and realized he would have to leave soon.

The door opened again and a middle-aged, balding man entered. It took Benton only five seconds to remember where he had seen him before. That afternoon. The man was the civilian passenger in the military car he had seen arrive at the base. Benton was surprised to see him there, but even more surprised when without any hesitation the man proceeded directly to Sievers's table and sat down.

"Ah, Colonel Thalberg," said Sievers, extending his hand, "good to see you."

Benton felt a coldness seep through him. An urge to run, to hide, to disappear clutched at him. The same feeling he had experienced when he stepped out of the van on Long Island. He looked quickly back out the window.

The two men began talking earnestly, but he was unable to hear any of their conversation except the occasional isolated word. The hum of talk from the other tables in the rapidly filling pub successfully masked their voices. But it was obvious that they knew each other quite well.

He *had* to hear what they were saying! Thalberg. The man who he was now certain was behind the attempt on his life. Thalberg. The military man who was involved in the missile program, yet who sat in a public place talking with one of the key opponents of that program. Who was working for whom?

Fighting the fear in his shaky knees, Christopher got up and approached the bar. He leaned against it, his back toward their table. He could hear snippets of conversation more clearly. He ordered another pint.

"...in Garlstedt when really they expect it here." It was Thalberg's voice. Benton had only heard him briefly before, on the telephone, but Sievers's German accent was very distinct.

"Of course I'm sure." Sievers. His voice became softer. Benton strained but could not make out the words. Thalberg said something, then Sievers replied. "Not until Friday...make it...Wetzen...." Thalberg seemed angry and impatient. "...expecting a call from General Forman at nine o'clock. I'll tell him, but he won't be happy, I can assure you." Again Sievers's reply was unintelligible. Why is it that Americans always seem to talk louder? Benton wondered. "Well, see what you can do. Otherwise, Friday. I'll be at the Adler in Hamburg then I'll take the train to Lüneburg. Good night." Thalberg rose and left.

Benton paid for his drinks, put on his jacket and walked unhurriedly out. He could see Thalberg's car disappear around the corner, heading in the direction of the base.

He felt on the brink of a discovery. Now he knew he *had* to get onto the base.

He rushed back to the camp.

1900 hours

BENTON HUDDLED close to the fire to keep the dampness at bay, while Robbins showed him the map of the base again. Although he had been looking for him, he had seen no sign of Sievers returning to the encampment. Indeed, as far as he knew, Sievers had not been there at all.

Robbins pointed at the map. "Here, on the eastern boundary, is where we've made the breakthrough. One of our people is an electrical engineer, and he cut the fence and constructed a bypass in the circuit so there was no break in the electric current. It was a professional job and has been so well camouflaged that they still haven't found it. We expect them to, eventually, but for now we can still enter the base here. The people who were arrested had smuggled themselves in on a lorry, so Security had no reason to inspect the fence more thoroughly than usual."

He put a navy-blue stocking cap on his head and handed one to Benton. "Here, pull this down as low as you can, it will make you less noticeable."

They walked away from the fire. Staying several hundred yards from the fence, they moved parallel to it and kept as many bushes and trees between themselves and it as possible. Near the fence, on both sides, most of the plant life had been removed, but the sky was completely obscured by clouds and a light mist limited vision to less than twenty feet. Christopher wondered if he would ever see anything in England but clouds, for the sky had been obstinately overcast since his arrival. Still, at this moment, he was grateful for their cover.

They walked almost a mile before they turned north. The fence had made a right-angle turn. There seemed to be some sort of small structure, perhaps a guard booth, at the corner, but Christopher was unable to distinguish what it was through the mist.

"Do you know Ulrich Sievers?" Benton asked softly after a few minutes.

"Yes. He's one of the leaders of the German movement. He's often in England speaking at demonstrations. Have you met him?"

"No, but I've seen him twice." He was unsure whether he should confide in Robbins the conversation he had witnessed at the pub.

"The Germans hope to elect him this year to the Bundestag. He's been a very effective opponent of the government and his rising political star augurs well for the success of the antinuclear movement in Germany."

"Well, I saw him at Hyde Park yesterday and then again this afternoon in Greenham Common."

"Here? Today? No, he hasn't been here. I would've noticed."

Benton considered for a moment, then decided to plunge in. "He was talking with Colonel Thalberg at the pub."

Robbins, who had been leading the way, stopped so abruptly that Benton almost crashed into him.

"That can't be possible! Are you sure you know what Sievers looks like?"

"Yes. I saw him give a speech."

"And Thalberg? How do you know it was Thalberg?"

"Sievers greeted him by name. He was the passenger in the car we saw enter the base earlier today."

"Bloody hell. Fuckin' bloody hell." He leaned against a tree. "What're they up to? Sievers gives us so much advice about strategy. It's hard to imagine him as an informer, or worse..."

"But why would he allow himself to be seen here with Thalberg?"

"No one knows Thalberg here. I told you I had heard *of* him, but that's only because of my insatiable appetite for reading everything about the missiles. I doubt if most of our people here have ever heard of him. It was probably his first visit to the base.... I'm trying to think what Sievers could possibly be up to. Did you hear much of the conversation?"

"Very little. A word here and there, but not much I could understand. They spoke about doing something in Wetzen on Friday. And they mentioned Lüneburg."

"Lüneburg is a northern German city near the East German border."

"Yes, I thought so. Thalberg also said something about Garlstedt, but they're 'expecting it here.' "

"Hmmm. That's quite fascinating. Garlstedt is a major missile base in Germany. Maybe they're concentrating more missiles there than here, contrary to what has been announced, or perhaps...perhaps..." He paused, then slapped his hand against his thigh. "I think I know! They're going to run the launcher test there and not here. We're expecting it here. That must be it! Was there anything else? Think hard!"

"The only other fragment I overheard was something about Forman calling at nine o'clock. General Forman. Also, for what it's worth, I don't think Thalberg and Sievers are particularly fond of each other—they sounded very annoyed with each other."

"Forman. General Forman," Robbins mused aloud. "Forman. The name is definitely familiar. Not in connection with Greenham Common, though, but with Europe. I'll have to check that one out."

2100 hours

"I'VE GOT SOME awkward news for you, Colonel."

"Yes, General?"

"We've found Janssen's body."

"Body?"

"Yes. Shot. No sign of Benton. The Suffolk County police found Janssen this morning out on eastern Long Island."

"My God! Then Benton *is* after us. What could he possibly know? What did Marcus tell him!"

"We've run him through the computer, but there doesn't seem to be anything tying him in with Washington, or anyplace else for that matter. But that doesn't mean a goddamn thing. Any undercover service can feed a computer whatever biographical information they want to feed it, giving an agent whatever cover story they wish. We don't know who he's working for, if anyone. And personally I don't think he is an agent. If he was he would never have called you. But the story that comes out is that he was a radical activist during the sixties. Civil Rights. Anti-Vietnam. All that bullshit. He has a Ph.D. in English literature from the University of Pennsylvania, probably student deferments kept him from being drafted so he could afford the luxury of protest.

"Perhaps Marcus talked too much to him and it sparked some left-wing liberal urge to go up against the establishment. But that's only a guess. I'm wiring his passport photo to you right now. I think you should assume he's looking for you. He arrived in Brussels Thursday morning and made a connection on to London two hours later. We're not sure if he's running blind or on your trail. Be careful to keep yourself guarded. I've also issued a directive to Brussels to send out agents after him. Trace and terminate. He'll not be able to cross another border without discovery.

"Now, what's the news from Sievers?"

"He says he doesn't think his people will be ready until Friday at the earliest. I insisted they be prepared by Thursday. Frankly, I don't like his attitude. Such arrogance."

"You won't have to work with him much longer. Actually, the word today is that the test *will* be Friday. I don't think it will be moved up.

"If you're finished there I want you to go to Wetzen right away. There's nothing more for you to do until the missiles are in your hands. Besides, your presence there might encourage Sievers to speed up all preparations."

"I doubt if my presence would ever be an encouragement to Sievers. Anyway, I told him I'll be flying to Hamburg tomorrow and will contact him from the Adler."

"Good. Make sure his people have rehearsed the exercise carefully. Remember, timing is critical. It has to be done within ten minutes."

"Yes, sir."

"One last thing. Tell Matecki to call me tomorrow when he returns to Brussels. I'll be flying in in the morning. We'll go to Germany together from there. Good night."

"Good night."

Thalberg replaced the receiver and looked across the room at Colonel William Matecki.

ROBBINS CHECKED the time, then signaled Benton to follow. They crawled silently up to the fence. Robbins showed him where they had buried the jump wire that carried the electrical charge uninterrupted across the break in the fence.

Benton was impressed at the careful job. Even though he looked where Robbins pointed he couldn't see the break. Robbins took hold of the lowest strand of barbed wire with both hands. Christopher winced, expecting to see a flash of light and sparks, but nothing happened. Robbins tugged and the entire section of wire between two vertical posts came free. Each end had been secured into the post with something that looked like a draftsman's plumb. The ends were wrapped with transparent tape so they could be touching the wire on the fence without completing the electrical circuit.

The men lay flat and crawled through the narrow space. Robbins reconnected one end of the wire to one post, but left the other end free. "The guards won't be back here for half an hour. Even so, they won't be looking that closely for a loose wire. That should give us ample time. If we got separated you'd never find this spot alone unless you could see the free end of the wire. Don't forget. Do *not* touch the fence at any other point. The charge would be fatal."

They repeated the procedure at the inner fence. Christopher felt uncomfortably vulnerable while they remained in the area between the two fences. If a guard approached now, he thought anxiously, we'd ... Then they were through.

Colin also left one end of the wire on the inner fence dangling. Christopher looked around, getting his bearings. According to the map they were about a quarter of a mile behind the aircraft hangars. Another quarter of a mile to their left were the large hardened shelters where the mobile launchers and their missiles were housed. Next to these structures was the administrative headquarters. The barracks were on the far side of the base.

Cautiously they made their way through the mist toward the hardened shelters. Thank God for the mist, thought Benton. He hoped it would thicken into a full-fledged fog. Now that he was actually on the base, he began to feel, for the first time, a pounding in his temples and a queasiness in his stomach. Nervous tension mounted rapidly in him. Like a moth to a flame! This was a crazy, foolish thing to do!

They crept toward the shelters. Spotlights illuminated the large doors. The one they were approaching seemed to be still partially under construction. There was a slight gap on one side that had not been finished. Careful to stay entirely within the shadows, they hurried over to the opening.

Robbins peered in. Quickly he motioned Benton to look. "Christ!" he muttered.

At first Benton could see nothing, then in the glow from the floodlights streaking through a similar opening on the far side, he could see what looked like a mammoth tractor trailer.

A Tomahawk cruise missile mobile launcher. A Transporter-erector-launcher. A TEL.

Just one.

The rest of the building was empty, though there would be room for several more TELs once it was finished.

They ducked down and slid around toward the back of the structure.

"I don't believe it!" Robbins exclaimed. "They're bloody playing with us. That shelter should have several TELs by now, even if it still is under construction. This supports what you heard this afternoon. There will be no test here. It will be in Germany! That must be where they have the bulk of the launchers and missiles. That explains what Thalberg said. We're squandering our energy while the real action is elsewhere."

Footsteps.

Leather on pavement.

They both froze as they heard someone approach the front of the shelter. The sound of the military boots seemed to echo and magnify in the stillness of the night.

The lock on the front door to the shelter rattled. Then, the guard apparently satisfied, the footsteps began to recede in the direction of the next missile shelter.

Benton cautiously peered around the corner of the building. He could see a lone soldier walking away, his shadow long and sharply defined by the floodlights on the far side of the tarmac.

The two of them moved back to the other side and circled around behind the administration building. It was a low-lying prefabricated structure, hardly more than an elaborate Quonset hut.

The only lights coming from the building other than in the entranceway and hallways, came from the third window from the near corner. Benton motioned to Robbins that he would have a look in there. Robbins signaled that he would go around back and see if anything else was visible. "Be careful," he mouthed silently, then moved off.

Benton crouched and glided swiftly over to the window. It was low enough for him to look inside without difficulty.

It was a typical office. A gray metal desk with swivel chair, some shelving on the wall behind the desk, two filing cabinets and two straight-backed chairs.

Two men were talking. One of them held a glass in his hand and his broad back was to the window. He wore a uniform and his fair hair was in a crew cut. Had the window been open Christopher could have reached in and touched him. In spite of his proximity he could hear nothing of what they were saying. The man on the other side of the room said something. It was Thalberg. Benton strained to hear him, but no words were distinguishable.

Suddenly the man by the window turned to set down his drink. Benton ducked out of sight and fell to the ground, hugging the building. There was a slight crunch of gravel as he hit the ground. He held his breath. His heart was pounding. He could hear the blood pulsing through his throbbing temples.

COLONEL MATECKI POURED another Scotch for Thalberg and set it on the desk as Thalberg replaced the receiver. Carefully, he sliced a wedge of lime and dropped it into a glass. He poured Perrier over it for himself.

Thalberg glanced at him, baffled that a hardened officer like Matecki would prefer "designer water" to whiskey.

"It looks like it's Friday," he said.

"Good."

"Forman wants you to call him tomorrow when you arrive. He'll be accompanying you to Germany."

Matecki sipped his designer water. "That old worrywart is going to hamper me. He doesn't even need to be at the Garlstedt base."

"Well, there's nothing you can do about it except try to ignore him and do your part. You might be the operations chief, but he is, after all, the general. Besides he will have the authority to countermand Oster if Oster gets nervous and decides to send out a larger security force with the convoy. Forman will talk him into a minimal-security run test." He downed half the whiskey and leaned back in the desk chair.

"One other thing. Benton is in England. He killed Janssen."

Matecki raised his eyebrows. "I always thought Janssen was a cocky son of a bitch." He set down his glass. As he turned he thought he saw a movement in his peripheral vision. There was a slight crunch of gravel. He stepped quickly away from the window and around the desk to the door.

"Someone's outside the window," he whispered.

Thalberg blanched.

"Keep talking, I'm going out to investigate." Matecki removed his service automatic and undid the safety. Silently, he stepped out into the hallway, shut the door behind him and glided toward the outside door. He could hear Thalberg nervously babbling in the office.

BENTON LAY PARALYZED for a moment, then when he heard the voice resume he cautiously raised his head again. Thalberg was speaking and gesturing, looking toward the corner on the far side of the filing cabinet. The other man was not in his line of vision.

He strained his ears again. Something didn't feel right. It seemed as though Thalberg was talking louder than previously.

Suddenly he knew. He had been heard. It was a trap!

He started to back away from the window. There was a footstep on the gravel. He spun around and saw a flashing movement over his head. An arm was descending and there was the thud of metal striking his skull.

His head swam and the world went black.

THE FAR SIDE of the building was in darkness, so Colin Robbins moved back to where he had taken leave of Benton. He heard something heavy scraping on gravel. He froze. Carefully he lay prone and peered slowly around the corner. A man in uniform was dragging what looked like a body along the ground and in the door. It was Benton. He was sure of it.

Robbins sat up and leaned his back against the side of the structure. He took several deep breaths and waited a few minutes. Then he crept over to the window and looked in. The man had dragged Benton into the room, and another, in civilian clothes, rose to help him. They shut the office door and heaved Benton's limp form onto a chair against the wall. There was blood on the side of his head.

Robbins ducked below the level of the window.

MATECKI WENT THROUGH the intruder's pockets. There was no weapon, but he found an American passport.

"Christ," he said, handing it to Thalberg. "It's Benton."

Colonel Thalberg looked carefully at the passport and handed it back. "So this is the infamous Christopher Benton! He is a very persistent and resourceful man. Or so it seems."

Colonel Matecki straightened up and began slapping Benton's face. Benton tossed his head from side to side as a slight moan escaped from his lips. Then Matecki threw the remains of the Perrier into his face. Benton's eyes opened. The slice of lime slid down his chest.

"Well, Mr. Benton. Welcome to Greenham Common!" said Thalberg. "How good of you to drop in."

"Save your sarcasm for someone who appreciates it, Colonel Thalberg!" Benton snapped.

"Come, come. You can't afford to be discourteous. The Suffolk County police and the FBI are looking for you on a charge of murder. You know how the government gets riled when one of their own is murdered. You are in deep trouble, my friend."

Matecki leaned down so that his face was inches from Benton's. "Look, you shit, you're a dead man." Suddenly he lashed out with the back of his left hand and struck Benton full force across the face. Then he grabbed his throat. "There's no way you're going to prevent Garlstedt." He pushed him sharply back, tilting the chair so that it leaned against the wall. "Who are you working for," Thalberg asked, "or are you on your own?"

Benton glared at him and said nothing.

"Look, we know Marcus got you involved in this. What did he tell you?"

"Is that why you had him killed?"

Thalberg snorted. "Believe it or not, that was an accident. But fortunately his death tipped us off to your involvement." He paused. Then he decided to be more direct. Pieces of the puzzle began slipping into place. "Did he tell you he was training me how to program the missile's guidance system?"

Benton thought, they're talking too casually, revealing too much. It was obvious they were going to kill him. He looked around to see if there was a means of escape. Where was Robbins? Matecki's knuckles again smashed into his face, whipping his head to the side and almost knocking over the chair. Christopher felt his jaw to see if it had been dislocated.

"Yes," he lied.

"Good. Good. Now we're beginning to get somewhere." Thalberg paced a few steps then turned to him. "What do you know?"

He had to bluff them. "We know Ulrich Sievers is working with you," he said, "and that you're helping him to hijack a missile." He frantically looked around. Where the hell was Robbins?

Thalberg looked at Matecki, then slowly turned back to Benton. "One final question, Mr. Benton. How many people know of our plans?" His voice was like ice. "How many are with you?"

Benton remained silent. Again Matecki's fist. "No one. I'm alone."

"Don't lie to us!" Matecki struck him again. And again.

Thalberg restrained Matecki's hand. "Of course you are aware, Mr. Benton, that we cannot afford to let you live, but it will be less unpleasant for you if you cooperate."

ROBBINS OPENED the door carefully, praying it would not make any noise. There was no one about. He could hear loud voices at the end of the hall and now and then the slapping sound of flesh against flesh. He didn't need an active imagination to picture what was happening.

He eased down the hallway. There was a fire extinguisher hanging on the wall in front of him. He bent down to slide under it, then paused a moment. Cautiously, he lifted it from its bracket and cradled it in his arms.

He moved forward.

Christopher was looking around desperately, evaluating his chances of trying to run. Suddenly the door crashed open, and Colin Robbins stood outlined in the light from the hall. He leaped in before the others could react, and threw the fire extinguisher at Colonel Thalberg. It struck him on the right side of the neck as he tried to jump aside. Thalberg crumpled to the floor.

Matecki swung toward Robbins, his gun in his right hand. Benton sprang from the chair and hit Matecki with both fists on the back of the neck. The force of the blow pushed Matecki forward. The gun fired and a bullet splintered into the desk top. Benton kicked him with all his might in the small of the back and he went down to his knees, grunting as the air left his lungs.

Thalberg stirred.

"Let's go!" Robbins shouted, and he flew through the door. Benton was right behind him.

They tore across the gravel toward the missile shelters, toward the fences, toward darkness.

The door banged behind them and they could hear running footsteps. Then they heard movement coming from the direction of the aircraft hangar, too. A shot crashed harmlessly into the ground beside Benton. They ran faster.

Then another shot.

Christopher saw Robbins waver for a split second. He had been hit, but it looked as though he would keep going. Then Christopher thought the bullet must have missed Robbins. But then he fell heavily to the ground. Without a sound.

Benton stopped. There was a spot of blood in the center of Robbins's back. He turned him over. Colin Robbins's unseeing eyes stared up past him.

Christopher felt the blood drain from his body as he jumped to his feet and forced himself to run, his legs pumping, his lungs bursting, fear threatening to overpower him. He ran from the sounds of death and violence behind him. The sounds of madness and destruction. He wanted to vomit, to scream in rage, to turn and strike out at his pursuers. But he ran.

He arrived at the fence, fell to the ground and snaked through the narrow gap. It was impossible to hold his breath, he was gasping uncontrollably for air. So what, he thought, if he was electrocuted. But then he was through to the far side of the outer fence. And he was safe. He knew Thalberg and his companion would not try going under the fence. They would head for the gate.

He ran past the shrubs and bushes into the sparse clumps of trees, not caring how much noise he made. He ran straight to the encampment. All the while Colin Robbins's sightless eyes staring at him. Urging him on. Haunting him.

"JESUS CHRIST!" Matecki stared at the body. "It's not Benton. We've got to get him!" They rushed on past the spot where Christopher had gone through the fence. Finally, they arrived at the southeast guard post. All was in silence.

"Either he got through the fence or he's still on the base," Matecki said. Thalberg was having difficulty keeping up with him. His right arm hung limply at his side. Now and then he would rub the top of his right shoulder and the side of his neck.

"We've got to find the bastard. He has to be stopped!" He was afraid he was going to get hysterical.

They stopped. "Go back to the office and get the car," Matecki said coldly. "I'll walk along the fence and see if I can spot a break."

Thalberg hurried off while Matecki walked slowly and calmly along the fence, inspecting it. The mist had mostly dissipated, but the fence was still enveloped in darkness. Finally he saw the detached wire. He was surprised that the break had not set off the alarm, but then he suspected they must have jumped the connection. "Very professional," he muttered, fingering the loose end of the wire.

There was only one place Benton could have gone, he reasoned, and that was back to the encampment, to the cars. He'd head for London.

Matecki broke into a run and arrived back at the administrative building only seconds behind Thalberg.

There was a cluster of guards around Robbins's body. One of them trotted up to Matecki.

"What's happened here, Colonel?" he asked.

"Two of the protesters have broken through the fence. We fired on them, but one got away."

"My God, Colonel! You've killed one. There's going to be quite a row!"

"Look, Sergeant, if your squad had been more alert you could have prevented this break-in in the first place."

Thalberg pulled the car up alongside the two. Matecki turned and jumped into the passenger seat. "Notify the main gate we're coming through. We're going after him."

"Yes, sir!" The sergeant saluted angrily and ran off to the telephone.

Thalberg stepped on the gas and with the tires spinning, spitting up gravel, they lurched forward, skidding from side to side.

BENTON OPENED the car door, got in and fumbled with the ignition. His hands were trembling. "Goddamn it!" he said as the key dropped to the floor. He groped around and couldn't find it. He turned on the overhead light, but still was unable to see it. Finally, he located the key under the seat, turned off the light, started the car and pulled out of the parking area.

The encampment was relatively quiet and he tried not to race as he approached the turnoff onto the main road. As he arrived at the road he could hear the ringing of a telephone in the guardhouse at the entrance to the base on his left. He swung out and accelerated.

What to do? What to do?

They'll be expecting me to head for London, he thought, as he approached the village center. There was no alternative though, but to take the London road. He sped down the hedgerow-lined road looking alertly both for road signs where he might recognize the name of a town he could head for, and at the rearview mirror. That they would follow him he was certain. They could not afford to let him go.

The expression on Colin's face rose before his eyes again. His stomach ached. He was nauseated. Another death. The third one I'm responsible for. The next one could be mine. His mind was racing. He was nearly in a panic. He had to calm himself somehow. But he had to get away, had to get back to London, had to stop them. But how?

He tried piecing the fragments together.

A TEL complete with missiles was going to be hijacked. From what he had overheard he figured it would happen in Germany. Probably Garlstedt. Or Wetzen. Or possibly Lüneburg? He must find out what was in Wetzen and Lüneburg. Or, perhaps that was where the missiles would be hidden. They must have made elaborate preparations. The missiles would no doubt be heavily guarded. And they certainly would be difficult to conceal. Everything must be worked out with clockwork precision and there must be many people involved. How was he going to be able to stop them?

He thought of Gabriele. He would have to tell her. But then, she was close to Sievers. A chill went through him. Perhaps she, too, was involved? Well, there was one way to find out.

Headlights appeared in the rearview mirror.

He was already traveling more than fifty miles per hour on this winding country lane, but he increased his speed. The headlights were gaining on him. He hit sixty-five.

Vision was limited because the road curved so fre-
quently. The six-foot hedgerows on either side prevented
him from seeing around any of the bends that came with
ever-increasing speed as he flashed by. The conical beams of
his headlights reflected back at him.

Suddenly, the fields around the road widened and he
could just make out an intersection ahead. He turned
sharply to the right; the tires screeching a protest, the car
skidded, rather than turned, onto the new road. He increased speed further, hoping to be beyond the view of his
pursuers by the time they arrived at the intersection.

He thought he had lost them, then they appeared again in
the mirror. They had a more powerful car than his rented
Escort, and he knew he could never outrun them on a
straightaway.

Up ahead there was a wooded area on the right. He turned
off onto an unpaved lane and pressed the accelerator to the
floor. The lane, hardly more than a bridle path, wasn't made
for such velocity, and he was forced to slow down consid-
erably. Turning a sharp corner, he came without warning to
a gate blocking the road. He jammed on the brakes, stopping inches in front of the wooden fence.

"Shit!" He jammed the gearshift into reverse, spun
backward and pulled around. He headed back the way he
had come. If they had followed him they would meet head-
on. But they would not be expecting him to be coming toward them. He could use this to his advantage. He turned
off the headlights and slowed the car to a crawl. The lane
curved sharply to the left. He stopped.

He could see lights bouncing off the trees as the other car
approached at high speed. He placed one hand on the door
latch, ready to leap out. The other hand rested on the headlight switch. The high beams, he knew, were on. Suddenly
the car came into view only thirty feet ahead. He pulled the
switch. The other driver swerved as hard as possible to his

left and the car skidded to Benton's right. It hit two sap-
lings and, as if in slow motion, rolled over onto its side.
Benton had started to open the door, but as the other vehicle brushed by, he shifted into first and peeled out as fast as
possible.

It would take them some time, even if they were not injured, to get the car righted and back on the road in pursuit. He returned to the intersection and took the road in the
direction of Basingstoke and the A30 to London. He looked
at his watch. It was past midnight.

COLONEL MATECKI CRAWLED out through the open window. His head ached, but he was unhurt. He pulled Thalberg out.

"That bastard," Thalberg moaned. His shoulder was
stiffening up and he had an abrasion on his forehead.

They looked at the car for a moment, then in unison
pushed it easily enough right side up. But it took their combined efforts for more than fifteen minutes to get it untan-
gled from the bushes, over a tree stump and back onto the
lane. Even then it was facing the wrong way. Thalberg's
bruised shoulder was too painful to drive, so Matecki took
over and he had to back the car for almost a mile before
there was enough space to turn around. By the time they
were back on the road they knew it was hopeless to continue the pursuit.

"Once he's on the A4 or the A30, with a twenty-minute
head start, we'll never catch him," Matecki said through his
teeth. "I suggest we get back to London. We'll have to put
out an alert at all embarkation points through Interpol. The
moment he tries to leave the country, we've got him."

Thalberg nodded. He was in pain. He was angry. He was
frightened. And he blamed himself.

Everything rests on Benton now, he thought bitterly.
Everything.

CHAPTER FIVE

London

IT WAS AFTER 3:00 A.M. when Benton parked the car on Lyall Street in Belgravia. The pavement was damp and glistened in the stillness. There had been very little traffic and Lyall Street was hushed.

He stepped out of the Escort.

He had decided not to return to the hotel. It would be too easy for him to be traced there. He walked through the deserted streets down South Eaton Place past the elegant columned Regency houses of Belgravia and finally to Ebury Bridge Road. He turned left on Warwick Way and a few minutes later was on Alderney Street.

He rang Gabriele's bell. The minutes stretched out as he waited.

"Mein Gott!" she said the moment she saw him, a shocked expression on her face. "You look awful!" He stumbled slightly as he started up the steps. Suddenly he realized how utterly fatigued he was.

At the top of the stairs they entered the room and she locked the door behind them.

Ah, safe, he thought. Finally. He sat in the armchair without a word, as she went to the sink and ran some water.

A minute later she began washing the blood and dirt from his face, dabbing carefully at the split in his scalp where Matecki had hit him with the gun. He looked into her eyes as she fussed over him and he saw the concern in them.

Then he thought of Colin Robbins lying dead on the plain, and he knew he had to tell her everything. The vision of Colin Robbins held him. It would not fade. And he wept.

She cradled his head in her arms and let the washcloth fall to the floor. She said nothing. But she held him.

After his sobs had subsided, she got him to stretch out on the yellow bedspread, took off his shoes, then went to the bathroom down the hall and drew a hot bath. She returned and helped him to his feet. They walked across the hall and entered the bath. Steam was rising and the cracked mirror was fogged over. She helped him undo his belt and removed his clothes. She tested the water with her hand, adjusted it, then steadied him as he stepped in.

He lay back, feeling the ache in every muscle of his body. The tension was slowly leaving him, but the horror was locked in his mind. He stared at the naked light bulb on the ceiling. Plaster was cracked and crumbling around it.

She sat on the edge of the tub, and soaped up his back, massaged shampoo into his hair.

"Gabriele," he finally managed to say without his voice breaking, "you're wonderful."

"Shhh," she said. "We'll get you cleaned up, then you can tell me all about it."

While he was rinsing off she went back to her room, turned up the gas fire and returned with her terry-cloth robe. "Put this on. It'll be tight, but it will help dry you, and keep you warm."

He dashed across the chilly hall behind her and into the room.

She smiled as he sat down on the floor in front of the heater, drying his hair. "You look so comical in that robe!" She put her hand to her mouth to stifle a giggle.

He looked down and saw his knobby knees protruding from the far-too-short robe. It had opened and his pale legs were visible. His shoulders were tightly confined and the sleeves only extended slightly below his elbows.

He smiled, too. He leaned against the foot of the bed and looked at her. Then he began the story from the beginning.

He told of David Marcus's accident in Philadelphia and the attempt on his own life. He told of New York and Janssen and running away. Of going to Brussels and calling NATO headquarters, then to England, and of how he got more involved each step of the way. And then he spoke of meeting her friend Colin Robbins and how helpful he'd been, and how they'd got on the base and he'd learned more about the plot. Then he told her how Robbins had rescued him, but was shot doing so.

She rose and began pacing the floor. "Those pigs," she said, trying to steady her breaking voice. She sat on the edge of the bed after a minute. She was in control of herself, but the shock was still there, lurking below the surface.

She reached down and began rubbing Christopher's shoulders. "We've got to tell Ulrich. He'll help us."

Benton turned to her, and took her left hand in his. "There's one more thing," he said, looking carefully at her. He had no choice. He *must* tell her. He *must* trust her. He believed he could trust her. He looked into her eyes. "Sievers is involved, too."

She stared incredulously at him. She swung off the bed and sat opposite him on the floor, held both his hands tightly. "That *cannot* be!"

Benton nodded. He told her of the meeting he had witnessed between Sievers and Thalberg and of the few words he had overheard.

"The way I've figured it out," he explained in conclusion, "is that they're going to hijack the missiles in Germany. Garlstedt is a missile base, right?"

She nodded.

"And the Adler? What is the Adler?"

"It's a famous hotel in Hamburg. Both Hamburg and Garlstedt are in Northern Germany."

"They'll get the missiles along with the launchers. How they'll do this I don't know. But Sievers has people lined up in Germany who will help. They've been instructed how to arm and program them. I don't know exactly what they plan to do when they have them, whether they're serious or not in using them. Perhaps Sievers is going to set up some people in the movement, who will be caught. One thought I had was that they'll hide the missiles with a core group of anti-missile people and then detonate them. That would serve the double function of discrediting the opposition, as well as killing many of them."

She stared uncomprehendingly.

"Lüneburg and Wetzen are important, too. Perhaps that's where they're going to conceal the missiles once they have them."

"Perhaps," she suggested, "Lüneburg is the target!"

"No, surely they wouldn't destroy a West German city?"

"Look, if they explode any nuclear missile in such a densely populated area as West Germany, then they might as well hit a city. The devastation will be felt throughout the country."

She put her head in her hands. *"Oh Gott, oh Gott,"* she mumbled. "This is so unbelievable, yet still it is just the sort of plot the CIA is capable of hatching. But Ulrich! It's incredible that he could be taking part in this. But the more I think about it, knowing him as well as I do, the more logical it seems. I knew him, yet I did not know him...."

"I think," Benton said, "that the fact that Sievers is involved would indicate that neither the American government nor NATO are involved. It's probably just a few hard-line anti-Communist military people who are behind the whole thing. Disgruntled colonels. Why else would they need to hijack the missiles or even need Ulrich's help? So

maybe we should just go to the American embassy and ask
to speak to the CIA? They could stop it.''

"We've got to do something, I agree. But I'm not convinced that your government isn't behind this. Of course the
missiles would have to be hijacked. They have to make it
look that way. So I don't think we can exclude the Americans or NATO from complicity. And if they are indeed involved, what do you think our pathetic appeal to the CIA
will result in? They've killed already. Our lives will be considered insignificant. No, we can't go to them. At least not
yet.''

"This isn't Russia!" Benton said. "They just don't kill
you for going to the CIA.''

She looked at him and sighed.

He looked away, feeling oddly naive.

"Then what do you suggest we do?" he said, exasperated. "What *can* we do?"

"We're going to thwart them, then expose them! We'll go
to Germany. We'll see if we can track down Colonel Thalberg at the Hotel Adler, then we'll go to Bremen and enlist
the aid of some friends of mine there. They used to be a very
radical group, but have since toned down their ideas about
violence. They're trying to change society without terrorist
tactics, but they know from experience how the terrorist
operates. They'll help us.''

3 January, 0500 hours
THE EASTERN SKY, Colonel Matecki noticed, standing at the
window of their suite in the London Hilton, had not yet begun to lighten with the approaching dawn. He put down the
telephone and walked through the doorway to the adjoin-
ing room.

Thalberg was in bed, already lightly snoring. There was a
bandage on his forehead. Matecki sat in the bedside chair
and touched Thalberg's shoulder.

"Oww!" Thalberg jerked awake. He rubbed his shoulder.

"Sorry, Sam," Matecki apologized, looking away. "I just wanted to tell you I've alerted Security. They've contacted Interpol and have issued an order to all embarkation points in the British Isles. Benton's photo is already being circulated. So we can get some sleep. We'll be notified the minute he is spotted. I've left orders that he's to be held in isolation and not questioned until we get there."

Thalberg grunted in acknowledgment and rolled over.

Matecki rose, turned out the lights and went back to his own room. In spite of the hour he did three sets of sixty sit-ups and then showered before climbing into bed.

0530 hours

"CHRISTOPHER," SHE SAID, "we've got to get some sleep." She got up and turned down the fire, set the alarm clock for noon and pulled back the blankets and sheets.

"I still haven't got used to these *verdammte* blankets," she said, untucking them at the feet. "When are the English ever going to learn that nothing beats a good eiderdown?" She turned to him and grabbed his arm, pulling him toward the bed.

He looked at the single bed. "I'll be okay. I'll stretch out here on the floor."

"Don't be silly." She laughed, pushing him back down on the bed. The bathrobe flew open, and he tried modestly to cover himself. "Come on." She pulled the robe off and threw the blankets over his naked body.

"Ahhhh," he murmured, sinking his head back into the pillow. He looked at her as she pulled off her pullover and blue jeans. She was wearing a woolen undershirt and briefs. No brassiere. She took off her underclothes and he was surprised at how full her breasts were. Her skin was soft and inviting, in spite of the goose bumps that covered her body, making the golden hair on her legs bristle and stand on end.

Quickly she extinguished the light and crawled in next to him, cuddling up close. He put his arms around her and rested his head on her breasts. She kissed him gently on the forehead and slowly pressed her fingers into the muscles of his back.

"Oh, that feels good," he murmured as she rubbed his back lightly with her thaumaturgic hands. Within minutes he was asleep.

She felt warmth rising from within her, slowly and sensuously encompassing both her and him. She felt the warmth flowing through her hands into him and back again.

She pulled him closer still.

And then she slept.

1200 hours

SUNLIGHT WAS STREAMING in around the edges of the shade. She awoke quickly when the alarm sounded, and turned it off. She looked at him, his hair spread out on her pillow. The blanket had fallen back, exposing his shoulders and part of his chest. He looked so good to her, so innocent in his sleep. Like a child. And yet not a child. A man. But a man with much softness to him. She leaned over and kissed his eyelids, the tips of her nipples just barely brushing across his hairless chest.

"Guten Morgen." She smiled at him as he opened his eyes.

He stretched. "Ohhhh." He looked at her, her long blond hair cascading around them, sunlight catching here and there in the strands. "Good morning." He opened his arms and she came into them, hugging him tightly. Then she leaned on her side.

"Time to get up. We have much to do."

"This is the first time I've seen sunlight all week," he said.

"Must be an auspicious omen." She smiled, springing to her feet.

He watched her move as she put the kettle on and began rummaging through a drawer for her clothes. She had broad shoulders and very boyish, muscular legs, but her breasts quickly contradicted the boyish impression. The hair under her arms was, like her eyebrows, quite a bit darker than that on her head, but her pubic hair was lighter, almost platinum. He thought it remarkable how many different colors emanated from her. His enjoyment of her was, however, speedily ended when he thought of yesterday.

Yesterday.

He got out of bed and began dressing. Most of the caked mud on his jeans and jacket had dried and he scraped as much as possible into the wastebasket.

"We should get you some new clothes so you look less conspicuous," Gabriele suggested.

"I have some new things at the hotel. But I think it would be wise to avoid going there."

She nodded. "We'll leave here soon. It's Tuesday. The *Prinz Hamlet* leaves every Tuesday for Hamburg. We'll get you some clothes and stop at the bank.

"We catch the train at Liverpool Street Station for Harwich. If I remember correctly, we need to catch the two-thirty train in order to get to Harwich in time."

The kettle was boiling. "Do you think you can make tea while I get dressed?" she asked.

"Sure."

"Remember how I showed you? We've got to start the day with a 'proper' cup of tea." She laughed.

CHAPTER SIX
The *Prinz Hamlet*

LIVERPOOL STREET STATION was a huge, decaying Victorian edifice. It was in the City of London, beyond the Bank of England and the stock exchange, beyond Threadneedle Street, where the elegant affluence of the economic center of the British empire had metamorphosed into the more plebeian cockney district of east London.

Gabriele had withdrawn all the money from her bank account, and after Christopher had returned the rental car, they stopped at Marks and Sparks for a new pair of jeans for him. He also bought a nylon anorak that was both lightweight and warm.

There were crowds of Germans waiting on the platform at Liverpool Street. The gate was still closed and they were endeavoring to maintain the semblance of an English queue, but the moment the train pulled in and the gate to the platform opened, the queue disintegrated and elbows began flying indiscriminately as passengers pushed their way on, hoping for prime seats.

Benton smiled to himself, imagining what the English must think of this display of Teutonic barbarism.

They were swept along amid a sea of *Bundeswehr* surplus parkas and yellow ponchos. German voices were chatting and complaining *über alles*.

"God, I hate German tourists," Gabriele expostulated as they were shoved from behind.

"See," Christopher said, laughing, "the Americans don't have the monopoly on being obnoxious!"

The crowded ride took little more than an hour as the train sped across the coastal fields of Essex. Their compartment was filled with smoke the whole time, and though Benton was an occasional pipe smoker, the cigarette-laden air had given him a headache by the time they disembarked at Harwich.

As the crowds began slowly filing through the immigration checkpoint at the dock prior to boarding the *Prinz Hamlet*, Benton became concerned.

"Gabriele," he said, "they're bound to be expecting me to head for Germany. What if they have an alarm out for me? What if I'm recognized?"

She smiled. "We radicals are always prepared! I have a surprise for you." She took two German passports out of her bag, looked at them carefully and gave him one.

"Uli always had me keep two extra passports that he had made in case he needed to leave the country under an alias. I think we can get by with this one, especially seeing as it's so crowded and the people are impatient. The officials will be looking for someone with an American passport, anyway."

She also gave him a pair of wire-framed glasses. "Put these spectacles on."

"Christ! I can barely see through them." He slid them down his nose and looked over them at the photo on the passport. It was Sievers with a full beard, glasses and beret. The baldness was not visible but the hair reached his shoulders.

She saw him looking quizzically at the picture. "They'll think you shaved and got a haircut. Just keep the glasses on and if you talk try it with a German accent."

"I vill dooo zat." He laughed. "But shit, I'm nervous."

They were nearing the counter. An official walking down the line was handing out embarkation cards that had to be filled out. Benton wrote in the name and address that were on the phony Sievers passport. Again he felt his stomach quiver the closer they got to the immigration officer.

Finally, they were at the counter. Gabriele took his passport and put it down in front of the officer along with hers, and the embarkation cards.

He glanced at their faces and then at the passports. "Traveling together?"

"Yes," said Gabriele.

Christopher heard an American accent at the counter to their right. He glanced over to see the immigration officer holding an American passport in his hand and comparing it with something under his desk top. It looked like a photograph. He stamped the passport, handed it back to the American student and waved him on.

"Pardon?" Benton said, looking at the officer, realizing, too late, that he had been asked a question and had not been listening.

"I said you should get a new passport photo now that you no longer have a beard," the man said with some impatience.

"Oh, *ja*, yes," said Christopher.

The man looked at him. Benton's eyes appeared larger than normal, magnified by the glasses. Then he looked again at the passport and then—oh shit! thought Christopher—he looked under the desk top.

The official stamped the passports and handed them back. "I think you look better with the beard, Herr Müller, if you don't mind my saying so," he said with a slight smile. Then he waved them through.

As they passed on they didn't dare look at each other. Benton was half expecting an alarm to be sounded, or his name to be shouted.

Nothing.

They headed up the gangplank, which swayed slightly as the ship rose with the movement of the sea. Clouds seemed to be gathering to the northeast.

"I thought I was going to have a heart attack," Benton said, as they arrived on deck.

"You! God, when you were looking away and didn't answer him I thought we had had it. But then he probably thought you had difficulty with English. *Ach so*, now we can breathe again."

They found the purser's office and booked a cabin. Then they sought out the cabin, which was amidships and inside. It was small. No porthole. Bunk beds, washstand and a tiny lavatory.

Gabriele set her pack on the floor. "I need a drink," she said, "let's go up to the bar."

He followed her out and up a narrow flight of stairs. The bar was already packed with people. Many had thrown their packs in corners or were actually spreading out sleeping bags on the benches along the walls.

They bought two bottles of Newcastle Brown Ale and walked out on deck. A gust of wind hit them forcefully as they stepped out to the railing. Behind them, despite the cold and wind, a few hearty souls were piling up their rucksacks and rolling out their sleeping bags.

"Most German young people travel as cheaply as possible," Gabriele explained. "They would never think of the luxury of a cabin, even if they could afford one—which a surprisingly large number of them can. They travel deck class. In summer you can hardly walk out here with all the sleeping people strewn all over."

They braced themselves against the wind and walked to the stern railing.

A last few stragglers were rushing up the gangplank as men on the dock prepared for casting off. The clouds seemed to be gathering more and more swiftly. Soon it would be dark.

The gangplank was hoisted away. The ropes were cast off, and as the ship inched away from the dock, two long blasts of its horn filled the air.

Swiftly they sailed eastward. A flock of sea gulls flew above, keeping pace with the ship, darting ahead, then floating lazily behind, diving into the sea and soaring up again with fish, or pieces of bread in their beaks, fragments from travelers' picnic lunches. Christopher thought of the sea gulls on Long Island after he had turned Janssen's gun on him. He had pulled the trigger. He was a murderer, even if it was in self-defense. And now, he thought, as they watched the land recede and the North Sea gather them up, he had entered an entirely new life. There would be more death. More violence. And perhaps he would not survive. He looked over at Gabriele.

There was no turning back.

As England became fainter and more distant, blending into the steel gray of the sea, they finished the ale and went below.

1800 hours
THE WAITING LOUNGE for continental departures at Heathrow was crowded with people.

Colonel Thalberg's Lufthansa flight to Hamburg would not be departing for another two hours. But Colonel Matecki's Sabena flight to Brussels had already been announced.

Matecki returned to the bar, where Thalberg was nursing his third whiskey. He looked disdainfully at the glass, but made no comment. Damn it, he wished his colleagues didn't drink so much. How were they going to keep their senses sharpened and their minds functioning one hundred percent for the next several days? And we need at *least* one hundred percent!

"Interpol still insists there's been no sign of him," Matecki said. "Of course vigilance will be maintained at this level for the next several days. If they do apprehend him I'll be over on the first plane. Security has given Interpol a cover story about him being a terrorist."

"Are you sure he'll try to leave England by conventional means? What about him hiring an airplane, or slipping across the channel on a private launch?"

"If he eludes us and arrives in Germany we've already notified the German Bundespolizei that he's an extremely dangerous terrorist. They'll be prepared and willing to shoot on sight. I've already called Sievers. You can give him the details when you arrive in Lüneburg. Sievers will know what to do if he turns up."

The final boarding call for Matecki's flight was announced. He picked up his briefcase and nodded to Thalberg. He didn't shake his hand, but walked out of the bar and through the gate to his flight.

Thalberg looked at his watch, finished off his whiskey and ordered another.

2100 hours

THEY HAD A SOGGY wiener schnitzel and *Spätzle* with lukewarm beets in the dining room, then went to the cabin. The swell had increased greatly, and it was not altogether improbable that they might encounter stormy weather before dawn.

"We have about ten hours ahead of us, you'd say?" Christopher asked, ducking down the companionway.

"Yes. Depending on the wind and the sea—usually it takes a little longer in winter." She unlocked the door to the cabin.

Christopher sat on the lower bunk and immediately stretched out. "I just had a wave of nausea," he said. "It always happens to me at sea, but when I lie down it passes."

She laughed. "Don't tell me I'm going to have to take care of you again tonight." She stood with her legs slightly apart and her hands resting on her hips.

Benton thought of Errol Flynn and old sailing vessels filled with swashbuckling buccaneers. "You're a strong woman, aren't you." He smiled. It was less a question than a statement. Her blue eyes deepened in color and seemed to sparkle. He felt a wave of tenderness and longing for her sweep over him.

Gabriele took off her shoes, then bent down and undid his. They clunked to the steel floor. A moment later, she climbed into the upper bunk, while he undressed and crawled under the blankets.

"Jesus, this is a tight fit!" she exclaimed. She jumped back to the floor. "Move over," she ordered.

"Move over! Where to? I'm already touching the wall."

She removed her clothes rapidly, lifted the blanket and lay on top of him. She laughed when he started to protest. "How else can two people stay in one bed when it's as narrow as this?"

"You have your own!" he said not too seriously.

"Oh, Christopher," she said, still laughing. Then, thrusting her hands down, she began softly rubbing his thighs.

He put his arms around her. Her entire body seemed to press into his. She looked into his eyes and then very delicately, at first, began kissing his face. Then she opened her mouth and covered his.

He opened his mouth, responding to each of her movements, while running his hands down over her buttocks and feeling the warmth between her thighs. She felt deliciously moist.

They maneuvered onto their sides and he began kissing her breasts, running his hand through the juices flowing through the soft hair as she spread her legs. She rolled back on top of him and guided him into her.

"Ohhhh," she sighed, "you feel so incredibly good." And she began moving, arching her back with her hands pressing against his chest. He touched the hard points of her nipples with his fingertips, then raised his head so he could dart out the tip of his tongue against them as they moved back and forth, toward him, then tantalizingly away from him.

She was looking into his eyes the first time she came, but though they seemed to plead for him to come with her, he held back. And then he began moving, slowly, always slowly, without increasing speed.

Her orgasms mounted and she began tossing her head, letting the strands of blond hair whip out around him, over his face, over the pillow, up to the bottom of the bunk above.

And she moved faster.

And her hair lashed at him, softly, sensuously, promisingly.

And he reached out for the touch of her, the smell of her, the taste of her.

"Oh...please...come...now..." she moaned, arching her back and staring deeply into his eyes, striving to swim into their depths. And, as if on command, he felt his response flow and throb, up and out of him, the walls of her vagina contracting around him, swallowing him up, until there was nothing left but the motion of the North Sea.

They awoke several times during the long night and rocked to the motion of the sea and their bodies.

And they slept. Their dreams intermingled, carrying them to the other shore of the world within, just as the *Prinz Hamlet* carried them in the world outside.

CHAPTER SEVEN

Hamburg

2330 hours

THE COLONEL'S TAXI pulled up in front of the Adler Hotel. He hurried through the drizzle and up the steps to the imposing entrance of the hotel, the damp January night chilling him.

Thalberg went directly to his room after leaving a message at the desk to be awakened at 7:00 a.m.

He unpacked his one bag, took a shower, opened the bottle of Johnnie Walker he had picked up at the duty-free shop in Heathrow and poured a stiff drink. Then he got into bed and dialed a telephone number in Wetzen.

"Thalberg here," he said.

"You have arrived in Germany, sir?" a woman responded.

"Yes. I'm at the Adler, room 423. I'll be coming down tomorrow. Tell Sievers to have me met at the Lüneburg Station at 1325."

"Very good, sir. We are all eagerly awaiting your arrival."

The line went dead.

He took another sip of his drink and turned on the television, watched headline news on the Turner network for a few minutes.

"Christ," he muttered to himself, "this is worse than reading *USA Today*."

Frustrated, he flicked around the channels. For a few minutes he watched *Annie Hall*, but somehow, Woody Allen dubbed in German just didn't sound very funny.

He switched off the set and got out of bed. He was dead tired, but too keyed up to sleep. For more than half an hour he paced, nursing his Scotch, before finally and mercifully exhaustion overcame him. He collapsed on the bed, and fell asleep.

4 January, 0800 hours

THE *PRINZ HAMLET* had sailed past the lighthouse near Cuxhaven at the mouth of the Elbe and proceeded at a slow steady pace on the smooth waters of the river. Though it was very cold there was no ice forming on the river. Hamburg's pollution kept the water temperature well above the freezing point. Most of the passengers had gathered their luggage together and were milling about on deck watching the flat north German farmland sliding by. Light snow covered many of the fields stretching out on either side of the river, but as the ship neared Hamburg the snow covering gradually dissipated.

Gabriele had been lying awake for more than half an hour. She was leaning on one elbow, looking at Christopher, now and then touching his face and neck with her fingertips.

He opened his eyes then closed them again. ''Gabriele,'' he whispered and snuggled closer.

''Christopher...Christopher... I like you so much more when you become involved.''

He looked at her.

''Don't worry,'' she said with a laugh, ''I'm not making claims on you. Not yet at least. I mean, involved with life. You've made some important decisions. You've decided you've got to do something to stop these people. That's political involvement. And you've decided to trust me. Who knows—'' her eyes twinkled, the lines at the corners of them deepening perceptibly ''—maybe they were good decisions.''

"Well, I don't know about that," he said, caressing her side with his left hand.

"It will be a formidable task to go against Sievers and Colonel Thalberg. We don't even know exactly what it is we're really up against. But one thing I do know..." She paused, then continued, "And I want you never to forget it—no matter what happens..." She kissed him lightly. Her breath smelled of him. "You *can* trust me. I know myself well enough to be able to say that with great conviction."

He looked into her eyes. How open she is! he thought. And how she has opened to me!

Inexplicably he could feel tears welling up in him, but he suppressed them. "It seems there's so much more I want to say to you, but I don't know where to begin."

"No need to now. We'll have plenty of time."

"What I do know is that you're showing me a part of myself that I had not known before... and that..."

"I know," she said, touching her fingers to his lips, "I know, you've opened me, too."

They embraced and slowly, sensuously and passionately fell, again and again, into each other.

THE SHIP SHUDDERED twice against the pilings as it docked at the pier. They got up hastily and dressed.

They went up the companionway and out onto the deck. The spires and rooftops of Hamburg could be seen in the distance as they joined the sleepy crowd disembarking sluggishly along the gangplank.

"We'll go through customs the same way as before. Let me do the talking. If you have to speak, pretend you have a cold. In spite of all the rumors of German efficiency, most of these entry points are really only casually supervised.

There are just far too many people crossing into West Germany every hour for them to be as vigilant as they like to pretend. Usually when I'm driving between the Netherlands or Belgium and Germany, there is no one at all along the autobahn checkpoints. So, don't worry. About all they will ask you is *'Haben Sie etwas zu verzollen?'* That means do you have anything to declare. Just say *nein*. You can do that, can't you?''

"Of course. I did have a year of German in college, so some of it does make sense to me."

"Okay, let's go. God, you look great. Can't you look more worn out and exhausted?''

"I thought I *was* exhausted after last night, after what you made me go through!" He laughed.

"On the contrary, boy, you look like you've had the best night you've ever had!"

"I have. I have!"

She laughed. "Oh, Christopher."

It made his stomach jump to hear the musical lilt her German accent gave his name.

"Just try to look like you've been seasick all night. That will psychologically encourage them to push you through faster. They don't want you to vomit on their orderly uniforms, do they?''

"I'll see if I can oblige."

They moved down the gangplank and walked across the dock to the customs station. Inside the hall there was chaos—or at least so it first appeared. But well-formed lines did exist at each counter where the customs and immigration officials held court.

Again, the closer they got to the official, the more nervous Christopher felt. He looked over at Gabriele. So cool, he thought, so unaffected by all this. As if this were all a dream. As if last night had never happened. Last night. God! He had responded to her needs in a way he had not thought possible. Never, in all his experience, had he felt this responsive to someone, this close, this open, this vulnerable.

She glanced over at him and saw him staring at her. She smiled. He has such depth, such power, she thought, and he doesn't even know it!

The official was having an altercation with the couple in front of them. Come on, come on, Benton willed them to hurry up. It was the delay now that was becoming excruciating.

Finally the others moved on. Christopher tried his best to look ill as Gabriele handed over their passports. The man looked at the photos and then at them.

"Was ist los, Herr Müller?" he asked.

Christopher didn't understand, but he knew he was being addressed.

Gabriele answered. *"Er war seekrank. Sein Magen macht ihm immer noch Schwierigkeiten."*

"Ach so," he said and stamped the passports. Then, as they passed by, he grabbed Christopher's shoulder. *"Moment, bitte!"*

Christopher froze, the blood draining from his face.

The officer reached into a drawer under the countertop. *"Nehmen Sie zwei von diesen Pillen. Bitte."* He opened a tubular bottle, tapped two pills into his hand and offered them to Christopher.

Christopher held out his hand and pocketed the pills. *"Danke,"* he replied and smiled in relief.

The man touched the tip of his cap and turned back to the line.

They walked out of the building and stood for a moment at the curbside.

Benton sighed.

"Christopher, you don't know how glad I am that that ordeal is over!"

"Me, too. I thought I'd die when he grabbed my shoulder. What are these anyway?" he asked, showing her the pills.

"Thomapyrin. A painkiller like aspirin. I told him you had been seasick. He was actually very kind and sympathetic. The thing that worried me, though, was whether they would accept the Müller passport. But obviously, Ulrich had a very professional job done. He really must have access to top forgers."

Christopher's eyes were wide open. "*You* were *not* sure?" he asked, astounded. "After you told me not to worry! Holy shit! I thought you were as cool as a cucumber."

"Cucumber?"

"An expression. An idiom again."

"I don't know if I like being compared to a cucumber! *Eine Gurke!*" She laughed.

"If I had known you were as nervous as I, I would have swum ashore!"

"That's exactly why I was so cool as your cucumber," she replied.

The relief of having passed through customs washed over him. He thought he would burst out laughing.

She grabbed his arm. "Let's get a taxi to the city center. We could check into the Adler for a few hours before we start looking for Thalberg. My cucumber is heating up fast!"

"Aha! Nudge, nudge, wink, wink, eh?" He thought of Monty Python.

She looked at him with a puzzled expression on her face. "You are a strange one, my Christopher." Her eyes were shining. "*My* Christopher."

His stomach did a somersault.

They sat holding hands in the beige taxi. The Mercedes easily absorbed the bumps from the cobblestones and trolley tracks that seemed to predominate on every street. Many of the houses and stores they passed were simple gray structures. Most of central Hamburg had been utterly destroyed during the war, and these uninspired *Neubau* dwellings made up the bulk of the architecture. Along the *Alster* some of the old shops had survived, and there was much charm to their arched fronts and to the promenade along the *Alster* itself.

Near the *Rathaus* Gabriele had leaned forward to the driver. *"Zum Hotel Adler, bitte."*

"Ach, ja." He glanced at them in the rearview mirror as if to judge their financial capabilities. "But perhaps you would like a cheaper hotel?" he asked.

"No, we want something really elegant!" Gabriele replied and she sat back and laughed.

The driver shook his head. They looked like students to him, but he supposed they were teachers. How else could they afford *das Adler*?

He stopped the car in front of the hotel. They paid the fare and stepped out.

"It's beautiful," said Benton, staring at the medieval facade.

"It's new," Gabriele told him over the noise of a trolley rattling along the street nearby. "Most of it was destroyed during the war. They rebuilt the facade to look like the original building, probably with whatever they could find of the original stones in the rubble."

They walked up the wide stairs and entered the lobby. To their right was a bank of elevators—brass doors surrounded by marble slabs. Oriental carpets were spread sumptuously throughout, with small groupings of eighteenth-century couches and armchairs placed around them. The entire room was dotted with palm trees and in one corner was a well-groomed display of exotic plants. To the left was the entrance to the hotel dining room, from which breakfast noises discreetly clinked and echoed. Straight ahead was the main desk.

Gabriele took his hand and started for the check-in counter.

He turned to her as one of the elevators beyond her opened. "Gabriele," he started to say. Suddenly he yanked her arm and pulled her back beyond a pillar. "Shhh..." he hissed, as she started to protest.

There were two palm trees next to the pillar, and he cautiously peeked through the branches. The thought of Tarzan flashed through his mind. The man he had seen step out of the elevator had arrived at the front desk. Yes. He was sure of it.

It was Colonel Thalberg.

He looked around frantically for more effective concealment.

"What is it?" Gabriele asked.

"I must hide!" He motioned with his head toward the desk. "Take a good look at the balding man at the desk. It's Colonel Thalberg. If he sees me, it's all over."

She looked through the palm leaves.

He thought about hastening into the restaurant, but it was possible Thalberg might head in there, too. It would be a cul-de-sac; he would be spotted.

She turned to him. "Sit here and don't even glance in his direction." She pushed him into an armchair with its back toward the desk. "Here." She picked up a magazine that was lying on a tea table and thrust it into his hands. "I'm going to have a closer look."

"Be careful."

"Don't worry, he doesn't even know I exist."

She wandered over to the desk. He could hear her ask the clerk a question, then the sound of footsteps, the colonel's footsteps, clacking against the marble floor. Hard leather against marble. Gabriele was talking to the concierge. The footsteps grew louder as they neared Benton. Christopher stared at *Der Spiegel* magazine, facing away from the sound.

He could see Thalberg's legs peripherally to his left as the man passed him. There was no hesitation. Thalberg continued walking to the front entrance. Benton lowered his head farther into the magazine in case the colonel turned back, but he didn't. The doorman opened the door and Thalberg stepped outside.

Gabriele touched his shoulder and he jumped. "We've got to follow him," she said urgently. "He's obviously preoccupied. He didn't look at me when I got to the desk, but still we must take precautions. You wait here for a minute. We can't risk him seeing you. After I get to the door, follow me, I'll signal you somehow."

She hurried to the door. After she had passed through, he stood up casually and followed.

Thalberg was just entering a taxi as she arrived at the door. She ran down the steps and hailed the next one in line. Looking back, she saw Christopher at the top of the steps and waved to him. He raced down to her and followed her into the cab.

Their taxi eased out into the traffic about five car lengths behind Thalberg.

"When we get to his destination," she said, "you stay behind again until I signal you."

He nodded in agreement.

Gabriele took an address book out of her shoulder bag, ripped a blank page out of the back and wrote a name and address on it. As the taxi zigged and zagged through the jumble of crowded one-way streets, she said, "If for any reason I have to follow him alone because the risk is too great that he would see you, and if we should get separated, go to Bremen and contact Eckhardt Schlegel." She handed him the paper. "He's very active in the Bremer Bürger Initiative and has many contacts in the various antinuclear groups of the area. He's often organized demonstrations at Garlstedt and Brokdorf. He's a good friend and will help you. Also, I will be able to contact you through him.''

He looked at the address, folded it and put it in his shirt pocket.

She also gave him some of the deutsche marks she had got in London.

The taxi stopped at the train station. The colonel was just emerging from the cab parked in front of theirs. He glanced around, then walked into the station. Gabriele leaned forward and asked the driver to wait. Then she got out and followed Thalberg.

Three minutes elapsed. Benton was getting fidgety.

Five minutes. He wanted to go after her. Protect her. But . . . if he was seen . . .

Seven minutes. He looked at his watch. I'll give her three more minutes, he thought.

The driver was tapping his fingers on the steering wheel impatiently. He said something. Benton shrugged.

Suddenly Gabriele appeared, breathless, at the window. "Let's go," she said. Christopher let out a breath and jumped out while she paid the driver.

"I stayed well behind him, so he wouldn't notice me," she announced. "He bought a ticket on the 12:47 to Lüneburg. We've got five minutes to get to the train." She brandished two tickets and gave him one.

They pushed through the crowds and downstairs onto track 3. "Stay toward the rear of the platform," she ordered. "He's traveling first class, so there shouldn't be much danger of bumping into him."

A minute later the train pulled in. People pushed past them, sweeping them along and into a second-class car. They got two seats together and Gabriele directed him to sit in the window seat.

"Bitte einsteigen." The announcement came from the loudspeakers along the platform. *"Der Zug nach Lüneburg fährt sofort ab."* Benton looked out at the clock above the platform. The minute hand moved one space from 12:46 to 12:47 and exactly simultaneously with the movement of the clock hand, the train moved effortlessly forward.

"I see German trains are prompt," he said, turning to her.

"German efficiency and pride," she replied. "It is *verboten* to be late."

"In England and America I think it is considered fashionable."

She smiled. "Strange notion."

The countryside south of Hamburg was monotonously flat. The farther they got from the city, the more the isolated patches of snow became a thin covering, overlayering the long-since harvested wheat fields.

The farmland gave way occasionally to clumps of trees and bushes and the ground began rolling and undulating.

"Soon we'll be crossing the Lüneburger Heide," she said. "*Heide* is something like heath. It's a beautiful place to take walks and picnics. But of course at this time of year it's rather desolate and not too colorful."

He thought how wonderful it would be to lie with her on a blanket in the warmth of the June sun, a picnic basket, a bottle of wine, the fragrance of wildflowers.... He pushed the image from his mind. There might not be a Spring on the Lüneburger Heide this year. Or next ... Or ... It was too difficult to envision it. His mind resisted.

She leaned her head on his shoulder. Her hair tickled his face.

At 1:25 sharp, the train pulled into the Lüneburg Station.

"I'll get off first," she said, "so I can see where Thalberg goes. You wait until the last minute. But remember, keep your eyes on me, and don't approach unless I motion you to."

"Don't worry," he said, smiling, "I can't keep my eyes off you!"

She laughed, throwing her head back slightly and to the side. It was a gesture he knew he would never forget. She kissed him quickly and ran up the corridor and down the steps to the platform.

He peered out the window. Disembarking passengers were jostling him as they went by. Thalberg was heading straight for the exit. Benton waited by the door. He saw Gabriele go past the ticket collector and into the building. He stepped off the train. He went down a flight of stairs and through a tunnel connected to the main hall. A dark-haired woman was talking with Thalberg and they turned and walked out of the waiting room. Gabriele stepped through the adjacent door. Benton went over to a kiosk near the door and idly looked at the magazine titles, while keeping one eye on Gabriele through the window.

Colonel Thalberg and the woman approached a parked BMW. The rear door opened and Ulrich Sievers stepped out. He shook hands with the colonel and motioned him to the car.

It was then that he saw Gabriele.

His eyes locked on hers. He stood absolutely still for a moment. And then he smiled.

Her eyes widened in consternation.

CHAPTER EIGHT

Wetzen

GABRIELE STARTED to turn back toward the station, but she mastered her momentary panic. If they saw her go back they would follow. They would see Christopher.

"Uli!" she said and went calmly over to him.

"What a surprise, Gabriele," he said. Both Colonel Thalberg and the woman looked at them with annoyed impatience.

He kissed her on the cheek. "What brings you to Lüneburg?" His voice was laced with suspicion. "You were in London only the other day."

"I have some friends who live nearby. I had a week off and was going to visit them for a day before going home to Bremen. I don't have any classes at LSE until the sixteenth."

"Oh, where do they live? Perhaps we can give you a lift?"

"No, no, that won't be necessary. I'll take a taxi. Besides it's near Salzhausen, twenty kilometers away." She was pleased with herself for being so quick-witted. She did know where Salzhausen was, some acquaintances of hers from the university had bought a farm there and opened a commune. Her story was so plausible she felt it almost convinced her.

Sievers turned to the other two. "This is an old friend of mine," he said, "Gabriele Witte. This is Samuel Thalberg and Helga Schumann." She shook hands with Thalberg and Helga. The latter was a small woman with dark hair, chopped in a type of punk haircut. She was very thin, nearly anorexic, and obviously only about twenty years old. Her eyes, Gabriele thought, looked empty. Nothing, not even boredom showed through. Thalberg looked the typical American businessman. He seemed nervous and impatient over this interruption, but she had an idea of the things going through his mind.

"Please," Sievers said again, "please get in the car. We will drop you off." It was more a command than an offer.

Thalberg got in the front seat and Gabriele and Sievers sat in the rear. Helga, behind the wheel, shifted into first and the car roared off.

Gabriele wanted so desperately to turn and look for Christopher, but she didn't dare.

She had to think fast.

CHRISTOPHER RAN OUT to the curb as the car disappeared. "Christ! Christ Almighty!" He was petrified. He didn't know what to do. He couldn't follow in a taxi, it would be too obvious. And if he were spotted, then he would be issuing Gabriele's death warrant.

He paced back and forth.

He would have to wait. He would stay at the station until she could return. There was no alternative.

But what if she could not return?

THE BMW HEADED SOUTH from Lüneburg toward Salzhausen. The medieval spires of the town were quickly behind them, and it was only a matter of minutes before they were traveling across farmland. Black-and-white Holstein cows were roaming in a pasture to their left, grazing off the few clumps of cold grass protruding through the thin covering of snow.

"Where are you going?" Gabriele asked Ulrich. "Are you staying nearby?"

It seemed that she had interrupted a train of thought.

"Huh? Yes. I recently moved into a commune near Wetzen. It's very effective. Everyone is very politically engaged. We are committed to ending American involvement in Germany and eventually Europe. The people here are much more serious than your friends in Bremen—wasting all that time on that Maoist criticism/self-criticism crap without ever *doing* anything!"

"Yes. We always did have that argument, didn't we? I was never willing to go as far as you. Well, I'm glad you're with people who appreciate you, who you can work and live with."

"It *is* very gratifying."

"It sounds fascinating. Why don't you take me there? I would love to see a successful and active political commune."

"But your friends? Surely they are waiting for you? It's a long drive, and by the time we'd be able to take you back to Salzhausen . . . well . . . it would be difficult."

"Don't worry about it. I'll call them later and tell them I'll be a day late. Really. It's not that important."

He thought for a moment. "Why not?" he said, half to her, half to himself.

BENTON LEFT the men's room and walked past the cabinet displays of condoms, ecstasy creams and inflatable "adult" dolls back into the waiting room. He knew he had to get control of himself. He had to act with the same calculating energy as Gabriele. How would she handle this?

He passed the ticket counters and went to the departures announcement board. There would be a train to Bremen within the hour.

If she was not back by then, he decided, he would go to Bremen. She had said she'd contact him at Eckhardt Schlegel's address. It was his only option.

THE SILVER-GRAY BMW had turned right off the Bundesstrasse 209 and wound along a dirt road for several kilometers.

Gabriele was carefully memorizing every landmark that
would lead her back here. That is, if she could get away in
the first place. She sensed more from Ulrich's attitude than
from anything he had said that she was, in effect, a "prisoner." Prisoner of war was how Ulrich would no doubt have
put it. She had to play along now—maybe she could convince them she would join them. It was an outside possibility, but her only chance. Besides, it was essential for her to
discover as much as possible about their base.

Before them was a large prosperous-looking farm—not at
all like the run-down abandoned farms most students
bought or rented for their communal experiments. A large
grove of ancient oaks and beeches rose majestically from the
surrounding wheat fields. Many of the fields were barren,
with bits of stubble interspersed amid the furrows; several
were covered with brittle, dried six-foot cornstalks. In the
shadows of the trees were several sheds and a large barn.
One of the sheds was ramshackle and was obviously filled
with farm implements—many of which, from what she
could see, looked broken down and rusted. The other sheds
and the barn were in first-rate condition. In fact, they
looked almost new, even though they were built along the
same design as most of the barns in that part of rural Germany. Attached to the largest shed was, incongruously, a
satellite dish antenna. The door of the barn was closed, but
since there was no odor in the air of cows or pigs, she knew
it was not used for animals. In fact, the entire place seemed
phony, like a movie set. It was a base camouflaged as a
farm.

The house, which stood before them, flanked by the sheds
on one side and the barn on the other, was substantial and
huge. Most farmhouses were large, but primarily because

he barn was traditionally attached to the house. This house
was at least thirty yards long and three stories tall. The roof
was tiled rather than thatched, and the building was constructed predominantly from brick. Each of the windows
were fitted with *Rolladen*, which were common on newer
buildings in Germany. They had probably been recently installed. They were metal shades that rolled down on the
outside of the windows, which were used at night in order
to block light from escaping and unwanted watchers from
seeing into the building. The entire compound, she noticed, could therefore be completely blacked-out at night, as
well as be adequately screened from view during the day by
the trees—leafless though they were. In summer, of course,
the foliage would provide total cover. It all seemed very well
thought out.

Helga turned the car around and backed into one of the
sheds. There were several motorcycles, a Volkswagen van
and a small truck parked inside. In one corner was a small
room. It was probably a communications center, she
thought, which would explain the antenna.

They left the car and walked over to the house. As they
approached, the heavy oak door swung open to admit them.

A tall blond man wearing blue jeans and a denim jacket
stood in the door. A machine gun was casually hanging by
a strap from his shoulder.

Gabriele pretended not to notice.

"This is Erich," Sievers said, pointing to the man. He did
not introduce them, he only pointed him out. Erich made no
attempt to shake hands, nor did it seem that he even acknowledged their presence.

"Colonel Thalberg," Ulrich said, pointing to a room on
their right, "this way please. Helga," he added, "show Gabriele to one of the guest rooms." Then he turned to Gabriele. "I will talk to you later, after our brief meeting here."

Gabriele nodded. There was something malicious in Ulrich's eyes, an unspoken threat, though he was smiling.

The colonel followed Sievers through the sliding oak
doors. She could see several people seated around a long
table. There was a murmur of talk as the two entered the
room, then the doors slid shut.

"This way, please." Helga pointed to a stairway ahead.
Gabriele followed her up two flights of stairs and down a
long corridor. Helga opened a door to a room at the end of
the corridor, and left her standing there as she went back
downstairs.

The room was small, but comfortably furnished with a
double bed, a large wardrobe, a small fall-front desk and
chair, an armchair and a washbasin. The bed was covered
with an eiderdown and there were *Gardinen*—white chintz
curtains—on the window.

She went to the window and looked out. It was a beautiful view. The fields rolled away to the east toward a line of
trees that seemed to mark the beginning of a forest. The
shadow of the house was stretching out away from her, toward the forest, as the sun neared the western horizon.

And in her heart she felt a longing, a leaning out. "Oh
Christopher..." she murmured to herself, "Christopher..."

COLONEL THALBERG SETTLED back in the chair. "So there
you have the final details. We'll be contacted by General
Forman exactly eight hours before the missiles leave the
base. He has worked out their route as well as the various
exercises the crew are supposed to run through. There'll be
plenty of time to get moving and carry out our plan successfully. I have been assured of both your eagerness and
your abilities." He looked around at the seven people. Ulrich sat opposite him at the far end of the table. In addition
to Erich and Helga, there were three men and another

woman. One of the men was in his forties, but the rest were probably in their late twenties. Disparate though they were, he thought, they did look a formidable bunch.

"Now, there is one problem. I think it's minor, but we must not take any chances. There's an American, a Christopher Benton, who has learned of the Tomahawk plan. We expect he'll try to stop us. We don't know exactly who he's working for—" there was a buzz of exclamations around the table "—but that's not important. Of course, once the missiles are in our hands, there is nothing anyone can do."

He opened his briefcase and took out a photograph. It had the grainy quality of all wire service photographs, but it sufficed. He passed it down the table. "This is Benton. Memorize that face. If you see him he is to be killed. It would be preferable to capture and interrogate him, but we've already failed at that, and time is short. So, don't worry about the interrogation. I'm sure his accomplices—if indeed he has any—will make themselves known to us soon enough."

He looked from face to face around the table. "Any questions?"

CHRISTOPHER LOOKED in all directions, hoping to see her rush along the platform toward him, but he knew his hopes were futile.

"*Bitte einsteigen, der Zug nach Bremen....*" The recorded announcement inviting passengers to board the train to Bremen came from the loudspeakers while Benton stepped onto the train. The doors closed and it began moving. He sat by a window in the half-empty carriage. It was a local train; there was no division into compartments, just a long aisle with two-passenger seats alternately facing and backing each other on either side. Small luggage racks stretched from steel columns above each bank of seats.

He looked out the window as the train left the station. Lüneburg seemed so small after Hamburg. There was a definite medieval flavor to some of the architecture, but he had no time to dwell on it. The train picked up speed and began racing toward Buchholz and Rotenburg and Bremen. Bremen, he thought, it will be dark by the time I get there. I hope I can find Gabriele's friend. I hope I can find someone who can help me. Help us.

THERE WAS A KNOCK on Gabriele's door and, before she could respond, it opened.

Sievers.

"Ah, I see you have made yourself at home," he said. He was carrying a tray with a pot of tea and two china cups.

She was sitting up on the bed.

"Some tea?"

"Yes, thank you." She got up and sat in the armchair. Ulrich set the tray on the desk, turned the straight-backed desk chair to face her and poured out the tea.

"I must say, Gabriele, it seems rather odd to bump into you like that after having just met you at the demonstration in London." He handed her the cup of tea. "You aren't, by any chance, following me?" He laughed.

She opened her mouth to answer, but he didn't let her speak. "Of course not," he said, holding up his hand. "Of course not. You wouldn't be interested in what I'm doing. I think we established that last year, didn't we?"

"Uli, you know why we couldn't go on together." She half sighed. "Your demands just didn't fit with me."

"Yes, yes. Let's not repeat old quarrels."

She sipped her tea. It was too weak. She looked at him. His overearnest expression. His cold eyes that never seemed to laugh, never in all the time she had known him. He was always so analytical. Too analytical. A one-sided person. Not like Christopher. No, she thought, she must not think about Christopher. She pushed him out of her mind, she had to get Ulrich to trust her. But how, she wondered, could she ever have spent more than six months with this man? She was amazed at herself, or at the self she had been only a year ago.

"What *are* you up to, Uli? Tell me, there's something going on here. An armed guard. The antenna. I'm not blind."

"Gabriele," he started slowly, "we have not always seen eye to eye. But politically we have much in common. Certainly on the issue of nuclear power plants and the deployment of missiles, we've always been in agreement."

"Yes, we have. But that was not enough common ground for a relationship."

"I'll not argue with you about that. We've done that enough times already. But maybe you would like to join us now. We have a foolproof plan that will completely surprise the Americans."

"Oh, really?"

"And I personally would like to have you join us. We could use you. I'm sure I can convince the others."

"Well, what is it?"

He sipped his tea, set the cup down and leaned forward. He paused. "First, you understand about these cruise missiles that they're deploying?"

My God, she thought, Christopher really is right!

"What do you mean?"

"Well, the key point to the strategy is that they can be launched from any position. They don't have to be confined to silos or launchpads on a base. They have what they call Transporter-erector-launchers—TELs—which are trucked around to any site with the missiles on them and launched from there. This is in order to minimize the risk of being a target for enemy missiles. How can the Russians wipe out the cruise missiles if they aren't on the base? They can't find them! It is, of course, an ingenious idea, one that the Soviets themselves already employ with their SS-20s."

His eyes, she noticed, showed how much he loved to hear the sound of his own voice.

"But we have an ingenious idea, too!" He paused. "They have to test their TELs. And they're going to do so within the next forty-eight hours at Garlstedt. We're going to hijack one of them complete with a full complement of missiles!" He waited to see what effect his words had on her.

"But how? It's preposterous! The Americans would have them too well guarded. You could never pull it off!"

There was a smug look on his face. "Oh, we have an elaborate plan, and besides, we've been helped by several disaffected American military personnel."

"Thalberg?"

"Yes. He and a few others. They'll let us know exactly when the test is to take place. Already they've been working with us for more than two months."

"It seems like such a dangerous idea. But even if you're successful what can you possibly hope to gain? You'll have every policeman in West Germany, as well as the entire NATO command looking for you. Someone will have seen you and the convoy, and you'll be caught within hours."

"Gain? Why, the fact that we've accomplished it will show those fools in Bonn and Washington how easy it would be to have missiles fall into the wrong hands. It will force them to reconsider the deployment policy. Besides, we will have demands to exchange for the safe return of the missiles. One of them will be the removal of the missiles already deployed in West Germany."

"But what can your threat be? They'll capture you, or kill you, or ignore you. Surely, for a test, the missiles will not be armed! Use your head!"

"Ah, but my dear Gabriele. That is already taken care of. They *will* be armed."

She examined the blue floral pattern on the teacup in her hand, trying to conceal the fear that she knew was in her eyes.

"Colonel Thalberg is here to program their guidance systems. We can launch a missile at Munich or Frankfurt or Brokdorf. So you see, NATO will have no choice but to acquiesce to our demands. Our threat is not a hollow one."

She stared at him, astonished. He was perfectly serious. And she knew her reaction at that moment would be carefully evaluated by him. If she rejected the invitation to join their plot, he would lock her up. Or worse. Certainly he wouldn't let her leave the house with this information. But how could she possibly convince him that she would go along with them? He was testing her. Her distaste for him was growing, and it would be impossible for her to conceal it. He could never trust her. But she must convince him she could be trusted. It was her only chance.

"I don't know," she said, "I don't know if it will work."

"Of course it will. They'll never expect anything so daring."

"But if you've got it all worked out, what could I do to help?"

"An extra pair of hands will come in handy. You can drive, or you can wield a gun."

She looked at her hands. She stood up and walked past him to the window. It was growing darker. She stared blankly out at the fields and the distant wooded area.

"Let me think about it."

He nodded, stood up and left the room.

As he passed Helga in the corridor he motioned with his head toward Gabriele's door. Then he went down the stairs.

Helga opened a closet and extracted a Heckler & Koch HK-54 submachine gun. Then she sat on a chair next to the banister at the head of the stairs. She looked toward the door of Gabriele's room. Another bourgeois student, she thought. These middle-class revolutionaries! What on earth was Ulrich up to? She looked down at the automatic resting in her lap. She made sure the safety catch was on and inserted an ammunition clip. There was a slight smudge on the barrel near where the clip joined it. She took a corner of her *keffiyeh*, the checkered Syrian kerchief she was wearing, and carefully wiped the barrel.

CHAPTER NINE

Bremen

THE HIGH ARCHED CEILING of the main Bremen railway station curved away on both sides as the train slowed to a stop on track four. Benton stepped onto the platform under the omnipresent clock that occupied the midpoint on each track. He jogged up the stairs quickly and went to the first telephone booth he could find.

He was in luck. Eckhardt Schlegel was at home and would meet him at the station in ten minutes. "I have a red VW bus," he said, "with Atomkraft Nein Danke stickers all over it. You can't miss it. I'll pull up by the taxistand."

"Thanks," Benton replied and hung up.

He walked through the large hall, observing people hurriedly running toward the tracks, or queuing up at the ticket window. A group of schoolchildren clad in yellow rain ponchos had just arrived on another train and were noisily pushing toward the exit. A sea of yellow. He followed them through.

There was a line of taxis in front of the station and several sets of trolley tracks and overhead electric cables converging about fifty yards ahead. To the right a bus was loading. Beyond the square that opened before him was an elevated highway and myriad lights from the buildings of the city. The tallest one he could see was the modern Siemens building, but even by Philadelphia standards, it was certainly no skyscraper. Beyond the nearest group of buildings were several spires from the cathedral and the town hall in the marketplace. He was looking at a map to get his bearings when the VW arrived.

Eckhardt was certainly not kidding, he thought. The vehicle was *covered* with antinuclear bumper stickers. From where he stood he saw a huge circular yellow one, about a yard in diameter, dominating the sliding side door, and another, equally huge, on the front.

He opened the door and jumped in. "Hello. Christopher Benton," he said, extending his hand.

Eckhardt took it and shook it warmly. *"Willkommen in Bremen,"* he said with a smile. "No luggage?"

"No. That's a long story."

"Well. Call me Pete, if you find Eckhardt too difficult. I'm a folk musician and a fan of Pete Seeger's. About fifteen years ago many of my friends began calling me Pete and the name has stuck." He inched the car forward, out around the taxis and onto the main road.

"You must be hungry. How long have you been traveling today?"

"It seems an eternity. Gabriele and I arrived in Hamburg only this morning on board the *Prinz Hamlet*, then we went to Lüneburg where we got separated. She had given me your address and told me to contact you. I thought she might try to get back in touch through you."

"Well, let's go to my flat and we'll have something to eat. My girlfriend is at the university tonight, and she'll be home later."

They took the road under the elevated highway and drove for several blocks past stores and restaurants. At a traffic circle, where there was a huge mural on the side of an apartment house, they exited to the right.

Christopher stared at the mural. It showed an elderly couple staring out their window. It must have been thirty

feet high and filled him with the eerie feeling of being
snooped upon. Pete noticed him looking at it.

"Extraordinary, isn't it? It's a big thing recently in Bremen. The city council pays artists to beautify ugly walls.
There's a lot of old bunkers in the city left over from the
war. They had planted dynamite all around one of the
bunkers. When they set it off the entire bunker jumped
about a meter into the air and came down again, about a
meter away, completely intact. When they found that no
matter how hard they tried, they couldn't be moved, they
decided they had to do something with them. They use them
now for storing city property. One of them has been made
into a practice studio for rock groups; an artist painted the
outside of it to look like an exploding bank vault with
money flying out all over the place. It always causes traffic
to slow down."

They made a few turns and then Pete parked the car.
"Here we are."

Christopher stepped out. They were on the corner of
Wulwesstrasse and Kohlhöckerstrasse. The streets in all
directions consisted of row houses, which seemed to be at
least one hundred years old. Obviously there had been little
destruction here during the war. Christopher remarked
about it.

"Most of Bremen has old houses like these. At least in the
inner city. Only a few bombs hit the city during the war. The
English and Americans concentrated on the shipyards and
Bremerhaven."

"From the little I've seen so far Bremen seems like a
beautiful place."

"That it is. The city center has sections that even date
back to the sixteenth century. There is one brand-new
building in the marketplace. When you see it you can tell
immediately that that's the one spot where an Allied bomb
missed the shipyards."

They walked past a bar on the corner and up the steps of
a large house two doors down the street.

The moment Pete opened the door Christopher was hit
with the overpowering odor of cats.

Cats, *über alles*.

It seemed like hundreds of them. The middle of the living room was dominated by the trunk of a birch tree, which
was wedged between the floor and the ceiling. Four or five
cats were sitting Cheshire-style on the branches.

Pete noticed Christopher's surprise. "I'm a cat lover," he
explained unnecessarily. "It began slowly, but they keep
reproducing faster than I can get them neutered." A black
one was rubbing against his leg. "This is Dubel. That's
Plattdeutsch for 'devil.' And that's precisely what he is, a
little devil." He picked him up gently.

"Good idea, *nicht wahr*?" he asked, tapping the tree. "I
needed a scratching post, but there are so many cats. So I
just brought in the whole tree. They love it."

In spite of the birch much of the furniture was nearing
total destruction from the cats' claws. Most of it looked as
if it had been found in the trash. Christopher surmised that
it probably had. But the most notable thing about the room
was the abundance and variety of musical instruments
strewn around. Guitars. Banjos. Tambourines. Bongos.
And several Middle Eastern instruments. It was apparent
that Pete had put whatever money he had into the instruments and not the furnishings.

"Have a seat," he said, motioning Christopher toward an
overstuffed armchair from which half the stuffing was protruding.

There were many political posters on the walls. One,
about a march on Bonn, Christopher recognized from Gabriele's room in London. Pete had put on a record and gone
into the kitchen, which could be seen from where Benton
sat. A moment later he returned with two bottles of Beck's

as the music of Taj Mahal began to fill the room. He noticed Christopher looking at one of the banjos.

"I made that one myself. Even had a bell-bronze sound ring cast for it."

"Looks like a professional job."

Pete grabbed it. "But listen. It's got an unbelievable sound." His eyes lit up as he began picking it in accompaniment to the record. After a minute he set it down and ran his hands through his unkempt dark blond hair. It contrasted sharply with his beard, which was dark brown on his cheeks and turning gray on his chin. Benton estimated he was about his own age.

"Well," Pete said at length, "tell me what you're doing in Germany."

"It's a long story." Christopher drank some of the beer. He would have to trust Pete. He would have to tell him everything, he had no choice. He began with how he met Gabriele. He related what he had learned at Greenham Common and the conversation he had overheard between Colonel Thalberg and Ulrich Sievers. Then he told how they had followed the Colonel from Hamburg to Lüneburg and that Gabriele had been recognized by Sievers and forced to go along with them.

"I don't think they know that Gabriele knows me. If they make that connection I fear for her life." He paused. Pete was staring at the bottle in his hand. "I wish she'd call us soon and let us know where she is...." Christopher felt a wave of dizziness. He was tired. He needed a bath and a shave.

Pete was silent, thinking, for several minutes. "Are you so positive these people really are serious? Sievers, I know, is a serious person. But I've seen him at several rallies and he's got a growing reputation. I find it hard to believe he'd work hand in hand with the Americans." He looked at a poster on the wall. "Of course, stranger and more bizarre things have happened in European politics."

"People have been killed." Christopher told of the attempt on his life. Of his landlord's death. And Janssen. And Robbins. "All I know is that somehow we have to stop them. I haven't felt anything this deeply in years. But...it's more than just a feeling. It's frightening."

Pete looked at him carefully, as if studying him.

"Okay," he said after a minute, "Gabriele knew what she was doing when she sent you here.... I've been involved for several years in the antinuclear movement. I've written many songs and I have a folk rock group that goes around Germany singing at rallies and demonstrations and marches. But lately our involvement has changed somewhat. One of the members of the group—the fiddle player—owns a small farm near here and we've met there many times in the past year discussing alternatives to opposing the government solely through peaceful nonviolent means. We still sincerely oppose the Baader-Meinhof approach. But we realize that we must protect ourselves. At first we began by wearing motorcycle helmets and gas masks to demonstrations as protection against the cops. Then we learned to carry sticks, billy clubs, to fend off blows from the cops. One of our group was once associated with Baader-Meinhof. He even served time on a weapons charge. He's been lecturing us on the use of weapons. Although we think of them as purely a defense measure, we feel we must be prepared for anything. But, I don't know, sometimes I have second thoughts. It's not that we shouldn't oppose what we feel is an inhuman policy, but it's...I don't know...maybe we do become too much like the enemy...and how does one really change anything...?"

He broke off and looked at his watch. "*Scheisse*, you must be starving! Let's get you something to eat."

Christopher followed him to the kitchen and sat at the Formica table. Pete opened the refrigerator and set the table with salami, cheese, margarine, pickles, tomatoes and onions. Then he put a cutting board and knife at each of their places. There were pots hanging from the greasy walls in between more political posters. He stood at the side of the table slicing a loaf of rye bread with a sharp knife and, with three cats rubbing against his legs, continued talking.

"Anyway, I know a lot of very concerned people and I'm sure we can get a few of them to join us and help thwart these bastards. I can hardly believe that Sievers has let himself be duped by the Americans into hijacking the missiles. They are obviously using him for their own purposes. It's a trap, I'm sure of it. The least that will happen is that it will set the movement back years. It sounds like the same fucked-up mentality that lay behind the whole Baader-Meinhof strategy. And I shudder to think what would happen if, even by accident, one of those nuclear warheads was launched or detonated."

"Is there any way we can alert the German police that an attempt is going to be made in the next few days?"

Pete thought for a moment. "Well...we could telephone in an anonymous tip, but I think the cops will be out in force anyway. They're always expecting the dreaded terrorists to attack. I suppose it won't hurt to alert them, but we don't have much evidence to convince them."

They were quiet for a moment, sipping their beers.

"I'm worried about Gabriele. I don't know what she's planning to do. Maybe she'll pretend to go along with them so she can find out where they're going to take the missiles. And then she'll contact us. But maybe she's trying desperately, even now, to get away from them. But we must wait until we get word."

"Gabriele is an extraordinary woman. I'm sure she has a plan. It could even be that she'll go along with them in order to sabotage them. That would make it imperative for us to wait to hear from her, and not rush in and spoil everything. She might need us ultimately to get her out, and if we act precipitately we may very well jeopardize her life. Her opposition to extremism, whether of the right or the left, whether of the government or the masses, goes very deep in her. I think what you say is important. We should wait until we hear from her, but then be prepared to act."

"I wish she would call."

Pete looked over at the telephone sitting silently on the table in the hall just outside the entrance to the kitchen.

"In the meantime," he added, "we must prepare ourselves."

He walked over to the telephone and dialed a number. After speaking for a few minutes in German, he hung up and returned to the table.

He picked up a slice of bread and spread margarine on it. Then he sliced a tomato and covered the bread with the slices. On top of this he expertly sliced thin slivers of onion and added salt and an abundance of freshly ground pepper. He placed the sandwich on Christopher's cutting board and made another for himself. "You eat it with your knife and fork, like so," he demonstrated. "Our sandwiches are not as elaborate or as massive as yours in America. After all, *we* are not the land of bountiful opportunities and limitless possibilities."

Benton laughed. "This is delicious," he said, sampling the open-faced sandwich.

They busied themselves with supper as Pete explained that he had called his friend Norbert, who had agreed to gather a few of the group at his house later that night. Pete hadn't told him what was up, but had said it was serious. Norbert, he explained, was a trusted and longtime friend, and he would be able to help out. Another friend, Sigismund, was the one who had connections with the Baader-Meinhof group. His special talents might come in handy now. "Though, I doubt," he concluded, half smiling, "that we can just locate Thalberg and Sievers and company and have a big shoot-out. Like at the O.K. Corral!"

The door opened and a woman entered. She had shoulder-length black hair in a sort of Buster Brown haircut, the bangs came down below the level of her eyebrows. Her face was heavily lined and there were dark circles under her brown eyes. She was probably older than Pete. There was a hardness about her that she seemed to have under control.

"Guten Abend," she said, removing her coat and scarf.

"Hannelore, this is Christopher Benton, an American. He's a friend of Gabriele's and is visiting Bremen."

"Good evening," she said in a thick German accent. She was wearing a heavy South American sweater with llamas marching in procession around her torso. It did not conceal the obvious fact that she was braless. "I'm Hannelore, Pete's *Freundin*—girlfriend you say in America. But I'm hardly a girl!" She shook Christopher's hand and sat down. Pete placed another cutting board on the table and served her some bread and ham.

They talked idly about Germany and America while they finished eating. Christopher didn't know whether to mention anything about what he and Pete had been discussing. He decided he would wait to follow Pete's lead. Anyone Pete would include in their plans would be all right with him. He was grateful it was possible for him to have confidence in people. Hopefully, he thought, he was right to trust them.

When they had finished eating, Pete suggested they go to the Hansen Kneipe, a tavern at the corner. "Pete, you're that bar's best customer," Hannelore moaned exasperatedly. Christopher had the impression that she disapproved of Pete's frequenting the place, but it was apparent she had no intention of dragging her feet, for she hastily threw on her coat.

A few minutes later, they entered the bar, which was nearly filled with people, mostly students. There was a jukebox blaring out a Lou Reed song and nearly all the tables and booths along the walls were full. The benches, chairs and tables were all made of wood, as was the floor. The windows were stained glass and there was a cozy, unkempt atmosphere to the place.

"The landlord here is a guestworker, from Turkey. He's one of the few migrant workers who've been successful in making money in Germany. Now he has no intentions of returning home, he is doing so well. The students from Bremen University like to hang out here—it's not as bourgeois as the average bars in town."

They sat at a table with a few of their friends, who were introduced to Benton with a great deal of hand shaking and head nodding. Most of them could speak English, but a few could not. The conversation was carried on in German unless Christopher was directly addressed by someone.

"Has Pete played his homemade banjo for you yet?" one of the men asked in hesitant English. "I think that's the first thing every guest at his place is subjected to!" He laughed, as did most of those at the table.

"Yes, he has," Christopher said. "First thing."

They all laughed again.

Everyone was drinking *Halbe* of Haake Beck beer. *Ein Halbe*, Christopher was told, means a half, a half liter. Which meant it was really the large-size beer, despite its misleading name. If one wanted the smaller size, one ordered *ein Kleines*.

Christopher began feeling uneasy amid the raucous chatter and banter and stories being told around the table. What if Gabriele tried to call now? Where was she? My God, he thought, and something in his stomach began gnawing at him, we should not have left the telephone!

CHAPTER TEN

Wetzen

THE DEEP, LUSH CARPET stretching the length of the corridor reminded Gabriele, as she stepped onto it, of the carpeting found in luxury hotels. It seemed out of place in a German farmhouse. But this was no ordinary *Bauernhaus*.

She reached the head of the stairs, but stopped when she saw Helga sitting on the landing. It was more the look in Helga's eyes than the sight of the gun that made her hesitate.

"I want to speak with Ulrich," she announced.

It seemed as though Helga hadn't heard her. Finally, she blinked and stood up. "Wait here," she said, then went down the stairs.

A minute later she returned and motioned Gabriele to proceed.

Ulrich was leaning against the threshold of a room on the second floor. It was in the center of the house.

"Come in," he said.

It was a large room. Four windows, flanked by the same style of curtain that was in her room, looked out over the front of the compound. An entire wall was filled with books. There was a bed, a sofa, two armchairs and a large mahogany table which was cluttered with books and papers. A detailed map of northern Germany was spread out in its center. In one corner was a television and next to it a radio transmitter. On the wall bordering the corridor was a gun case filled with several shotguns, rifles and automatic weapons. She forced herself not to stare at it.

Colonel Thalberg was sitting on the sofa looking through a file folder. She sat in one of the armchairs opposite him.

"I take it," Ulrich said, sinking into the other armchair, "you've made your decision whether or not to join us."

She looked at Thalberg, then back at Ulrich and nodded. "I think I must. You know how strongly I oppose deployment. But, of course, I don't have much choice, do I?" She tried making it sound like a jest. "You won't very well allow me to walk out of here after telling me your plans."

Sievers smiled, but it was a smile that didn't touch his eyes. "We won't force you to join us. But, as you say, if you don't we'll have to keep you here until it's all over."

"Well, I will join you, but I must confess, I do have some reservations. I don't want to be involved with any violence."

"Don't worry, Gabriele, this will hardly be less 'peaceful' than any of the usual demonstrations. It will just be more effective."

Colonel Thalberg placed the folder next to him on the couch. "May I interject something here, Herr Sievers?"

"Go right ahead."

"We don't need her. The plan is worked out. She will be superfluous. Besides, I don't see how we can trust her. I don't understand why you even asked her to join us."

"Colonel!" Sievers acted offended. "I have lived with this woman for several months. I can certainly vouch for her. We may have had problems in our relationship, but she is a talented, resourceful woman. There is always room for resourcefulness and talent, isn't there? I've chosen each member of the group for exactly these reasons. You said you wanted people with those qualities."

Thalberg didn't like it. There was always danger when you added a new recruit this far along into an operation, no matter how good they were. He had seen it in Chile. He had seen it in Nicaragua. But he had given Sievers a free hand in recruiting the Germans. He picked up a whiskey glass from the table and made a noncommittal wave with his hand. He was too tired to argue. "Whatever you say." Christ, he thought, I do hope Forman sends the go-ahead tomorrow. I don't think I could stand an extra twenty-four hours of waiting. I'm getting too tense.

"Then it's decided. Good. Let me introduce you to the others and we'll explain what your role can be." Sievers rose and led Gabriele out of the room and downstairs.

Erich was seated in a chair by the front door, looking at a magazine, his machine gun on his lap. Gabriele suspected that he wasn't reading, but merely holding the copy of *Konkret* to affect casualness. He struck her as being anything but casual. Like a bouncer in a bar. An automaton. A machine that was made for a simple job.

They went past him through the sliding doors and sat at the large conference table. Two other people were there, going over papers and examining a map pinned on the wall. Near the map was a freestanding blackboard with chalk diagrams, *x*'s and *o*'s and arrows scribbled on it.

"Klaus," Ulrich said to one of them, who was eating a sandwich, "go to the barn and get the others." Klaus seemed very young, perhaps only seventeen or eighteen. He was large but Gabriele had the feeling he was still growing. He wore blue jeans and a heavy double-knit pullover. His longish hair framed his boyish, almost pretty, face. He smiled shyly at her and left.

"This is Bernhard," Ulrich introduced her to the other, a man who was old enough to be Klaus's father, for he must have been in his late forties. But he looked like a laborer, whereas Klaus gave the impression of coming from a well-educated bourgeois family. Bernhard's arms were powerful, his hands large and meaty. When he spoke his accent was heavily Hessian, and it seemed that he would have been happier speaking Plattdeutsch.

A few minutes later two others arrived with Klaus. Alex and Antje. Perhaps they were married, thought Gabriele, but no, Ulrich would not have tolerated that in the commune. Antje was extraordinarily pretty. Pale, Scandinavian blond hair, a tight, compact well-proportioned figure and a face that showed deep intelligence. She draped her parka over a chair and took Gabriele's hand. Gabriele knew she would like Antje and wondered how she could be duped into working for Ulrich and Colonel Thalberg. In rejecting her background she might have lost her perspective, but then who could tell?

Alex wore *Zimmermannshosen*, the black corduroy, bell-bottom pants with two zippers that were the trademark of carpenters in the medieval guilds. Many students wore them nowadays to display solidarity with the working class. Like Antje, he was in his mid-twenties and had very fair blond hair. It was so thin that it would not be long before he started losing it.

"Our plan is simple," Ulrich was saying. "When we learn of the convoy's departure we're going to stage a little accident. We already know from our sources the convoy's destination. Not even the people on the base know this yet. Only the lead driver will have that information, and only after the convoy has left the base. We have carefully chosen the best spot along the route—" he pointed to a road on the wall map "—which is conveniently nearby. Of course the convoy's route has been decided on by our people. We force the convoy to stop, take hostages and persuade the rest to lay down their weapons. Then we take over the TEL and drive it here. The barn was renovated so as to accommodate it.

"Some of us will be concealed in the lead truck, which will stage the accident, blocking the road and forcing the convoy to stop. The others will be in a VW bus that will come up behind. You will be the driver of the bus, Gabriele. That way you won't have to carry a gun or get more closely involved. Clear?"

Gabriele thought for a moment. "What makes you think they won't resist?" she said finally.

"The moment the convoy stops we'll have guns aimed at the lead jeeps and weapons carriers. We will also gas the troop carrier, thereby rendering unconscious the bulk of the security force. We take several hostages and force the others to surrender and leave the vehicles. Don't worry. No one will get hurt!"

Gabriele knew he was lying, that he had no intention of taking hostages. He would shoot first. But she had to feign abhorrence of violence and relief at Ulrich's reassurances. Otherwise he would not believe her. He knew anything else would not be in her character. She looked into his eyes, and she knew he was perfectly capable of killing her. He had found his destiny at last, and he was ready to act on it. Would she have the courage to act when the crunch came? The next twenty-four hours were going to bring some hard lessons. Of that she was certain. She suppressed a shiver.

"Mein Gott!" she said, looking at her watch. "I have to call my friends, they'll wonder what's happened to me!" She knew, too, that Ulrich had probably wondered, or would wonder, why she hadn't asked to call them. Now he might trust her story and let his guard down. Or was that wishful thinking?

"Ah, but of course. I was going to suggest it myself. After all, we don't want them to worry and call the police because you have disappeared."

There was a telephone at the far end of the table. Ulrich pointed toward it.

She picked up the receiver and dialed 0421, the code for Bremen. Thank God, she thought, she knew Eckhardt's number by heart. She finished dialing. Please, please, be there! The phone was ringing. She looked over at the others. They were talking among themselves, ignoring her. Obviously everything was planned down to the last, minutest detail. She felt like a piece on a chessboard. But was she deciding on her own moves, or was she being moved? Ring. Ring. No answer. God, please! Ring. Ring. Ulrich, she could see, was eyeing her. Reluctantly, not knowing when she would have another opportunity to call, she replaced the receiver.

"That's odd. No answer," she explained and returned to the other end of the table. "I'll try again later."

"Come with me," Ulrich said. "I want to show you the rest of the compound. Then we should probably turn in. Tomorrow will be the start of a very long and demanding day."

She followed him out of the room. Alex went with them. They took their coats from the rack in the hall, and Erich opened the door for them. It was chilly and damp as they walked across to the barn, but not uncomfortably cold. The branches of a giant beech sighed over their heads as they shifted in the wind. As they approached the barn she realized how tall it was. The doors seemed no wider than nine feet, but their height went right up to the roof, at least twelve feet above.

"The TELs on which the cruise missiles are transported are rather tall. So we had to ascertain that we had enough head room in the barn. Very cleverly done, wouldn't you agree?" he said as he unlocked and swung back the door.

When it had fully opened they stepped in. Klaus switched on an overhead light and she looked up to the cantilevered ceiling.

"Very professional," she said, "it must have cost you much money and time to do this."

Ulrich smiled. "We have our resources," he replied smugly.

She also saw two jeeps, one on either side, with formidable guns mounted on the back. There must be a full-scale arsenal here, she thought, looking around.

He noticed her scrutiny. "Precautionary," he explained.

After Ulrich locked up, they walked over to one of the sheds. Ulrich pointed out the VW van that Gabriele would drive, and the radio room. "We have an extraordinarily powerful transmitter. Also, there are baffling and interfering devices that make it nearly impossible for anyone to trace the transmitter's source."

They went back to the house.

"When does the test take place?" Gabriele asked when they had reentered.

"Tomorrow. Possibly Saturday, but as of now it is expected tomorrow night. We'll be signaled eight hours before it is to begin, so there will be plenty of time to set up."

They hung up their coats in the downstairs hall.

"You should get some sleep," he said.

"Yes. But perhaps I can try my friends one more time?"

CHAPTER ELEVEN

Bremen

THE BEER WAS EXCELLENT. Christopher liked it better than Beck's, which was apparently Bremen's major contribution to Western culture. Christopher went to the bar and bought a round for the table. He had lost track of how many rounds had already been consumed. The Bremers had the custom of drinking a shot of *Korn* just before the beer. Ah, he thought, what a wonderful invention! *Korn* was a type of schnapps that was common in northern Germany. There were three varieties: *Apfelkorn*, which was one-hundred proof alcohol with the flavor of apples, *Sauerkorn*, which tasted of lemon and straight *Korn*, which tasted like pure wood alcohol. He brought back eight *Halbe* and eight *Apfelkorn* precariously balanced on a round tin tray.

"*Wunderbar,*" several people expostulated, as he returned to the table. "Your friend is a good man!" someone said to Pete approvingly.

Everyone smiled; they were becoming rambunctious. But then the bar was already swinging into boisterous conversation and loud music blaring from the antiquated jukebox.

Hey babe, take a walk
on the wild side....

"*Zum Wohl!*" They raised their glasses of *Apfelkorn* and downed them in one quick motion. Even Christopher was beginning to feel expert. His head, at any rate, was beginning to swim.

At the urging of several people Pete left and ran home. Several minutes later he returned with his banjo and one of his guitars. The latter he gave to one of his friends, Ralf, and after they persuaded the landlord to unplug the jukebox, the two of them began playing "Mr. Tamberine Man."

It struck Christopher as nearly comical hearing their German-accented voices singing in English. He wanted to laugh, but was just sober enough to remain polite. But they were all thoroughly enjoying themselves.

Freedom's just another word,
for nothin' left to lose....

Christopher sang along. From the heart. He began to feel good. The beer. The *Korn*. The music. These people. Yes, these people singing amid the chaos surrounding them all. He thought of the politics of the Cold War. Of war-devastated Germany divided by the conquering Allies. Of the Berlin Wall. Of JFK. *"Ich bin ein Berliner."* Of the buildup of missiles. Of the converting of one of the centers of European culture into the probable battlefield for the inevitable Armageddon. Armageddon, when the major powers, striving to preserve the Metternichian balance of power, finally and irrevocably would unbalance the world. But the music dominated, for now. And he was getting drunk.... He liked these people.

In the clearing stands a boxer,
and a fighter by his trade....

They must have gone through a dozen songs. American folk songs from the sixties, as well as German antinuclear songs. Finally, Christopher leaned over to Pete and suggested that perhaps they should return to the house. Possibly Gabriele would try to call. And it would be bad if they missed it.

Pete was enjoying himself, but he nodded in affirmation.

They did a final song, then after much argument against their friends' pleas that they stay, Pete, Hannelore and Christopher broke away.

When they entered the house Christopher asked if he could take a bath. Pete showed him to the bathroom, gave him a towel and said he would tell Hannelore Christopher's story while he bathed.

Christopher looked in the mirror while the tub was filling. It was odd, he thought, how half of him could feel so tipsy while the other half was stone-cold sober. He knew that if he had to, he could act coolly and effectively at a moment's notice despite the alcohol in his blood.

He hadn't shaved for three days, and he noticed that the stubble was just beginning to look like a beard. He decided to let it go. It would help to serve as a partial disguise in case his photo was circulated in Germany. Once Thalberg and company knew he had eluded them and was out of England, they would undoubtedly expand the search to the Continent.

He undressed and lay back in the tub.

Relaxation.

In the distance the telephone rang.

He sat up. The sober half, as he had foreseen, taking over. He waited tensely to see if he would be summoned to the phone, but, as the seconds lengthened, and he knew he would not be called, he relaxed again.

A few minutes later, after he had again leaned back and stretched out, there was a knock on the door.

"Come in," he said.

It was Pete. "Gabriele just rang up," he said, closing the door behind him and leaning against it.

"You should have called me to the phone!"

"I thought of it, but it was apparent she wasn't alone and whoever was there, I'm sure, would have been suspicious if she had spoken English."

"Uh-huh."

"She called me Martha. Martha! So obviously she was being observed. All she said was that she was in Wetzen and couldn't make it for a couple of days. She was busy Friday and she would be in touch."

"Did she have any message for me at all?" Christopher interrupted impatiently.

"I don't think she could have addressed you. As I said, someone must have been in the same room with her. I did tell her that you were here and that you were worried about her. All she said was 'good.' "

Christopher lay motionless in the tub, thinking.

"Finish your bath. We have to make some plans."

"What can we do?"

"First, we'll find out where Wetzen is. I'm going to call Norbert and have him come here tonight. We mustn't leave this phone again in case she has the opportunity to make another call. We'll work out something and we have to be ready to act. Obviously whatever is going to happen will take place tomorrow in the vicinity of Wetzen."

He stopped for a moment, his hand on the doorknob, then turned to Benton. "I'm doing this only for Gabriele. Personally, I would do almost anything if it would mean the end of deployment. I've been working for it nonstop for a long time. But Gabriele is in danger. She's a good friend and I trust her judgment. We've got to get her away from these people." He opened the door and left before Christopher could reply.

GABRIELE THREW HERSELF onto the bed. She lay motionless for several minutes staring at the ceiling. Then she rose,
undressed and, wearing only her undershirt, slipped under
the eiderdown.

She must get to the telephone again, she thought, as she
began drifting off. Tomorrow, as soon as she knew the exact time and place of the attack, she must call Schlegel again
and tell him. Then she could either try to escape, or go along
with them. She knew Christopher was in Bremen now.

Funny, she thought, how close she felt to him, so quickly,
so easily. She thought of his tenderness, his sensitivity.
Never had she known a man who could be *that* gentle. It was
as if he was part woman himself. He let the feminine part of
himself touch her just as deeply as the masculine.... She
thought of the expression in his eyes when she was astride
him....

She fell asleep.

ULRICH SIEVERS STEPPED carefully down the narrow
wooden steps into the cellar. He ducked through a brick arch
and turned into a small alcove. Antje was seated at a table
in front of a tape recorder and a switchboard. A pair of
headphones and a notepad lying near her hand.

"You were right," she said, then she turned a switch and
the tape wheels began rolling.

"Martha?" It was Gabriele's voice.

"Gabriele, is it you? We've been worrying about you." A
male voice.

A smile flashed across Ulrich's face for a second, to be
replaced with a look of cold dark hatred as he listened to the
conversation. And then, when the man said that Christopher Benton was there and worried about her, Ulrich
slammed down the palm of his hand on the table so hard
that the headphones jumped.

"Stop it right there," he ordered.

Antje turned off the machine.

"Rewind it, I'll be right back!" He turned and ran up the stairs.

He returned with Thalberg. The Colonel was wearing a robe and had obviously been preparing for bed.

"Listen to this, Colonel." Sievers signaled to Antje and she switched on the tape recorder.

Ulrich looked shaken, although he tried to mask it, but Thalberg grew intense, at first, and then elated.

"Oh, this is really good. So, she's collaborating with Benton! We tried to discover if he had any accomplices. Now we have one of them here in this house. And she will lead us to him!"

He turned to Sievers. "I want this Benton."

"Do you have a trace on the number?" Ulrich asked Antje.

"Yes." She handed him a notepad. "A number in Bremen," she said. "Address is Kohlhökerstrasse 17. The phone is registered in the name of Eckhardt Schlegel."

Ulrich looked at the pad, then tore off the sheet and gave it to Thalberg.

"Great," Thalberg said, "this simplifies things. We don't even have to lure them here." He picked up the telephone and dialed a number in Brussels.

NORBERT BARZ STEPPED out of the house and walked across to his Renault.

"No. No, Rudolf," he said, holding his retriever back, preventing him from jumping into the car. "You've got to stay home tonight."

The dog looked at him with eager eyes, which rapidly turned disappointed as Norbert closed the door of the car.

He started the engine and looked at his dog sitting in the yard in front of the house. He was a wonderful dog, loyal, friendly, adaptable. Norbert loved his house, too. He looked

at the eighteenth-century structure. Dark oak beams criss-
crossing through the red brick walls. The thatched roof,
which he had redone the previous summer. It was a beautiful old farmhouse and he had worked long and hard for it,
both in saving the money to purchase it and in the hours of
labor put into its careful restoration. Next year, he thought,
as he steered down the driveway, he would have to get central heating. These Bremen winters were too damp, he would
wind up getting rheumatism.

The village of Sudweyhe, in the lowlands south of Bremen, was a provincial farm town, hardly more than a
crossroads. He had moved there two years before, although he still worked as a teacher in Bremen. City life was
too hectic. He was basically a man of the soil, and although he did little more than have a small vegetable garden and a chicken coop, he felt more satisfied living in
seclusion than he had ever felt while living in the city.

He drove into Neustadt, the post-war extension of Bremen, where, as its name implied, all the buildings were
newly built, boring and conventional, gray and white, aris-
ing phoenixlike from the ashes of the Third Reich. He
crossed the river into central Bremen and the *Ostertor*
quarter. The *Ostertor* was by far the most dynamic section
of Bremen. The street, which gave its name to the area, was
lined with small shops, restaurants, bars, jazz clubs, even a
repertory cinema. Mostly students lived in the area, either
in bed-sitters or communes. Separating the *Ostertor* from
the city center was the *Wall*, an ancient moat that had been
converted into a public park—trees and flowers planted
around it, ducks swimming on it, people lounging, in warm
weather, on the grass that surrounded it as it wound its way
around the ancient boundary of the medieval city.

By the time he arrived at Pete's it was already midnight.
The others had arrived before him. He was introduced to the

American and then he sat down on a beer crate, the only "chair" left unoccupied in Pete's cluttered living room.

Sigismund was sitting on the couch along with Hannelore and Christopher. Pete and Götz Fischer were in the two chairs. Norbert wiped the moisture from his glasses as Pete began explaining the reason for his summons.

"So, what it all comes down to," Pete concluded, "is that we have to decide what can be done to assist Gabriele and publicize this plot."

"I'm ready for anything," said Sigismund, "I've got sufficient weapons and ammunition hidden away that we can use if necessary."

Götz nodded in affirmation, brushing back his shoulder-length hair. He was so young, Norbert thought. These young idealists, always ready to plunge in headfirst. He, on the other hand, did not like the sound of it at all. His life was comfortable. He felt relatively happy. Why endanger himself?

"I think," Norbert interjected, "we ought to be very cautious and see what happens. If they do take the missiles, we should simply tell the authorities to comb the area around Wetzen. They'll find them."

"But," Hannelore said, her eyes darting from one to the other of them, "that might only provoke them to make good their threat. Those medium-range Tomahawk missiles, if they're armed with nuclear warheads, could obliterate not only a city, but also our whole movement. And have any of you considered what the result would be if they decide to use them not against a city, but against one of the nuclear power plants? Can you imagine the consequences then?"

Pete and Götz nodded.

Christopher was at a loss. He knew they were discussing their strategy, but there was nothing he could contribute to this German conversation until they told him their decisions. He listened, understanding only isolated words.

"The police," Hannelore continued, "and the special Anti-Terrorist Commando Unit has the propensity for rushing in with an iron fist, as we know. Besides, we don't want Gabriele to be hurt, either by Sievers's group or by the police. What is needed here is a bit more finesse. A surreptitious undermining of the whole plot. Perhaps we can prevent it before it even gets under way."

"But we can't unless we know their exact location and the correct timing," Pete said. "Christopher said he learned that they're planning a test at Garlstedt. So we know that much. But what route are the missiles to take, and where along such a route would it be most convenient to spring a trap?"

"If they're planning to hide them in Wetzen," offered Norbert, "then perhaps they already know that the route is going to bring the missiles near them. They're obviously going to be carried on large vehicles. You can't drive a missile carrier very far along the autobahn without being noticed. I think they plan to do the hijacking close to the area where they plan to conceal them, so as to minimize the time they will be most vulnerable to counterattack."

"Yes! That's it!" exclaimed Hannelore. "That's why you are such an important part of this group, Norbert. I'm sure your analysis is correct. Besides, their possession of the missiles gives them no advantage until they are armed and programmed, and I would venture to predict that they will want to get them as quickly as possible to a secure, quiet spot where this can be done."

"Well," said Pete, leaning back in his chair, stroking the cat on his lap, "I'm sure Gabriele will try to contact us again as soon as she knows. We'll monitor the telephone and in the meantime be prepared to move out."

He turned to Sigismund. "We'll go to your place and load up the VW with whatever 'supplies' you have."

"Good!" he said, smiling.

"The rest of you stay here. Hannelore, perhaps you can explain to Christopher what we've said and what preparations we are going to make."

She nodded.

"There are plenty of mattresses in the practice room. Throw some sleeping bags on them so you can all rest." He and Sigismund rose to go.

Norbert didn't really like it, but the others were in agreement that they must act. And in spite of his contentment with his life, he was just as committed as the rest of them and he had long ago vowed solidarity with them. Anyway, perhaps everything would be decided without their involvement. But if worse came to worst he knew he would not fail them—after all, he never forgot that his farm, his well-being, even his solitary existence were all connected to the rest of society, and the Sieverses of the world were threatening all of them.

He took a beer from the refrigerator, went down to the cellar and spread out a few of the mattresses that were lining the walls. He, Pete and several others had spent days, the year before, collecting these old mattresses from the trash, and had "soundproofed" the walls with them so as to transform the cellar into a practice room and studio. He leaned over the trap set and picked up one of Pete's guitars. He played a few tunes, then lay back staring at the ceiling as he nursed his beer.

CHAPTER TWELVE
Wetzen

MATECKI REPLACED the receiver and turned to General Forman.

"They've located Benton. He's with a cadre of radicals in Bremen."

Forman looked at the address Colonel Matecki had written down, then picked up the telephone. The number he called was in Bremerhaven. A voice with a Texas accent answered.

"We've got a little job for you, Morgan," he said. "Take Spinetti with you. You might need backup firepower." He gave the address in Bremen and explained what had to be done.

When he finished he buzzed Captain Packer on the intercom.

"Get everything ready. We'll be leaving first thing in the morning for Garlstedt."

Forman looked at Matecki and smiled.

"At last," he said. "At last."

HE SET DOWN the empty glass on his desk.

"That bitch!" Ulrich said aloud, then went on thinking silently. And she thinks she can get away with such an amateurish attempt to infiltrate our finely tuned organization! He rose from the straight-backed chair and paced the floor. It'll be enjoyable to teach her that she can't make a fool of me. I'll make her squirm.

He turned abruptly and walked to the door.

Helga watched him closely as he walked past her. They looked at each other, but neither spoke. He proceeded silently down the corridor and stopped outside Gabriele's door. He listened for a moment, then slowly twisted the knob, opened the door and stepped silently inside.

The light from the hallway fell across Gabriele's bed. He could see her sleeping form; the eiderdown was just below her shoulders, and the straps of her undershirt were visible.

She stirred slightly and he closed the door.

Without hesitation he removed his clothes.

THE DRIVER WAS THIN and muscular, in his early thirties and proud as hell to be an American. His grandfather had emigrated from Italy and although his father was born in the United States, he still had an Italian accent. But he, Anthony Spinetti, was one hundred percent pure American, and he would do anything for his country. He was proud, too, that no matter how difficult the task he had always volunteered for every dangerous mission when he was with the Marines. And now, as a member of the elite security division of NATO, he had dedicated himself to promoting American interests in the Old World.

He turned the wheel of the silver-gray Audi and left the autobahn after the quick fifty-kilometer drive from Bremerhaven. He glanced at his superior officer, James "Whitey" Morgan—Whitey, because of his prematurely gray hair closely cropped into a crew cut. Somewhere during his career his appearance had reminded someone of Whitey Herzog and the nickname was attached to him.

Morgan opened the case on his lap and made sure the two Colt .45s were loaded. He handed one to Spinetti, who took it and placed it in his shoulder holster. A silencer and three extra ammunition clips went into his pocket. He holstered his own Colt and then lifted his Smith & Wesson .38 special.

It always felt good to handle this favorite gun. He spun the cylinder and placed it in his coat pocket.

Spinetti was good, he thought, he could be trusted, but somehow...somehow, he was just a little too gung ho for his taste. Morgan had been working undercover for several years, and he just couldn't overcome his basic distrust of and dislike for most of these young, eager, efficient types that were being sent over. But, he smiled wryly to himself, I guess I was a little like that at the beginning, too....

The Audi slowed to a crawl.

"That's it." Morgan motioned with his head to number 17. Spinetti leaned over and peered through the passenger window. Then he wheeled the car around the corner and parked there.

Morgan took the photo out of his inside pocket and unfolded it. They both examined it for a moment.

"He's the primary. The one we've gotta get," he said. "Memorize his face real good. But if anyone is with him we have orders to take them out, too."

They took out their Colts, affixed the silencers and stepped out of the car. Spinetti left the key in the ignition.

"Okay, boss," he said, "let's blow these fuckers away."

Morgan winced.

PETE AND SIGISMUND had just set the third and final crate in the back of the van. Sigismund handed him a loaded Walther PPK and slipped a Mauser Parabellum inside his belt under his jacket.

"Be careful," he warned, "it's loaded." He demonstrated how to disengage the safety.

"I have several more PPKs with plenty of ammunition. In the crates are two French MAT 49 submachine guns I had smuggled in from my contacts in France. Also there are several rifles and even a few grenades."

"Scheisse!" said Pete, "you're prepared for a bloody war!"

Sigismund winked and smiled, dimples creasing his thin, pockmarked face.

"Let's go."

They shut the sliding door, got in the van and headed back to Kohlhökerstrasse.

SHE WAS DREAMING. Christopher was there. He was coming to her.

She opened her eyes.

It was not a dream. It was not Christopher.

The eiderdown was being lifted up and she turned to confront the shadowy figure.

"Gabriele," Ulrich said, slithering under the cover and pressing close to her.

"Ulrich! What are you doing?" She was shocked and afraid. He was aroused. She could feel him, hard and rough. Pushing at her.

"No. Ulrich, no!" she pleaded.

"Oh come on, Gabriele, since when have you become so shy? You've joined us now. I'm just going to seal the pact by fucking you."

"Please, Ulrich, don't!"

"Don't tell me there's someone else?"

Her mind was nearing panic. She must think fast. He was testing her. She was sure of it.

"No. Of course not."

"Then stop resisting," he said and he began yanking the shirt up over her head.

Oh God! No! Christopher! Help me. She wanted to run. She wanted to push him off. He was so coarse. So vulgar. So hard. So insensitive.

He pressed his hands under her buttocks and spread her open, then he began ramming at her.

She lay completely passive, staring up at the ceiling past his head, his breath moist and warm against her neck, strands of his thin hair brushing her face.

He had penetrated her. God, it hurt. I don't remember him ever hurting like this before, she thought. He's too big. Far too big.

He moved, pushing harder, harder, then back and forth, pumping. She thought she would be ripped in half.

Oh God! She moaned.

"You like that!" he said, panting. "You haven't been fucked by a real man in a long time, *nicht wahr*?"

He leaned on his elbows looking at her. She didn't look at him, she couldn't look at him. He was moving furiously, and she had to do something before it killed her. The pain was too much. Finally she began moving, rocking her hips, arching her back. Get it over with, you bastard, she thought, damn it!

"Come on then," she said, "fuck me. Do it. Pump it into me. Show me what a real man you are!"

Her words pushed him over. "Ahhh..." He let out a convulsive sigh as he came.

She could feel him pulsate, feel the semen, warm and sticky, begin to ooze out of her. Tears were rising. She wanted to cry. So desperately. But she didn't dare. He must not be allowed to know anything about her.

They lay still for several minutes, his heavy breathing slowly subsiding.

Oh please go. Go soon. I need to be alone.

He pulled out of her.

"That was a good start," he said, rising up and sitting astride her stomach.

His penis hung in front of her face, slightly limp, but still hard.

Suddenly he grabbed her behind the head and pulled her away from the pillow. With one hand he held his penis and forced it into her mouth.

"Come on, suck it," he ordered, his left hand pinching the tendons on the back of her neck.

No. No. She couldn't believe it. This wasn't a test. He was simply raping her. He pushed into her throat and began rocking back and forth.

Now the tears began to flow. She couldn't stop them, nor the humiliation.

He jammed harder. She began to gag and some vomit came up. She thought she would suffocate. He was strangling her. Abruptly he dropped her head back to the pillow as he ejaculated, sperm landing on her face, her eyes, her nose, mingling with the vomit on her lips.

She was sobbing.

He looked at her. She was so pathetic, he thought. So pathetic.

He got off the bed and picked up his clothes from the floor.

"Good night, my sweet," he said and patted her wet cheeks roughly.

He opened the door and walked out stark naked, his clothes over his arm. He passed Helga, who smiled at him.

"Get Bernhard to take over for you and come to my room," he said.

She stood up, cupped his testicles in her hand, wiping off some of the stickiness with the other hand. Then she hurried down the stairs ahead of him.

CHAPTER THIRTEEN

Bremen

CHRISTOPHER AND HANNELORE were seated at each end of the couch. She had been telling him how she and Pete had first met. She was hitchhiking and Pete had driven past her in the opposite direction. He continued on for about a mile, then turned around and picked her up. Took her all the way up to Blumenthal even though he had been heading for Hemmelingen! Evidently it was love at first dialectical argument. They always argued and discussed Marxian dialectics and had pretty much, over the years, learned to agree about disagreeing.

There was a knock at the door. Götz, who was in the kitchen, called that he would answer it.

He opened the door. He saw the men standing there, and the expression on their faces made him react instantly. He pushed the door shut with his shoulder. *"Hannelore!"* he shouted. *"Run! Quickly!"*

She rose from the couch.

Pfft!

A hole ripped into Götz's neck.

Christopher leaped to his feet. He *knew* that sound!

Pfft!

"Gunfire!" he shouted, his eyes panicky. "They've come!"

"Quick!" Hannelore said, grabbing his hand and running into the bedroom. She locked the door behind them and pointed to the window. He raced across the room and

tried to open it. It wouldn't budge. Then he realized the window opened outward. They could hear footsteps behind them in the living room. He stopped trying to slide the window up, undid the catch and swung it open.

Hannelore had opened a drawer and pulled out a hunting knife. "Come on!" she ordered as she jumped easily out the window. He followed, landing softly in a frosty flower bed about six feet below. As he landed he could hear the door to the bedroom crash open.

Oh my God! Had Gabriele given them away? The question flashed through his churning mind. How had they discovered where he was so soon?

Hannelore was creeping along the wall ahead of him toward the kitchen window, the knife held in readiness.

NORBERT HAD HEARD the commotion on the floor above and scrambled out of the sleeping bag. He rushed over to the foot of the cellar steps as the footsteps above resounded throughout the building. In the corner were some tools Pete used for his VW. He found a tire iron and scurried underneath the cellar steps.

The door at the top of the stairs flew open and banged against the wall.

PETE STOPPED the VW in front of the house. The parking space they had vacated was still there, and he thought how lucky they were. At the same instant he noticed the door to the house was ajar.

He turned off the ignition and pointed to the door.

"*Scheisse!*" Sigismund swore, pulling the Mauser from his belt and jumping out of the car. Pete followed him and they crept stealthily up to the steps.

Sigismund peered over the threshold and gasped when he saw Götz's body lying about ten feet back from the door, almost at the entrance to the kitchen. From the grotesque way he was lying in a pool of blood, there was no doubt that he was dead.

Sigismund ducked back out as he caught sight of a man heading into the cellar. He leaned against the wall to the side of the stoop.

"They've killed Götz," he said to Pete.

Pete felt the blood drain from his face and his knees became weak. He thought he would faint.

THE KITCHEN LIGHT cast the elongated shadow of the gunman into the backyard. Hannelore stood and moved closer. Morgan saw her movement and fired through the window.

Glass shattered around them as Hannelore, who had seen him whirl toward her, hit the ground. There was blood on her face.

"Run!" she gasped. "I'm not hit, it's the glass."

They both took off toward the back of the yard and the neighboring garden on the other side of the fence. She leaned against a tree next to the fence. "Over you go," she ordered.

Morgan pushed the window frame aside and jumped in a low crouch into the yard. He followed in pursuit.

Christopher had just vaulted over the fence. Morgan caught only a glimpse of him, but he knew right away that he was the one they wanted. He stood next to the tree and leaned his arm against it for support. Taking careful aim with both hands at the fleeing figure twenty-five feet away he very slowly began squeezing the trigger.

The arm and the gun were stretched out, only inches from Hannelore's face. Gripping the knife tightly, she slashed, with all her might.

She could feel the knife, as it cut through the fabric of the coat and the flesh of the forearm, come to a jarring halt as it struck bone.

There was a grunt of pain as the gun dropped to the ground, and the man pulled away. The knife was embedded in his arm. He glared at her with hatred in his eyes as she grabbed for the gun. Reaching over with his left hand he yanked the knife from his arm. For a moment it looked as though he would strike out at her, but the blood that started gushing from the severed veins prevented him. He dropped the knife and attempted to stem the flow by pressing his hand over the wound.

Hannelore, holding the gun steadily, raised it and sighted along the barrel.

He looked into the barrel of his own gun, then leaped deftly to the side just as she squeezed the trigger. A flash of light erupted from the gun as a bullet brushed by him, creasing his left shoulder. Without further hesitation, he dived over the fence and ran into the shadows of the yard on the far side.

Hannelore spun around trying to take another shot, but her target was dodging evasively toward the alley alongside the house facing the other street. Christopher had just gone that way, she knew. She might hit him by mistake. She turned around and rushed back to the house, the gun in her hand.

NORBERT COULD SEE the heels of the leather shoes through the cracks in the stairs. The man descending had almost reached the foot of the stairs, and Norbert shifted his weight to get a better grip on the tire iron. He would wait until the man had stepped into the middle of the room and then, when his back was to him, would jump out and strike him.

As he shifted he inadvertently bumped the tire iron against the stairs. The man jumped off the last step and spun around, aiming his gun through the stairs. Norbert looked helplessly at him and knew he was about to die.

A shot rang out.

A red blossom sprang from the man's forehead and he fell backward, dead before he hit the floor.

Norbert staggered out from under the stairs and threw up.

Sigismund raced down the stairs, his Mauser ready for a second shot. He looked at the body then turned to Norbert.

"Are you all right?"

Norbert looked up from the floor, wiping the vomit with his sleeve, unable to answer.

"How many are there?" Sigismund asked impatiently.

"I...don't know.... At least another one.... I heard him...in the kitchen."

Sigismund darted back up the stairs.

CHRISTOPHER PASSED through the alley and scrambled under a hedge in the front yard of the house to his left. He was gasping for breath.

And then he heard someone else gasping. It wasn't Hannelore, who he had thought was right behind him.

He lay utterly still as a man rushed by. The man was cradling his right arm in his left. Christopher waited a moment, then followed him at a distance. The man went around the block toward the front of Pete's house. At the corner he got into a parked Audi and drove off.

Christopher stared at the vanishing car, repeating the license number over and over to himself, committing it to memory.

Then he ran around to the front of the house and up the steps.

PETE AND SIGISMUND were in the kitchen.

"Oh my God," Christopher said, looking down at Götz's body.

The other two turned sharply, Sigismund half raised his gun, but when he saw Christopher he lowered it.

"Close the door," Pete ordered urgently.

Norbert was coming up from the cellar. He looked ill.

Pete was tugging at Hannelore's arm, helping her through the destroyed kitchen window. There were a few cuts on her face where the flying glass had struck her. She wet a dish towel at the sink and wiped gingerly at the scratches.

They all stood there silently for a moment.

"Are there any others?" Sigismund asked.

Pete translated for Benton.

"One got away in an Audi," he said. "I've memorized the license number. Give me something to write on."

Pete handed him the pad next to the telephone. He jotted down the number.

"Bremerhaven," said Pete, looking at it. "It's a Bremerhaven registration."

They walked together through the rooms, then paused over Götz's body.

"He tried to warn us," said Hannelore. "They killed him for it. He was so damn young.... I'm glad I wounded the one who got away. It must have nearly severed his arm. I wish I had shot him, too." Her face was grim. No one doubted her sincerity.

Norbert and Christopher seemed to be the most shaken.

Sigismund led them downstairs and they went through the pockets of the man he had shot. "He's got an international driver's license, issued in Baltimore. Spinetti is his name, Anthony Spinetti. There are a lot of Americans stationed in Bremerhaven. The American base there. It makes sense."

"They were after me."

They all turned to look at Christopher. "Yes," he spoke the obvious, "somehow they had learned I was here."

There was silence.

"The only person who knew was Gabriele. But I can't believe she told them, unless it was under duress."

"They probably overheard her telephone call to me," said Pete, "and that would make her situation there very dangerous.... Anyway, we know for certain how absolutely serious they are. Deadly serious. They've killed Götz. They were going to kill Christopher. They probably would have killed all of us. Obviously they will let nothing stand in the way of their strategy."

"But *Americans*," said Hannelore, "it's Americans who are ultimately behind this whole thing. I wonder if Sievers is a willing accomplice, or a dupe."

"We've got to do something about the dead," said Norbert, his face still ashen.

"We'll take them to a secluded spot and make an anonymous call to the police," Hannelore ventured. "But we must wait until tomorrow to call them. The police will connect Götz with us and we must avoid any inquiries until after tomorrow. We need time. If the American government or the CIA is behind this operation, then they might very easily have the German police under their control. I don't trust anyone."

"She's right," seconded Sigismund.

He and Pete grabbed Spinetti's arms and legs and dragged him upstairs.

Slide... thump.

Slide... thump.

Slide... thump.

The sound of the body being dragged along the stairs, the head thumping on every step, magnified in Christopher's brain. He knew he would never forget that sound.

Then they straightened out Götz's legs while Hannelore took two sheets out of a closet to wrap the bodies.

"Sigismund," said Pete, "you stay here with Hannelore and Christopher. Keep your gun ready in case another attempt is made. Norbert, you come with me. We'll put them in the VW and take them up to Blockland."

They carried the shrouded bodies hastily to the van. It was late and cold. No one was about. No lights came from any of the neighboring houses. Their movements, as awkward as they were, would hopefully go unnoticed. Even if they were seen there was little to be done about it now. All the while Pete kept repeating silently to himself, do not think. Do not think. Just act. It's the only way to survive.

HE COULD NOT STOP the flow of blood. It still spurted from his arm, and he knew that if he didn't do something soon he would lose consciousness. Morgan pulled the Audi off the road. He took off his tie, wrapped it around his upper arm and, holding one end with his teeth, pulled it as tightly as possible. The flow subsided. He looked at the blood covering the seat, the gearshift, the steering wheel. The arm was nearly useless. He couldn't go back and shoot them all, which was what he most wanted to do. Neither could he return to base and report his failure.

He examined his left shoulder where the bullet had grazed him. It was no more than a scratch. There was little blood, but it burned like hell. He moved his arm, pivoting his shoulder. Yes, it was still functional. He tried handling the Smith & Wesson and found that it felt comfortable enough in his left hand. It was awkward, but he would be able to shoot.

But whatever he did, he had to act fast. His right arm would have to be attended to by a physician as soon as possible. His hand was already numb. He had to go back. He had to put revenge from his mind. He would not have the strength to go up against them all. But his assignment to kill Benton *absolutely* had to be carried out.

Benton.

He wheeled the car around and headed back toward Kohlhökerstrasse.

HER SOBS WERE finally subsiding.

Gabriele ached all over. But the physical pain was nothing compared to the psychological. The sense of violation. And she had never been so vulnerable before in her entire life.

Her mind yearned for Christopher. She wanted him to come and hold her and comfort her and extract her from this horror. She had never suspected at any moment of her adult life that she would want or need one person so completely. But she knew it was all up to her now. Her alone.

Something had gone wrong. Ulrich was not including her in the plan. She was indeed his prisoner. She had to escape, it was her only chance. She was determined to survive.

Gabriele slowly got out of bed and turned on the overhead light. Her body looked foreign to her. It was something apart, separate from her. She looked in the mirror. Her face was sore, the nauseous taste was still in her mouth. She turned on the hot water tap, then threw handfuls of water on her face, washing away the vomit, washing away *him*.

She put on her pullover and looked into the hall.

No one.

She stepped out, goose pimples immediately covering her bare legs. She walked toward the bathroom. Bernhard was sitting on the landing staring up at her. She pulled the bottom of the sweater lower to cover her crotch. Then she entered the bathroom.

Will they ever let down their guard? Gabriele wondered, filling the tub. If only she could get out of the house, she could take one of the cars or motorcycles and get to Bremen—to Christopher. Or even without a vehicle, she could go through the fields to the woods. They would never find her once she got loose. She loved the forest and had spent the summer each year hiking in Switzerland, in Scandinavia, in the Black Forest. They were her home. She knew how to hide herself, how to survive, for days if necessary.

No. If she could get to the woods no one would ever find her.

The water was as hot as she could stand it. She lay back in the tub, gasping with the rush of burning heat all over her, through her, scalding her, cleansing her, purging her.

HANNELORE CAME UP the cellar steps.

Sigismund and Christopher had just finished washing the blood from the entranceway. Neither had spoken, their task benumbing them.

They followed Hannelore into the kitchen as she placed several items on the table. Spinetti's wallet, gun and ammunition.

"Notice," Hannelore said, fingering the silencer of the gun, "this gun is the mate to the one I took from the assassin in the garden." She pulled it out of her belt. "I would bet anything the two Colt .45s are United States Government issue." She looked at Christopher. "There is no doubt we can lay Götz's death at the feet of Uncle Sam."

"I'm sure you're right," he said. "Someone tried to kill me last week with a gun that looked very much like this."

She handed Spinetti's Colt and the extra bullet clips to him. "I've got my souvenir. Here's yours. I suggest you learn how to use it and feel comfortable with it. When the one who got away realizes his partner didn't, he'll be back." She switched off the light. "Come."

They went into the front room after locking all the doors. She lit a candle, dripped wax onto a plate, stuck the candle to the wax and set it on the floor in one corner.

"You two keep watch by the front window. Stay out of sight, but call me if you see any movement whatsoever. Use the gun, if necessary. But don't shoot each other. Christopher, if you're too nervous give the gun to Sigismund." She could see by the expression on Christopher's face that he

was somewhat insulted at her lack of confidence in him. She
knew she was overreacting. They would be all right.

"I'll be at the bedroom window. I expect he'll come that
way. It's darker, and besides, he knows how to use that alley now. Remember he'll be favoring his right arm. He'll be
holding a gun in his left hand."

They looked at each other, then moved off, stationing
themselves at the windows.

BLOCKLAND.

It was a *Naturschutzgebiet*. A bird and wildlife sanctuary north of Bremen, beyond the university. Students often
took lengthy bicycle tours on weekends through the area
along the dikes bordering the canals and streams.

Pete drove the van slowly along a dike. The gravel road
was no wider than the van, but he wasn't expecting to meet
any other traffic at this time of night. To their right the low-
lying land covered with tall grass and cattails stretched into
the night. He knew that many birds nested there, but there
wouldn't be many in January. Still, if there were two bodies lying hidden from view in the grass, the wildlife of the
area would eventually give away their presence. It wouldn't
do to have a flock of scavenging birds flying in circles all day
tomorrow. He considered weighting the bodies and putting
them in the canal on the far side of the dike to their left, but
he thought of Götz and decided he couldn't do it.

The road came to an end, at least for vehicles. There were
four concrete posts spaced close together so that only bicy-
cles could continue farther. On the other side there was a
small copse of trees on a slight incline between the path and
the swampy bird sanctuary.

He stopped the van.

Norbert slid open the door. Gently they grasped Götz by
the feet and shoulders and crossed through the posts, turn-

ing right, off the path and into the copse. They tripped several times on the underbrush, but finally managed to get to the far side. They set the body down and went back for the other. Again, another stumbling walk through the brush.

When finally they had set down their burden, they gathered together leaves and branches and piled them loosely over the bodies.

"This will have to do," Pete said. "Certainly it will be no more than a day before someone, or some animal, discovers them. But that's probably all the time we'll need, anyway."

For a minute they looked down at the mound. Then quietly they pushed their way through the scrub back to the van.

GABRIELE DRIED herself off repeatedly, then returned to her room.

Bernhard stared at her, as she passed, but said nothing.

She closed the door behind her. There was no key, but it probably wouldn't keep Sievers out even if she could lock the door.

The sheet was a mess. She stripped it off the bed, then threw the eiderdown over the bare mattress. She turned out the light, crawled under the eiderdown and closed her eyes.

She would never be able to sleep. She looked at the luminescent dial on her watch lying on the bedside table. Four in the morning. She lay with her eyes open, imploring sleep to come, but every time her eyes closed they sprang open again.

Every creak and groan in the house made her jump into alert wakefulness. Finally, her head aching from the effort, she slipped into a fitful doze.

PETE HAD JUST DRIVEN around the traffic circle at the border of Schwachhausen when he saw the flashing lights of the police car behind them.

"Scheisse, Scheisse, Scheisse," he said.

Norbert looked at him, petrified.

"What if they find the weapons?" he asked, trying to control his voice.

"Just keep calm," Pete said, pulling the car over to the side of Parkallee, "this is just one of their routine checks. It pisses me off how they pick on every older vehicle with Atomkraft Danke Nein stickers on it. They hope we're drunk so they can suspend my driver's license. *Scheisse!* It's harassment."

"But they might search the car!" Norbert's eyes darted back and forth as two officers stepped out of the patrol car and approached them.

"Then, of course, we'll be arrested. Stay quiet. Let me handle this."

Pete rolled down the window as the first officer arrived next to the driver's door. The other policeman stood next to Norbert, his hand resting lightly on his holster.

"Papiere, bitte!" the first cop demanded.

Pete handed over his license, registration and *Personalausweis*—the personal identity card that all Germans must carry. Norbert gave his to the second cop.

They examined the papers. Then the second officer took them, returned to the police car and radioed in the information.

"Herr Schlegel, have you been drinking this evening?"

"No. I mean, well, a few hours ago I had, perhaps, two beers. Is that why you stopped us? I know I haven't broken any traffic regulations."

"Will you agree to take a breathalyzer test?"

"Natürlich," he said, stepping out of the van. Must get them away from the van, he thought, they mustn't become too curious about those crates!

Norbert watched as Pete preceded the policeman back to the patrol car. The officer on the radio looked at his colleague and shook his head. "No warrants out for them," he said.

Pete was convinced that the cop was disappointed. He had to fight back the desire to shout at them, to attack them for their prejudicial tactics of hassling students and those too poor to drive Mercedes Benzes or Audis or BMWs. It seemed the cops only made these checks on Volkswagens or old Fiats or broken-down Deux Cheveaux. The bastards!

But he had to play along. Any resistance in his attitude and they would surely search them.

The first policeman handed him a plastic container with a tube attached, and instructed him to blow into it. There was a clear liquid in the container, and Pete knew that if the alcohol content in his blood exceeded a certain minimum level the liquid would turn color.

He blew. One long expulsion of air.

The officer took the container and held it up to the headlight of the car. *"Nichts."* Nothing. His voice, too, was laced with disappointment.

The police handed back their papers.

"Gute Nacht," one of the officers said with a slight nod of his head, and then he turned and got back into the car.

Pete walked slowly and deliberately back to the van, fighting the urge to run. He got behind the wheel, handed Norbert his I.D. without saying a word and unhurriedly drove off.

The cops followed them for several blocks, probably to ascertain that they were returning home. All the while Pete strained to remain calm.

Finally, near the station, the police turned off, and they both sighed. "I thought I was going to faint," Norbert said after a few minutes.

Pete parked the VW on Wulwesstrasse, took a board he usually kept in the van as a sleeping platform for camping and set it across the back seat area, effectively covering the three ammunition crates. God, he thought, if those cops had searched the car... All they would have had to do was shine their flashlights through the side windows.... That was too close.

"We're damned lucky we weren't arrested," he said as he locked the van. They looked through the windows to verify that nothing was visible from outside, then went up the steps to the house.

Sigismund met them at the door to the living room. "I saw you drive up. Everything work out okay?" he asked.

Pete looked at Norbert. "Yes," he said.

"Hannelore's doing sentry duty at the bedroom window. I'm at the front. Christopher's fallen asleep on the couch. Why don't you two get some sleep?"

Pete nodded. He was exhausted. It was hard to imagine that only a few hours earlier they had been drinking heavily and singing songs. He was astonished that the alcohol had not registered on the breathalyzer test, but then he felt none of its effects now, anyway.

"Wake me if you start falling asleep and we'll switch."

Sigismund nodded.

Norbert and Pete went into the bedroom. Hannelore turned to look at them from her post at the window. "We're going to get some sleep," Pete explained. "If you need to be relieved, wake us."

"Okay." She turned her watchful eye back to the garden.

They lay on top of the bed and within minutes both had fallen asleep. Pete was snoring lightly, Norbert's breathing was a heavy rhythmic undertone.

MORGAN HAD BEEN SITTING in the car on the parallel street for several minutes. He could see the alley between the houses that led to the backyards of the houses on Kohlhökerstrasse. He was grateful it was the only alley on the street, otherwise he might not have recognized it.

His arm still ached, but numbness was creeping up, taking over from the throbbing below the makeshift tourniquet. His fingers seemed to be totally immobile now. If he didn't get to a doctor very soon he might lose the arm. No more time to waste.

He opened the door and stepped into the street.

HANNELORE WAS EXHAUSTED.

Twice she had caught herself nodding off.

If it happens again, she thought, I'll have to wake Eckhardt and have him take over. No. She must keep going. She wanted this bastard. Her hatred was nearly consuming her. She thought of the time six years before when she had returned from Turkey and was busted crossing into Germany. The insults and the indignity of the body searches she had endured at the hands of the authorities. Eighteen months in jail for a lousy twenty grams of hashish. These emissaries of the state were all killers, were all life destroyers, whether it was the border guards, or the police, or the jailers, or the paid assassins of the United States government. There was no doubt in her mind about this one. From Bremerhaven. Living in Germany with the consent and compliance of the German government, probably even invited here. *Scheisse,* she hated them all. The official destroyers who sapped the spirit of a country...

There was a movement! Yes!

Near the tree where she had struck him with the knife, a form had slipped over the fence.

Hannelore drew back into the shadows alongside the window. She held the gun ready and peered out.

There he was.

Easing out from behind the tree and gliding swiftly and silently along the side wall. Obviously a professional. His right arm was held horizontally across his middle. There was a gun in his left hand.

Just as she'd expected.

He moved up to the kitchen window, but then backed off quickly when he saw he was about to tread on fragments of broken glass.

Very observant, she thought, and very careful.

He skirted the broken glass and crouched outside the bedroom window. There were several beer crates piled against the side of the house a few feet beyond the bedroom window. He silently took the top one and set it under the window. He placed another one on top of it and another next to it, forming a makeshift stepladder.

She pulled back farther into the shadows and pressed herself flat against the wall as she saw him step up and look in the window. His face was less than a yard away, but she was just out of his line of sight. He looked at the sleeping forms on the bed.

Slowly, very slowly, and without a sound, he eased the window fully open and stepped up higher. Holding his left forearm against the sill, with the gun pointed straight down at the floor, he began hauling himself over the ledge.

This was the moment! He was completely at her mercy. What satisfaction this would bring her!

She stepped out from the wall and stood before him.

Morgan looked up at her.

"You fucker!" she said in English.

He started to raise his left arm and as he did so he began slipping backward.

She pressed the barrel of the silencer into his right eye and pulled the trigger.

Pfft!

His left eye staring wide and incredulously at her, he fell back out the window and with a thud landed on his back in the garden. His legs twitched spasmodically as she stared down at him.

Norbert had stirred, and half opened his eyes looking at her. Pete had not budged.

"Go back to sleep," she said calmly.

Sigismund opened the door. "I heard something," he said.

"You did. I've got him. It's over. Now we have another body to dispose of."

He followed her to the window and looked out. "Christ!" he whispered. "You did an efficient job!"

He clambered out using the beer crates. "Go to the kitchen, I'll heave him up there so we don't wake the others."

He carried the crates over to the kitchen window. He pried the gun from Morgan's left hand and gave it to Hannelore. Then he threw the body over his shoulder and carried it to the windowsill. He heaved it up so that it landed half over the sill and was dangling into the kitchen. Then he climbed up and the two of them dragged the body over the sill and onto the kitchen floor.

"It's going to be daylight soon," Sigismund said, "so we'll have to keep this one here, at least until tonight."

They half carried, half dragged the corpse out of the kitchen and down the cellar stairs. There was an old, unused coal bin in the back. They placed the body in the corner.

Sigismund went through the man's pockets. There were several rounds of ammunition for the Smith & Wesson, a wallet and a folded piece of paper. That was all.

Hannelore unfolded the paper and saw it was a photograph of Christopher. She raised her eyebrows and handed it over to Sigismund without comment.

They returned upstairs.

Sigismund took a sleeping bag and laid it on the floor next to the couch where Christopher was sleeping. Two cats stared at him from the incongruous birch tree. They had been perched there throughout the night.

Hannelore went into the bedroom. She was surprised that she felt so calm and relaxed.

She locked the window before squeezing onto the double bed. Snuggling up to the oblivious Pete, she threw one arm over him and, contentment stealing over her, fell into a deep sleep.

CHAPTER FOURTEEN
Wetzen

Friday, 6 January, 0700 hours

THE PHONE WAS RINGING. Ulrich reached across Helga's naked form and lifted the receiver.

"*Ja?*"

"Eight hours," a voice said. "Route 209, as per plan."

"Right."

The line went dead.

He swung his feet to the floor and rubbed his face with his hands. He stretched, stood up, threw on a robe and walked down the hall to Thalberg's room.

He knocked and entered without waiting for an acknowledgment. The colonel looked up at him from the bed.

"Two-oh-nine," Ulrich said.

Thalberg looked at his watch. "Good. They leave the base at three this afternoon. They'll be nearing Sottorf between six-thirty and seven."

"We'll begin preparations at ten. You might as well sleep as long as you can," Sievers said, then returned to his own room.

0900 hours

THE UNITED STATES AIR FORCE jet from Brussels came out of the low-lying clouds and touched down on the wet runway in Bremerhaven. Colonel Matecki, General Forman and Captain Packer were the only passengers.

Lieutenant Colonel Richard Oster, surrounded by several aides, met them as they disembarked. He saluted. "Welcome to Bremerhaven, General," he said, addressing Forman.

The general returned his salute.

"This is Colonel Matecki and Captain Packer," he introduced the two to Oster. "The colonel will oversee the preparations for the exercise. Captain Packer is my aide."

"This way, sir."

They followed Colonel Oster to two waiting limousines. Forman sat with Oster in the lead car. Matecki and Packer followed in the second.

"The drive to the base won't take very long, General," Oster said, as the car crawled off the tarmac. "But perhaps you can fill me in on the finer details of the exercise. Everything, of course, is all set, as you had instructed."

"Very good." He looked through the darkened window as they left the airport. "We'll commence the exercise at 1500. The route is mapped out to take the convoy through a variety of roads, both autobahns and back roads, in an effort to simulate as far as possible the uncertain conditions that would prevail during an actual alert. They'll be on the road for approximately eight hours, and visit three possible launching sites before returning to base. We have many options that are programmed into the computer. This morning I selected at random one of those options." He extracted a sealed manila envelope marked Top Secret from his attaché case. "When we get to the base you will open this and follow the instructions precisely. As I said, Colonel Matecki will supervise operations. I'm merely present as an observer."

"What about protection for the convoy?"

"No more than the usual contingent of military police. I've even decided against having a troop carrier...."

"But, General..." the colonel started to protest.

"No—" Forman held up his hand "—that won't be necessary. We want the test to be run as close as possible to real combat conditions. And in a combat situation there would be little opportunity to protect the TELs. They'd be sent out to launch their missiles. The minute they did so they'd no longer be possible targets. The only reason I've agreed to any security at all for this secret test—and you must remember it *is* secret, none of the demonstrators will be expecting this, so I doubt if there'll be any trouble—is the German government with its terrorist paranoia is on my neck. They'll of course be informed of the test, once it's under way. But I don't want them interfering with it like a flock of goddamn mother hens."

The cars crossed a heath and turned onto a private road. Signs in English and in German warned trespassers that it was forbidden to travel farther.

They arrived at a sentry box at a large gate. There were armed guards stationed formidably every fifty feet along the double fence that stretched away on either side.

A black military policeman approached the window. The driver gave him a clipboard. He examined the order affixed to it, looked into the limousines and saluted.

The gate opened and the two vehicles sped onto the base.

1000 hours

THE DOOR OPENED. Gabriele jumped up instantly, pulling the cover protectively around her. She was still wearing her sweater.

"Gabriele." It was Antje. "It's time to get up." There was no warmth in her voice. "You are wanted downstairs." She closed the door.

Gabriele got to her feet and dressed. There was no guard on the landing as she headed downstairs. *Scheisse,* she thought, did I miss a chance to escape?

There was the aroma of coffee wafting from the doorway opposite the conference room on the ground floor. She felt hungry. She looked inside.

Helga and Erich were in the kitchen drinking coffee and eating rolls with salami and cheese. Helga smiled maliciously. "Ulrich wants you," she said. There was an ominous undertone to her voice. "He's across the hall."

"Do you mind if I have some coffee first?" Gabriele asked contemptuously.

"Help yourself." Helga shrugged, making no move to offer any.

Gabriele poured a cup of strong black coffee. She ate a roll with cheese in silence while drinking the coffee, then poured a second cup and took it with her into the conference room.

"Ah, good morning, Gabriele," said Ulrich, rising. He was seated at the table with Thalberg, Bernhard and Klaus.

"I trust you slept well?" he said with a sneer.

"I didn't know the word *trust* was a part of your vocabulary," she replied.

"Achh...Gabriele, what a wit you are!"

He walked toward her. "Our plans are all set. You'll be interested to know that the hijacking takes place not far from here on Bundesstrasse 209 at seven tonight. But first—" he started out the door "—come with me, I want to show you something."

He motioned her to follow. She hesitated, uncertain. "Come on, I won't hurt you!" He grinned.

They went down the cellar steps and he led her into the alcove with the switchboard and tape recorder.

She looked around the dimly lit damp cellar with a sense of foreboding. The smell of potatoes and mildew pervaded the air.

Sievers started the tape recorder.

"Christopher is here." Eckhardt's voice leaped out at her from the speaker, and then her own voice. "Good." Oh, my God! They had taped the conversation. They knew everything!

She slumped defeated onto the chair as he switched off the machine.

"I thought you would like to know that we had the telephone number traced and that two armed exterminators were sent to Kohlhökerstrasse 17 in Bremen last night, while we were making love, to kill him. So if you have any thoughts of rescue, discard them."

Suddenly and without warning, he grabbed her hair and yanked her backward. Both she and the chair went sprawling. He pulled her to her feet. "You fucking bitch," he snarled, then struck her with his fist, full on the mouth.

She thought she would pass out. She fell against the switchboard, knocking a telephone off its hook.

Then he hit her again. And again.

Vainly, she tried protecting herself with her arms. "Stop it. Stop it!" she managed to shout. "Haven't you abused me enough already?"

"Abuse!" His eyes looked as if they would burst from their sockets. "You think I'm a fool! You always did!" He wrapped his fingers around her neck and lifted her off her feet.

She lashed out and kicked him in the groin with her knee. He released her and doubled over.

She ran to the foot of the stairs, but he lunged out and tripped her. She lay on the floor, but before she could get up he stood above her and kicked her in the stomach. She rolled over, trying to elude him.

He kicked her viciously in the back. She gasped. She thought she must be paralyzed.

"You bitch." He grabbed her ankles and dragged her across the stone floor to a wooden grate opposite the switchboard. He opened the grate and dragged her into the potato cellar and cast her against the wall.

"You sniveling, whimpering cunt. I'll deal with you when we return. You should be good for a few more fucks before I cut your throat." He kicked her again in the left breast, took the gun from his belt and hit her, sharply, at the base of the skull. Then he rose, shut the grate and locked it.

1200 hours

COLONEL MATECKI CLIMBED up to the launch platform of the TEL. He reached out and touched the cream-colored nose cone of the missile, caressing it almost tenderly. It was beautiful to see, stretching out its full six yards before him.

He stepped farther along the launch rig and reached the panel on the sleek side of the missile. He took a wrench, especially designed for the job, from the holster clipped to his belt. Six sunken bolts were holding the panel in place. Only one tool could operate them. He set to work, slowly and carefully extracting the bolts and removing the cover.

The colonel took a stainless steel key from his pocket and inserted it into the armament mechanism. As it turned, a projectile slid out of the adjacent receptacle. He removed it completely from the locking mechanism and stepped back on the scaffolding.

There was a large black case at his feet. He opened it and picked up a seemingly identical projectile to the one in his other hand. Matecki exchanged the two projectiles and, taking the new one, slipped it into the receptacle in the missile, pushing it until he heard the click. Then, as he rotated the key, it slid back into its compartment.

He removed the key and set the cover back over the compartment.

Though he knew the extra caution was unnecessary, his excitement was heightened enough that he replaced the screws to the panel with even more care than he had removed them.

Colonel Matecki climbed down the gantry and walked across to the other side of the TEL. He repeated the entire process on missile three.

When he had finished he stood for a moment admiring his handiwork.

The nuclear warheads of missiles one and three on the TEL were now fully armed.

1430 hours

SIEVERS HASTILY DESCENDED the cellar steps and looked through the grate into the larder where Gabriele still lay.

After unlocking the slatted door, he stepped through, and knelt on one knee to listen carefully to her breathing while feeling her pulse.

She was still unconscious, but there was no telling when she might come to. Again he raised the gun and struck her head in the same spot. That should keep her for a few more hours, he thought.

He rose, locked the grate again and pocketed the key. At the top of the cellar stairs he turned off the lights and bolted the heavy door behind him.

1630 hours

SIEVERS ROLLED UP the map. "Any last questions?" he asked.

There were none.

They filed out of the room. Ulrich and Erich set the alarms for the windows and doors, and then they proceeded across the compound. The sky was clouding over heavily, dark black clouds rolling in from the northwest. A storm seemed imminent. Hopefully, Thalberg thought as he looked at the sky, it will hold off until after the missiles are safely here.

The eight entered the shed. Bernhard went to one of the jeeps and checked the ammunition supply. Alex checked the other. It had all been done every day for the past week, but they went through the routine anyway.

Klaus would drive the follow-up VW with Helga and Erich. Antje and Ulrich would be in the truck that would stage the "accident." They spoke among themselves about the various contingencies that might possibly develop, checked their weapons and supplies. Everything was, as expected, in order.

"Colonel Thalberg, this way please," said Alex when they had finished the preparations. He showed him into the radio room and instructed him on the various bands they would be using. "This monitor will keep you posted on the action in all four vehicles. You'll have an open line to us at all times. By switching this control here—" he demonstrated its operation "—you can talk to General Forman at headquarters. And finally—" he pointed to another speaker "—this monitor is tuned to the Air Force frequency that they'll be employing this evening. You can hear what they're saying, and you can use this switch—" again he illustrated its use "—to jam their transmissions, thereby cutting off all communication among them, as well as back to their base, once the operation has begun."

He paused and looked at the colonel. "I'm sure you're familiar with this equipment. Is everything clear?"

Thalberg sat in the console chair and examined all the dials for several moments. "Yes," he said, "quite clear."

1700 hours

HER HEAD ACHED. It had never ached so badly before.

Gabriele was still lying on the floor crumpled against the wall. She opened her eyes and looked around.

All she could see were vague shadows through the grate in the main part of the cellar. High on the wall opposite was a small window. Actually it was probably a coal shute, she thought. It was far too small to crawl through, but some light did come through.

Tentatively she raised her head. She fell back gasping. The pain was excruciating. Her head. Her back. Her breast. She didn't think she would ever be able to stand.

There was the taste of blood in her mouth. She moved her tongue. It felt raw and ragged. Two teeth were loose.

As she lay perfectly still, mentally assessing her body for damage, knowing that it would be an eternity before the pain of the past day would ever subside, she began talking softly to herself. "I *will* survive! I *will* survive...."

She rolled over and groaned. Then she straightened up and leaned on one elbow. Tears formed in her eyes from the effort.

Slowly, agonizingly slowly, Gabriele rose to her feet. She had hardly risen to a crouch when a wave of dizziness threatened to flatten her again. She reached for the wall with both hands as she began to topple and propped herself against it. Regaining her equilibrium, a vile taste remaining in her mouth, she rubbed her hand across her lips. They were caked with blood. With her tongue she felt the loose teeth again.

But the blood was not only from her mouth. Her face was swollen. She ran her hands through her hair and winced as she touched the wound in her scalp, a large swollen tender area. Her left breast and her stomach were on fire. Gabriele raised the pullover and looked. There were red marks that were already turning black and blue. The left breast seemed much larger than the right one and she realized it was swollen, too. She touched it and drew in her breath sharply through her teeth as a jolt of pain shot through it. But the worst pain was in her back. At the level of her kidneys. She carefully tried pivoting her back and immediately stopped as the pain stabbed down her left leg and up to her left shoulder.

But she could still walk. Stooped and belabored, but movement nevertheless. She shuffled over to the old door. Of course it was locked.

"Is anyone there?" she shouted through the slats into the damp darkness. But it was not a shout. Her voice frightened her, it sounded more like a death rattle.

Gabriele listened carefully. The house seemed silent.

They must have gone.

She started pacing the cell, shuffling in circles, trying to get the blood flowing again through her joints and to limber up her muscles.

She looked around to see if there was anything, any tool at all in the cell that could be used to break down the door. But the empty room only confirmed the hopelessness of her situation.

The cell seemed to mock her, to laugh in silent complicity.

The only things in the room were a wooden barrel of potatoes, a small pile of coal and two bundles of newspapers stacked in one corner. She slid the bundles over to the coal shute, climbed up and, bracing her hands against the damp, crumbly surface of the wall, looked out.

The sky, through the trees, was almost dark. She could see nothing other than the road leading away from the front of the house. Neither the barn nor the sheds were visible from her vantage point. She strained her ears, but could hear nothing except the distant murmuring of the wind in the barren branches of the beeches.

Gabriele returned to the door and listened intently.

Silence again.

She sat on the bundles of paper and looked around. I've got to think . . . got to think. . . .

She looked at the barrel. It was old and heavy, made of solid oak. She started taking out the potatoes. When it was half-empty she pushed it on its side and dumped out the remainder. Those at the bottom had been there for ages. They were dried out and shriveled. She rolled the barrel hard against the door and kicked it. Then she rolled it back and shoved it again into the slats of the door, again and again, throwing her weight behind that of the barrel. Finally, there was a splintering sound. One of the slats had split. She abandoned the barrel and kicked it several times, lengthening the split with each kick.

Finally the slat split in two. After several minutes of tugging she eventually pried one of the halves loose from the door.

She sat on the floor exhausted. Her fingers were bleeding. Several splinters were embedded in them. For a few minutes she tried removing them, but only succeeded in extracting the largest one. She looked again at the slatted door. She knew she could eventually get through, but she would have to go through the process of breaking at least three more slats.

She took the broken slat and used it as a lever, sticking it between two slats near one of the horizontal braces and prying as hard as she could. A wave of nausea and dizziness came over her again and she paused, leaning her head against the grate.

Taking a few deep breaths she started again. Finally, she felt the second slat cracking. The wood was old and the slat broke free easily from the nails holding it in place.

Encouraged, she kept at it until two more slats were dislodged. The task seemed interminable, but now there was an opening just large enough for her to squeeze through. Still holding the remnant of the first broken slat in her hand she wriggled through the space and fell through into the cellar.

For a moment she lay gasping, catching her breath, listening to the pounding beat of her heart. Her head throbbed.

Suddenly there was a loud rumbling sound. The house began to vibrate.

She sucked in her breath and crawled hastily back into the cell, clutching the slat pathetically in front of her for protection. She slid crablike to the farthest corner, waiting for someone to come down the stairs and discover the broken slats.

But the rumbling was outside, not in the house.

She climbed onto the bundle of papers and looked out. In the driveway, moving away from the house, were the armed jeeps, the VW bus and a larger truck. *Away*. Thank God! They were on their way to the ambush!

Gabriele stepped down and went back to the door. She crawled through it again and went as quickly as possible up the cellar stairs. She listened. Again silence.

She tried the door. It was locked. Of course.

Don't panic. Keep calm.

The switchboard! She stumbled back down the cellar stairs. She made sure the tape recorder was off and lifted the receiver. Yes. Remarkably, there was a dial tone.

She dialed the number in Bremen again. I don't even care if anyone's listening now, I'll get through! *If* there is anyone there to answer.

The phone was ringing. Three, four times.

"Hello? Schlegel here."

It was Pete.

"*Mensch*, are you all right?" she asked, out of breath.

"Yes."

"And Christopher? They sent someone to kill Christopher!" She felt her knees tremble awaiting his reply.

"He's all right. They made the attempt and there was bloodshed, but Christopher was unhurt."

"They've just left. They're going to ambush the missile convoy someplace on the Bundesstrasse 209. Near here. I've been beaten and locked up in the farmhouse. It's near Wetzen. We turned right off the B-209 coming from Lüneburg after we had passed Drögennindorf. The dirt road is difficult to find, but it's in good enough condition for large vehicles. They're planning to bring the missiles back here; there's a fortified farmhouse and a modified barn where the missiles will be hidden. It's a regular compound. The grounds are probably wired to give them warning if anyone approaches.

"That's all I know. I'm going to try to break out of the house now. Oh, yes, one other thing, there are eight of them, including Sievers and Colonel Thalberg."

"Drögennindorf, you say," repeated Pete. "I'm writing this down. Look, we'll be there as soon as possible. If we can, we'll try to stop them. Otherwise we'll go to the farm."

"Please be careful. They're heavily armed. They're killers."

"We know. Don't worry, we're armed too.... Here's Christopher."

"Gabriele!"

"Oh, Christopher!"

"I've been going crazy worrying about you!"

"And I you. It's okay, I'm all right now. I'm being held prisoner, but I'll be out of here by the time they return. Christopher, I almost died when they told me you had been killed."

"Have they harmed you?"

"Yes. But I'll survive.... Christopher, I . . . need you."

"We're coming."

"Hurry!"

She hung up before he could hear her voice break.

ULRICH DROVE the truck down the dirt road. It would be completely dark any minute, which would help make them less obtrusive. Although they had covered the guns mounted on the two jeeps, it was impossible to disguise that they were military vehicles. However, they would not be visible for long.

They passed through Sottorf and Etzen and proceeded for several miles up the hill toward Rehrhof. Near the crest was a barely noticeable turnoff. The jeeps and the truck pulled off out of sight of the road. The VW bus continued on into Rehrhof, turned onto a side street in the middle of this small village, made a U-turn and parked facing the road.

When they had turned off the ignition Helga radioed in to Sievers in the truck and Thalberg at base. "Beta in position."

"Acknowledged." Sievers.

"Acknowledged." Thalberg.

She leaned back, lit up a cigarette and offered the packet of *Roth Händle* to Klaus behind the wheel and Erich in back. "Now we wait," she said, and inhaled deeply on the cigarette.

One of the jeeps was driven diagonally across the asphalt and hidden behind several trees about twenty yards farther up the road. The other was left where it was while Sievers swung the truck around so it would be ready to stage the "accident."

"Alpha positioned," Sievers radioed to the colonel.

"Gamma positioned," from Bernhard.

"Delta positioned and being prepared for offensive," from Alex.

Colonel Thalberg acknowledged all three and leaned back in the swivel chair. He opened the bottle of Johnnie Walker and poured out a shot. Just a small one. Then he threw a switch and spoke into the microphone.

"The trap is set," he said.

"One hour." Captain Edward Packer's voice sounded surprisingly loud through the monitor.

Thalberg smiled, raised the glass to the monitors and drained it.

CHAPTER FIFTEEN
Bundesstrasse 209

THEY FILED OUT of the house and into the red Volkswagen van. Pete was at the wheel. Hannelore and Norbert sat in front with him, and Sigismund and Christopher in the rear.

They drove to the *Ostertor* and through the city center. Bremen was gearing up for a Friday night. Fashionably dressed concertgoers were clustering around the Goethe Theater as they drove past.

Because of the one-way system, they had to go several blocks out of the way to approach Osterdeich in the right direction.

Several minutes later they entered the autobahn at the Hemelingen entrance and sped off in the direction of Hamburg.

"We'll get on the number seven south and exit at Garlstorf," said Hannelore, looking at the map. "We can cut through Salzhausen to Wetzen, and see if we can locate this farm from there. It's a small enough place. If not, then we'll get to the 209 at Drögennindorf and follow Gabriele's route."

They drove in silence, each involved with his or her own thoughts. Sigismund made sure the weapons were all operational and loaded. He had affixed several hand grenades to a belt that he would wear if things got hot. It was almost as if the threat of violence and danger had brought him to life; he felt he was living more intensely than he ever had before. Even though he had learned much from the time

he had spent with the Red Army Faction, the arguments and
nitpicking had disappointed him. Now he was involved in
something decisive and it enthralled him.

Norbert was thinking of his farm, and Götz and the
senselessness of his death. He did not want to be making this
trip, but he went along freely. He debated inwardly why he
considered it necessary to accompany his friends on this futile mission. No good could possibly come of it, but a part
of him knew he had to make the effort.

Hannelore, like Sigismund, felt life flowing through her
with an incredible force. She had looked death in the face
and she had killed. She wondered at her reaction. Never in
her life had she thought that she would feel so free. She had
always been dedicated to what she believed was right, the
truth as she saw it, but now for the first time she had the
opportunity to act. She had nothing to lose. Everything to
gain.

Pete was worried. He feared the unknown and the danger, but there was never a question that he should back
down. The cause was more important than any personal
considerations. And he would always be ready to submit his
will to the public good, though it was never fully clear to
him what the public good was.

Christopher was with Gabriele. He realized that he didn't
want to lose her. For the first time he had found someone he
felt he truly wanted. He was reluctant to admit to himself
that perhaps he was falling in love. Love was a word he
never used, and he retreated from it again now. All he knew
was that something in him was touched that had never been
touched before, something that he hadn't even known existed. And he wanted to grow deeper in it. At the same time
he was aware that though it was Gabriele who somehow held
the key, it was not only what was happening between them
that affected him so deeply. Something larger was taking
control of him. Something that had begun to manifest it-

self in these past ten days. Yes. He would never again be the same. A new Christopher Benton was being born. *If* he survived.

GABRIELE HAD GONE through the entire cellar, but there was no alternate exit to the door at the head of the stairs.

In a far corner she found a massive pile of junk. Old furniture that had obviously been stored there when Ulrich's group renovated the house.

She spent an hour dragging chairs and tables aside. Looking through cartons of kitchen utensils and dishes. Setting aside framed paintings, looking for something, anything, that could be used to get her out of the cellar. After an arduous effort sliding an antique washing machine to one side, she found some old rusted tools on the floor near the wall.

She went through them.

Thank God! There, on the floor, was an ax. She clutched it gratefully, praying that the handle would not break when she swung it into the heavy door.

THE CONVOY HAD LEFT the base shortly after dusk. It traveled rapidly along the autobahn and exited onto a secondary road.

Other drivers on the road slowed and looked surprised and awed when they saw the TEL. Perhaps it was the realization that the deployment policy in West Germany was indeed a reality. This was an exercise German citizens would no doubt be witnessing with more and more frequency in the months and years ahead. That is, if it was only an exercise. But the soldiers waved at the gawking drivers, and it was obvious, the drivers thought, that this was not the real thing. Many waved back.

The convoy stopped briefly in a field near Rotenburg and went through a few maneuvers. Primarily parking and stabilizing exercises for the launchers. Then they continued on successively poorer-quality roads.

After a short run along an unpaved road the procession emerged again on a state road. The *Bundesstrasse* 209.

"Convoy to base. We've entered the B-209."

"Roger."

Colonel Matecki glanced at General Forman, who was seated in the war room. He was staring intently at the operations map on the wall, seemingly mesmerized by the movement of the pinpoints of light across its surface, which marked the location of the convoy.

Soon. Very soon, Forman thought.

HELGA THREW the cigarette through the opened vent window. She picked up the microphone. "Still no activity."

She lit another *Roth Händle* and continued staring up the road. The van was stuffy, filled with smoke from the strong cigarette.

A light rain began to fall. She wondered idly if the temperature might drop sufficiently for it to turn to snow.

THE VAN LEFT the autobahn at Garlstorf, passed through Oelstorf and Salzhausen, then turned south toward Wetzen.

"Soon, Gabriele, soon," Christopher muttered softly to himself.

Pete switched on the windshield wipers.

GABRIELE COULD WAIT no longer. The thought that they might return and find her still in the cellar petrified her. She *had* to try the ax now.

She mounted the stairs. With all her might she raised the ax in both hands above her head and crashed it into the center of the door.

A jarring pain seared through her back, but she ignored it and pulled the ax out of the door. She swung again.

And again.

With each stroke the door splintered and shattered. After five agonizing strokes she was through.

She ran across the floor to the conference room. No one there. Then up the stairs as fast as possible to Ulrich's room.

The door was locked, but Gabriele was in gear. It took only three full swings of the ax and she was through.

She wanted to destroy. The first feeling that surged through her as she burst into his room was to vandalize and destroy everything she could. But she suppressed the urge and instead approached the gun rack.

She took an automatic machine gun and a handgun. Neither was loaded. Hastily she pulled out desk drawers until she found, at the back of one of them, several ammunition clips and boxes of bullets.

She tried one of the clips in the automatic. It didn't seem to fit. She sat down for a minute on the desk and carefully examined the clip. She turned it around and after a moment of fiddling with it she snapped it into place on the weapon. She practiced removing it and replacing it several times. Then, after trying the safety, she hung the weapon over her shoulder by its strap the way she had seen Erich carrying his.

Next she took a bullet from a box and tried it in the revolver. It fit. She loaded it and stuck it in her belt. She filled her pockets with bullets, grabbed three more clips for the machine gun and ran downstairs.

Her parka was still on the hook in the hall. She threw it on and stuffed the automatic clips in the large bellows pockets. She approached the front window and looked out.

"HERE THEY ARE."

It was Helga's voice in the monitor. She spoke in English for Colonel Thalberg's benefit.

Thalberg listened as Sievers acknowledged her. He tapped his fingers nervously on the console, then put his hand on the interference switch and waited for the signal.

Sievers and Antje drove the truck out from the cover of the trees and parked it blocking the road. They removed the valves from the tires and set a smoke bomb on the seat.

Antje lay on the ground in front of the truck, bathed in its headlights. Slanting drops of rain gleamed and sparkled in the cones of light above her still form.

Ulrich raised his arm in the direction of the jeeps, then concealed himself behind the truck, his HPK ready.

Klaus pulled the van out of the side road after the last American jeep in the convoy had passed. He followed at a distance of half to three-quarters of a mile.

SERGEANT EDDIE MCCOY HAD just looked at the clipboard at his side. The route was clearly drawn out. They would continue along the B-209 to Sottorf and then turn south toward Wriedel. Here they would leave the road entirely and travel overland into the *Heide*, where they would go through a second dry-run exercise. By the time they swung back on the autobahn and returned to the base it would be close to midnight.

There ought to be enough time to hit a couple of bars when we get back, he thought. I sure as hell could use a beer.

Up ahead a thick fog was descending.

"Aw sheet!" he said.

"What's that, Sergeant?" It was Corporal Leroy Washington, who was driving the jeep.

"Foggy stretch up ahead, Lee. It'll slow us down for sure. I was just thinkin' about tyin' one on when we get back."

"Fuckin' right!"

He couldn't tell if Lee was referring to tying one on or to the descending fog. He assumed it was the former.

"Wait," the corporal said, "that ain't no fog, that's smoke!"

McCoy strained to look through the drizzle that the wipers were smearing across the windshield of the jeep. "Yeah. You're right. Looks like a truck. Sheet! It must be on fire, lookit that smoke!"

He picked up the microphone. "Looks like an accident up here," he reported to the vehicles behind. "We're slowing down." He felt, oddly, that something was not quite right.

The jeep slowed as it approached the truck. Washington flashed on the high beams.

"Christ, there's someone injured there," the corporal said, and stopped the jeep several yards from the woman lying on the ground.

McCoy jumped out of the jeep as the armed vehicle immediately behind them and the TEL ground to a halt.

"Are you okay?" he asked, cautiously approaching the woman.

She rolled over and half opened her eyes. It looked as though she was trying to say something. He got down on one knee to try to hear better.

"It's all right," he said and reached out to her.

It seemed, suddenly, that all hell had broken loose.

THERE WAS NOTHING open in Wetzen.

A small grocery store with two gas pumps outside was evidently the focal point of this crossroads. But it was not even a crossroads. The small auxiliary road that passed through the center of town didn't bend or turn, or, for that matter, even slow down. It just went straight through, passing a few houses and the tiny general store/gas station. There was not even a post office.

"*Scheisse,*" said Hannelore. She lowered the window. "Pete, there's a house with a light up the road about a hundred meters. Pull over there."

He did as she directed and stopped the car. She stepped out and went quickly up to the door. She knocked, and then, after a minute, knocked again.

It seemed forever before the door was opened. An old man stood before her.

"*Ja?*" he asked gruffly. It was obvious he didn't particularly like strangers. He looked at Hannelore, and as his eyes traversed her from head to foot it was also obvious that he wasn't pleased with what he saw.

"*Pardon,*" she said, trying to be as polite as possible. She could hear a television blaring in the background. "Excuse me, but we're supposed to visit some friends who live on a farm near here, and, in this weather, we seem to have lost our way."

He looked up toward the sky as if to see what the weather could possibly have to do with it, then back at her without replying.

"They live in a large house," she continued. "There's a barn and several other outbuildings, so it must be a rather big place."

His eyes narrowed. For a moment she had the feeling he was about to slam the door in her face.

"That's the old von Pappenheim place," he said after a pause. She had to strain to understand him, for he spoke in a dialect. "The entrance is from the B-209, but you can get there by driving two or three kilometers due east until you get to a dirt turnoff on the right. No one knows about this back entrance, and it's almost impossible to find because it hasn't been used for years. But if you can't find it you'll have to go around via Drögennindorf. That's where the main entrance is to your student commune." The last two words were spoken with a definite sneer.

"Thank you," she said gratefully.

He said nothing.

She turned to go.

The door slammed behind her.

They carefully watched the odometer and the side of the road. The old man was right. Just two and a half kilometers along they found the turnoff. It was hardly more than a break in the fields. They turned onto it and bounced and pitched along for another kilometer. Although it was primarily farmland, there were several dips and climbs over a series of small hills. The abandoned road was so rutted that the crates clattered around noisily in the back of the van as they drove.

"Are you sure this is the right way?" Pete asked.

"We'll soon find out," Hannelore responded.

Suddenly the road came to an end, joining another to form a T. The newer road was somewhat wider and in noticeably better condition.

"Which way?" Pete asked.

Hannelore studied the map. "The only thing I can figure is that since Wetzen is now behind us, if we turned left we would probably be heading away from Wetzen toward Lüneburg. So I think we ought to turn right. Left is where this road connects to the *Bundesstrasse*."

"Okay, to the right." Pete turned the wheel.

They hadn't gone more than a few hundred yards when the road curved to the left and they could see several very tall trees ahead. They neared the trees and soon they could make out the buildings amid them.

"Good navigating, Hannelore!" Norbert said. "This must be it."

Christopher and Sigismund leaned over the seat and looked through the windshield at the outlines of the buildings partially concealed in the grove. The farm was in darkness.

"You know, if they return before we leave, we'll be trapped. We'd better park on the path we came on, and then scout the place on foot. They certainly wouldn't use the other road because larger vehicles than this one would never be able to negotiate it.''

There were muttered agreements.

Pete reversed the car to the intersection. He turned off the main dirt road and went along the older path until they were out of sight.

They got out and looked around. There was enough scrub and bushes that it seemed even in daylight the VW would not be visible from even thirty yards away.

Sigismund issued them their weapons and flashlights. They paused and looked at one another for a moment, but no one spoke any encouraging words.

They set out together in silence.

GABRIELE HAD HER HAND on the latch to the front door, but something made her hesitate.

Slowly she withdrew her hand.

Her instinct for survival had become finely tuned. There must be an alarm or a warning system in operation, she thought. Perhaps the door was booby-trapped. They would never leave the place without some security measures in force.

She looked carefully around the edges of the door. It didn't take long to find the thin wire connecting the door hinges. She followed it along the molding at the base of the wall. It disappeared into a hole drilled into the corner. She walked into the conference room and looked closely at all the windows. The *Rolladen* were closed and locked. Even if she broke the windows she could not get through the steel plates of the *Rolladen*.

Hastily she ran from window to window. It was the same for all of them on the ground floor. She was beginning to get panicky. She felt fear rising, and tried breathing deeply in order to quell it.

A door from the kitchen at the back of the house was also securely locked, and again she spotted the telltale wire. What she was unsure of was whether tampering with the wire would only set off an alarm, or a booby trap.

Finally, on the wall behind the kitchen door, she found the master switch for the security system.

It was a digital combination system consisting of nine numbered buttons.

She leaned against the wall in frustration.

She walked back to the front door and stared at it while drumming her fingers against the ax handle. She *must* do something, she knew. And soon.

Very soon.

COLONEL THALBERG LISTENED intently.

He heard the American's voice come through the loud-speakers. "We're slowing down." Then for several moments there was silence.

Suddenly, from the other monitor, Sievers's voice spoke a single word. *"Now."*

Instantly, Colonel Thalberg tossed the toggle switch and there was the simultaneous rush of crackling static hissing loudly from the convoy monitor. The sound of the jamming was nearly deafening. He turned down the volume on his monitor, but knew that the oscillations that were emanating from his transmitter would remain at the preselected volume.

The colonel was surprised when he heard the rush of air escaping from his lungs. He hadn't realized that he'd been holding his breath.

"GOODBYE." YES. That was the word the injured woman said to him. It seemed a strange thing to say, and Sergeant Eddie McCoy couldn't quite understand why she said it.

A puzzled looked crossed his face. The expression remained there as a sudden burst from a machine gun nearly cut him in half.

Sievers released the trigger, but continued sidestepping toward the jeep. He fired a short round through the left side of the windshield and heard the cry of the driver as he was hit.

Antje was on her feet by the time McCoy's body had hit the ground, almost in the same spot where she had lain. She crouched and ran quickly around the left side of the jeep just as Sievers's shots had eliminated the driver. The upper part of his body fell halfway out of the jeep only seconds before she rushed past him. She had already pulled the pins on two hand grenades, and the moment she rounded the rear of the jeep she rolled one of them under the armored vehicle that was there. The second one she tossed onto the roof of the cab before anyone in the truck had had time to react. She leaped to her right, landed on the shoulder of the road and rolled rapidly farther into the bushes.

The explosion was deafening. Bits of metal and glass hit her, and she knew immediately that the backs of her hands were badly lacerated. There was also the feel of something warm on her neck. Blood. She touched it gingerly and extracted a bladelike sliver of metal.

Sievers was lacing the truck with several rounds from his Heckler & Koch automatic. He smiled as he watched the bullets rip into the armored plating and the remnants of the cab. No one had even the slightest chance to man the machine gun mounted on the platform behind the cab.

The moment they had heard the firing ahead, both Alex, on one side of the road, and Bernhard on the other rolled their jeeps slightly forward from behind their cover. They swung over the seats and onto the platforms and opened fire with the machine guns, Alex aiming at the support vehicle immediately behind the TEL and Bernhard on the one following it. Within seconds Alex had saturated his target with round after round of ammunition. Not a single shot was fired back at him.

Klaus stopped the van ten yards behind the rear of the convoy while Helga and Erich leaped out to attack the last jeep.

The man in the passenger seat jumped out and ran across the road near Bernhard's position.

Erich shot out the jeep's tires while Helga ran rapidly up to the driver's door. She fired blindly into the cab. The jeep lurched forward and collided into the rear of the armored vehicle in front, where a soldier was firing the mounted machine gun at Bernhard. He was thrown off balance for a moment by the collision and fell to his knees. When he stood he was hit several times across his chest by a burst of fire from Bernhard. He slouched behind the gun, his torso slumping over it, but kept firing.

Meanwhile the officer at the side of the road had begun firing at Bernhard. Suddenly, caught in the cross fire, Bernhard was hit. He fell backward and landed against the front seat.

Helga tossed a grenade at the wounded gunner on the armored truck. He continued firing his weapon, and it seemed to Helga that even after the explosion had destroyed the vehicle, his gun fired a last few rounds.

She went past the burning vehicle and crouched alongside the large tractor-trailer truck that was the launch control center. She climbed up on the running board and pressed the barrel of her automatic against the neck of the driver.

"Freeze," she said.

The man was as white as a sheet. He raised his hands. "Don't shoot! Please, don't shoot!"

The corporal alongside him also raised his hands.

"Slowly, very slowly, open the door and get out," she ordered.

The driver climbed down from the cab and onto the road.

"Lie down!" she snapped.

He complied without hesitation. She kept her gun aimed at the passenger while speaking to the driver.

"Spread your arms out above your head." She removed the gun from his holster, then she turned to the other one. "Okay. Slide toward me. Slowly!"

The corporal did so, his hands held above his head.

"No sudden movements now." She motioned him to lie next to his comrade. She took his gun.

Ulrich was kneeling in front of the hood of the TEL. He peered over the edge of the right front fender. The soldier in the passenger seat had rolled down the window and was leaning out, looking toward the rear of the convoy and at the shooting that was going on at Bernhard's jeep. It was difficult for the soldier to see because the combined length of the TEL and the LCC was between him and the action. He knew he should be able to see the perpetrators, but other than the truck blocking the road up ahead, nothing was visible.

There was a movement. A dark figure, silhouetted against the flames of the burning vehicle, stepped out right in front of him. The soldier raised his .45 and pulled the trigger.

Another shot rang out and he slumped back, dead, in his seat.

Ulrich staggered as he felt the bullet brush his cheek. He fired quickly and accurately and saw the man fall. Then he jumped onto the foothold beside the passenger door, pulled himself up in one easy motion and fired three shots into the cab. He opened the door and dragged the passenger's body out, then ran around to the other side and pulled out the driver's body.

He moved back along the side of the TEL, reloading as he went, and came up to Helga, who was standing guard over the two men lying at the side of the road.

"The TEL is taken," he said haughtily through sharp breaths.

"The LCC, too," Helga replied. "Where's Antje?"

"She's forward by the armored car. She took it out single-handedly."

"I think they're having some trouble in back. Erich is pinned down in a shooting match with one of them."

"I'll check it out," he said, and hurried off. He passed the LCC and signaled to Alex in the jeep to his right, then he cut across in front of the two silenced armored support vehicles.

There was staccato firing from the bushes to the right, and he saw the burst of flames spouting from the barrels of two automatics trained on each other.

The farther one came from behind a tree. Must be Erich, he thought. The nearer one came from a ditch close to the road.

He crept forward, pulled the pin from a hand grenade and bowled it, just as he used to do in his bowling club when he was a teenager, toward the man. The grenade rolled along the pavement, skipping slightly, and fell into the ditch on the back of the soldier.

There was an explosion and it seemed that along with clumps of earth, bits and pieces of flesh flew in every direction. Ulrich had fallen to his face and when he arose he was spattered with gore.

Erich came out from behind the tree. "That bastard was obstinate," he said. He trotted over to the ditch and looked in as Ulrich walked to meet him.

"Christ!" said Erich, turning away from the ditch.

"Everything secured back here now?" Ulrich asked.

Erich nodded. "He was the last." He motioned toward the ditch.

They signaled to Klaus. He drove over to them in the VW while they inspected their losses.

Bernhard was dead. Erich got into the jeep and drove toward the front of the convoy with the body of their colleague lying on the rear platform.

Ulrich went back to Helga. "The convoy is ours. We've lost Bernhard." Helga blinked, but otherwise showed no outward reaction.

Sievers squatted on his haunches between the two men, took an envelope and handed it to the driver. "After we leave," he said in English, "you are to wait here for ten minutes. Then get up and leave. Give this envelope to your superiors. It contains our demands. Tell them," he said, "tell them—" he raised his pistol and pressed it into the back of the head of the corporal lying on his other side "—what you saw." He pulled the trigger and a stream of blood arched up and out of the wound in the corporal's skull, making a splattering sound as it formed a puddle in the gravel. The puddle expanded slowly, diluted by the rain.

The driver, clutching the envelope in his fist, began to weep. "You…killed…him…." It looked as if he was going to vomit.

"Shut up," Ulrich snapped, "unless you want to join him! We can just as easily pin this letter to your body!"

The man shut up.

Sievers rose. "Helga, you drive the LCC. I'll take the TEL." He signaled to Alex and Klaus to take up the rear behind the two larger vehicles. Then he went forward to Erich.

"Where the hell's Antje?" he asked impatiently.

No one knew.

Sievers ran quickly back to the truck. The smoke had dissipated. She was not there. He turned around, walked past the jeep and then spotted her on the ground about ten yards from the armored car she had taken out. He ran over to her.

"Are you wounded?" he shouted. He hadn't thought she'd been hit, and she looked so normal lying there with her hands to her head. He noticed the sliver of metal in her hand and rolled her over.

She was dead.

Her face was white. He hadn't known flesh could look so white. And then he saw what he hadn't at first noticed because of the puddles of rainwater around her. Her jugular had been severed. The puddles were pink.

He walked over to the truck, reached into the cab and picked up the microphone. "Let's go," he said to Klaus and Alex.

Without waiting for a reply he motioned to Erich, and the two of them placed Antje's body in the rear of the jeep next to Bernhard.

Erich started off in the jeep, Ulrich behind him driving the TEL. Helga left the prisoner and climbed into the LCC and within seconds they were speeding along the road. The two large camouflaged vehicles, the object of their mission, were flanked by Erich and Alex in the jeeps and Klaus taking up the rear in the VW.

Klaus pressed the transmit switch on the microphone. "We're starting out."

"Very good," Colonel Thalberg replied, "see you in twenty minutes. Over and out."

Ulrich smiled and looked at his watch while listening to Klaus's message. They had lost two people. That was bad, but the entire operation had taken less than five minutes. And there had been no unexpected innocent passersby. Twenty minutes to the base.

And then this ordinary Friday night would no longer be ordinary.

"GENERAL FORMAN, General Forman," the lieutenant shouted shrilly to the general across the war room. "The frequency is being jammed. We've lost all contact with the convoy!"

General Forman walked over to him, Oster and Matecki at his side. "Keep trying to raise them," he ordered. "Don't worry, it's probably the weather creating the interference."

"Not this strong, General. I've never heard anything this powerful that wasn't deliberate interference," said the radio operator.

"Don't you think we should alert the police?" Oster asked.

"Give it a few minutes, Colonel. Give it a few minutes. It's probably nothing." He turned to the radio officer. "Keep trying to raise them," he ordered. "Keep trying."

CHAPTER SIXTEEN

Wetzen

THE ENTIRE COMPOUND seemed deserted. But since all the windows of the house were shuttered, there was no way of knowing whether anyone was in the building.

Hannelore and Sigismund slipped through the shadows to look at the sheds, while Norbert, Pete and Christopher approached the main house. Pete went around back. As he turned the corner there was an abrupt, loud, splintering sound, immediately followed by the blast of a siren.

Hannelore and Sigismund wheeled around and ran back toward Pete. Christopher and Norbert stopped for a moment, then hurried around the other way.

Pete was pulling someone through the shattered ruins of the kitchen door into a small garden area. There was a cord of wood leaning against the wall alongside the door and it partially obscured Christopher's view. He broke into a run.

Yes. It was Gabriele.

He could see immediately, as he ran toward her, that she appeared to have changed. It looked as though she had put on weight in her face. Then he realized it was swollen. There were bruises and one eye was almost shut.

"Christopher!" she said, spying him.

He arrived in front of her. She took the last two steps toward him and fell into his arms. "Christopher..." Her voice broke, but she fought back the tears. There was no time. Not now.

He held her. His chest felt as though it would burst.

The siren was still wailing. "Quick," she said. "They'll be back any minute. Besides, there must be someone in the radio room." She started to move away from the house. "We've got to hide."

They followed her as she led them in a large semicircle around the barn. They started across an abandoned field, jumping over the now-empty rows where rye had grown.

"Gabriele, we have a van behind that field over there." Pete pointed beyond the field they were crossing. "That's also the direction they'll be coming from."

"Yes," she said, "this way then." She cut diagonally, closer to the dirt road, heading for a distant field of dried-out cornstalks and the scattered trees beyond.

Christopher was running at her side. Occasionally they exchanged glances, but neither one spoke. Behind them the incessant ringing of the alarm was breaking apart the night. It seemed so out of place in the deserted quiet farmland. Snowflakes began mingling with the rain.

A rumbling sound in the distance slowly became louder, competing with the sound of the alarm. Sievers was returning.

They arrived at the edge of the cornfield and without hesitation plunged through. As soon as they were hidden from view they stopped and turned to look back. Through two rows of stalks they could clearly see the big trees and the buildings. To their left was the dirt road converging on the house. Through the trees a light suddenly shone as a door opened.

"Look!" Hannelore pointed.

"It's the radio shed," said Gabriele.

The rumbling had intensified and had finally begun to overwhelm the siren. The ground vibrated and they all instinctively crouched lower.

Headlights illuminated the trees, and a few seconds later the first vehicle came into view. It was an armored jeep followed by a second one. As the rumbling heightened the TEL appeared. The Transporter-erector-launcher, complete with four nuclear medium-range Tomahawk BGM-109 cruise missiles. The missiles themselves, out of sight inside their launch tubes, were no longer than six yards. The truck appeared to be a typical armed forces tractor trailer, but it was plated with high-grade steel 0.25-inch-thick, bonded to 0.375-inch aluminum, which provided effective protection from small arms. Effective, at least, when the occupants expected an attack. The ten-ton tractor, which had been built in West Germany, featured an eight-speed drive system that could drive all eight wheels. It was camouflage-painted in greens, browns and blacks. The fifty-five-foot-long trailer's main feature was the launcher, which could elevate the missiles to a firing angle of forty-five degrees, with its electromechanical lift mechanism.

Behind the TEL was the launch control center. This tractor-trailer system was also camouflage painted, but the length of the entire tractor trailer was only the same as the missile launcher unit without its tractor. The LCC was used to monitor the target. Information fed into it from reconnaissance aircraft tracking its movements could be relayed to the guidance system in the missile during its flight so as to make the necessary adjustments in its flight path to compensate for any evasive movements by the target. This would ensure near-perfect accuracy.

Finally, the VW van came into view as the convoy halted.

WITH THE ENGINE still running, Sievers jumped from the driver's seat of the TEL. Thalberg ran up to him.

"The woman has escaped!" he shouted above the din created by the vehicles.

"What!" Sievers shouted in rage. It was only then that he could hear the sound of the alarm. He looked toward the house, angry that Gabriele's escape should diminish his euphoria at this moment of triumph.

"How the hell could she have got out?" he demanded.

"Through the back. It was only minutes before you arrived. I heard the alarm and ran out, although I was reluctant to leave the console. I saw nothing at first, but then I went around back and saw the kitchen door was splintered."

"But how did she get out of the cellar?" Sievers was angry, but there was no time to indulge his anger now. They had to conceal their trophies. It wouldn't be long before the whole area was surrounded by the police searching for them.

"*Quickly!*" he ordered, pointing at Erich. "Get the barn doors open!"

Erich ran to comply.

Ulrich drove the TEL around in as tight a circle as the wheels would allow, and then, following the hand signals of the others, backed it into the barn. Helga did the same with the LCC. They closed the barn and put the jeeps and van into the nearest shed.

"Okay," said Sievers to the others, "Alex, you go with the colonel to assist him. Klaus, take care of our comrades' bodies. And Helga—" he turned to her "—this is our moment!"

They entered the radio room. Within two minutes they had radioed out their message. They didn't await a reply. They knew that not only would Washington and Bonn know of their deed within minutes, but that also the world's press would be reacting to the news. The *Frankfurter Rundschau*, Axel Springer's *Bild Zeitung*, *The Times*, *Le Monde*, *Pravda*, the *New York Times*, the *Washington Post*.

Ulrich unlocked the front door of the house. He went into the kitchen, turned off the alarm and inspected the splin-

tered door there. Then he went through the broken door to
the cellar. It was obvious that she had had no outside help,
because the two ruined doors had both been destroyed from
inside.

He stalked up to Helga. "That bitch," he said. "She escaped on her own, but she can't have gone very far. We've
got to stop and kill her before she can contact anyone."

"I'm going with you," said Helga.

He nodded in agreement as they put fresh clips into the
magazines of their HK-54s.

They stepped through the back door and headed toward
the fields.

GENERAL FORMAN GLANCED from the clock on the wall
back to the frantic face of the radio officer. The latter was
trying, unsuccessfully, to raise the convoy on every frequency.

Fifteen minutes, thought Forman. They must have
cleared it by now.

"Okay," he said. "Emergency alert. Contact the German police. Give them the last known position of the convoy. Send out a squadron of Army choppers to the area.
Lieutenant, keep trying to raise them." He turned to Colonel Matecki.

"General!" the lieutenant interrupted him before he
could speak, "General, listen!"

He switched on the monitor and removed his headphones. The German-accented voice of a male speaking
English broke into the chaotic atmosphere of the war room
and brought instantaneous silence.

"This is an announcement from the Anti-Nuclear Proliferation Front," he was saying. "We have in our possession
four cruise missiles armed with nuclear warheads, which
were formerly the property of the right arm of American
dominance in Europe—NATO. The missiles together with

their launcher have been liberated for use by the ANPF. They will be used against specified targets in Western Europe unless we receive guarantees that *all* American nuclear missiles are removed from Europe within one week. We know this is a formidable undertaking, but if the removal of the missiles has not commenced within twenty-four hours, we shall launch one of the Tomahawk cruise missiles. And we shall launch one each day until the removal has begun.''

There was a pause.

''They're insane,'' Oster exclaimed. ''Those missiles are useless. The warheads are not armed, their guidance systems are not programmed!''

''Do not,'' the speaker quietly continued, as if in reply to Oster's outburst, ''we repeat, *do not* make the mistake of assuming we will not use these missiles. And don't think that they are useless to us. They *are* armed, and they are at this very moment being programmed to seek out very easy targets. Stationary targets of large population centers that cannot avoid the detection of the missiles' contour-matching digital-map guidance centers. We will not even need the use of the LCC since the targets we have chosen are incapable of making evasive maneuvers. You can see that we are knowledgeable about the missiles and how to use them.

''The governments of the United States of America and West Germany are asked to announce their compliance with our demand at 0200 Central European time tonight on all radio stations.''

The communication abruptly ended.

''Christ Almighty!'' Oster gasped. ''How could they arm the missiles?''

''Contact the police immediately,'' ordered Forman, ''and send out those choppers without delay.'' He turned to Oster. ''We've got to call the President and the Chancellor.''

Oster nodded, his face drained of color. His career, he reasoned as he picked up the red telephone for the first time as base commander, was in a shambles. He unlocked the telephone and with trembling hands punched a three-digit code. "Get me General Torbert," he said, his voice a rasping whisper.

Forman and Matecki exchanged glances. Nearly imperceptibly General Forman nodded.

Colonel Matecki left the room.

COLONEL THALBERG AND ALEX had opened the panel to the missile's guidance control center.

While Alex checked the gyroscopes, the colonel looked at the strips of numbers he had on a card and then punched them slowly and accurately into the small computer console. Then he added the coordinates of their position in Wetzen.

Alex closed the compartment and tightened the bolts while Thalberg went to the next missile and entered the same coordinates along with a different set of target instructions. He smiled to himself as he worked. David Marcus's lessons were good, he thought; it was even more easily accomplished than Marcus had boasted. He glanced over at Alex. The dumb ox. All of them. These idiot idealistic middle-class revolutionaries. They thought they were going to change the world according to their image. How surprised they were going to be. But, of course, they wouldn't be around to be surprised.

Alex watched him punch in the numbers. He thought the numbers were the coordinates that would send the missile to Munich.

Colonel Thalberg smiled and nodded at Alex. "Almost done," he said.

Alex smiled back.

The fool! Thalberg thought.

CHAPTER SEVENTEEN
Washington, D.C.

1600 hours

THE PRESIDENT of the United States always took a brief nap in the afternoon. The standing order that was strictly observed was that he was not to be disturbed for any reason whatsoever unless it was a matter of national security. He valued his sleep. After all, how was an older man like him going to be able to function well and carry out the strenuous duties of his office if he was denied his rest?

General Oswald, or "Ozzie," Torbert was the only five-star general in the United States Army. He was the chairman of the Joint Chiefs of Staff and was one of the few men who had access to the President who was allowed to awaken him. He didn't like doing it at all. But he dialed the number.

The telephone on the night table buzzed softly. Instantly the President reached out and raised it. "Yes?"

"Mr. President." A man spoke in a calm but urgent voice. "I'm sorry to have to wake you, but we have a problem here."

Larry Tice, special assistant to the President, paused. He was a young man. Energetic, affable, efficient and devoted. "General Torbert is on the line. It seems there is a crisis in Germany."

"Put him on." The President sighed. He raised himself to a sitting position and punched the pillows into a more comfortable backrest. He glanced at the digital clock, as the distraught voice of the general came over the line.

"Mr. President, Torbert here. Sorry to disturb you, sir."

"That's all right, Ozzie." The President's voice was smooth and mellow. Reassuring. Soothing.

"Well, Mr. President, there has been a hijacking in West Germany of four of our cruise missiles, complete with launch vehicles."

"Good God!"

"It seems to be a left-wing antinuclear group behind it. They demand the removal of our missiles from Europe within one week, or else they will destroy four targets in Western Europe."

"That's ridiculous! Absurd! Even if we wanted to, it would be logistically impossible to remove the missiles within a week. But how on earth could anyone break onto a base and steal the missiles in the first place?"

"These missiles were not on a base. They were going through a test exercise to determine how easily transportable they are. It was more a test of the Transporter-erector-launcher."

"Well, surely they were dummy missiles? Or at least unarmed missiles?"

"We use real missiles, but of course, as you say, they were not armed. We would never send armed missiles off base for an exercise. However, these terrorists claim they have armed the missiles themselves. I can't see how they could have accomplished that, but of course maybe they've had inside help or been supplied with classified information. Furthermore, they insist they have programmed the missiles' guidance systems. Perhaps the Soviets are involved. At this point in time we don't know."

"Well, General, you're right, this *is* a problem. But there is no question of us complying with their demands. I will not be blackmailed. But what do you suggest we do? Is there any way we can find these misfits and destroy them?''

''I don't think it will be too difficult to locate them. After all, they certainly couldn't have got very far from the scene of the hijacking in twenty minutes, which was the time elapsed when they made their announcement. In a kidnapping, of course, they could keep moving their hostage around and no one would notice. But in this case I think it's apparent that they're going to have to stay put.

''But even after we pinpoint them, I don't know if we can do too much. Even if we bombed them or attacked them with conventional warhead missiles, they could probably still launch one, maybe two missiles. Besides, we don't want to risk their detonating all the missiles; that would have quite a devastating effect on central Europe.... Unless they are bluffing...''

''We'll convene an emergency session of the Joint Chiefs with the secretaries of State and Defense and the National Security Adviser. By the way, did we lose any men during the hijacking?''

''Yes. Quite a few, sir, it was a massacre.''

''Well, have the usual messages of condolences prepared, bravery and courage in the line of duty and so forth. But, don't have the next-of-kin notified yet. This is to be kept secret as long as possible.

''Now, if you'll excuse me, I'll have my assistant arrange this emergency session. I'll see you there. Goodbye.''

''Goodbye, Mr. President.''

The President punched a button on the telephone. ''Larry,'' he said, ''get State, Defense and the NSA to the Cabinet Room as soon as possible. Also the Joint Chiefs.''

He hung up, buzzed his valet and got out of bed.

CHAPTER EIGHTEEN
Wetzen

KLAUS LAID THE BODIES of his two comrades on the ground in the rear of the smaller implement shed. He covered them with a tarpaulin and rejoined Alex and Thalberg. The two had just finished programming the on-board guidance system.

"Because of the relative proximity of the targets," Colonel Thalberg explained, "and the fact that they are cities and obviously not changing position, we'll not even need to use the LCC. The function of the LCC is to relay signals from a reconnaissance aircraft, which is observing the evasive movements of the target, to the missile after launching, so it can adjust to maximize the possibilities for a direct hit. We've programmed the missiles to detonate upon arriving at the centers of Munich, Frankfurt, Brussels and Brokdorf."

The two Germans looked sharply at each other.

"Wait a moment," said Klaus, "Brokdorf's a nuclear power plant. That would be utterly suicidal. The damage would be irreparable."

"Precisely," said Thalberg. "When the authorities learn of our intention to destroy Brokdorf, and when they consider the consequences of such an audacious attack, they will immediately back down. Of course, we have no real intention of launching that fourth missile. Hopefully, we won't have to launch any."

He told them what they wanted to hear. They nodded, but it was obvious that they were skeptical.

"Now, we've got to prepare missile number one."

Thalberg checked the circuits on the booster engine while Klaus operated the hydraulic lift, raising the launcher partially into firing position.

"All we have to do now, is pull the TEL out of the barn into the open. Raise the platform fully, stabilize the TEL pads and launch it." He showed them the correct sequence of switches to operate on the control panel.

He stepped back and looked at their handiwork. "Munich," he announced. Then he smiled to himself.

Hamburg

HAUPTMANN DIETRICH HOLZAUER was stamping out his cigarette in the ashtray on his desk. He took the pack of cigarettes out of his shirt pocket and lit another.

Scheisse, he said to himself, looking at the full ashtray. I've got to cut down. This job is going to kill me with lung cancer before any terrorist shoots me!

He was the operations chief of the Antiterrorist Commando Unit, which had been formed in response to the escalating attacks of the Red Army Faction. He always had so much extra duty on weekends, or so it seemed. He looked at his watch. Soon his wife would call, when she had checked into the hotel in Munich. She was taking the children to the Alps for a ski vacation. Christ, he missed them already. And only this morning he had been glad that the demands of his work gave him an excuse not to go with them. It was always like this. The children drove him crazy, but he couldn't imagine being without them. And Heike . . . I hope she calls soon, he thought.

The telephone on his desk interrupted his thoughts. It wouldn't be Heike. She would call on the regular line. This was the emergency line.

He picked it up. "Holzauer," he said. Then, hastily taking the cigarette from his mouth, he leaned forward in his chair as he recognized the chancellor's voice.

"This is a national alert," the chancellor said superfluously. "Four NATO missiles have been hijacked by an antinuclear terrorist group. Deploy all your forces in a full effort to find them. The hijacking took place near Etzen. That's between Lüneburg and Soltau on the B-209. Send out helicopters, jeeps, everything into the area. They've got to be within a thirty-kilometer radius of Etzen."

"Yes, sir!" Holzauer said.

"We'll be in constant communication with you. Set out at once. I'm going to be in touch with the American president within minutes in order to work out a strategy. But first we must find them. I'm counting on you!"

"We'll be right on it, sir."

They hung up.

Holzauer punched another button on the phone. "Schöndorf," he said. "Full alert. Assemble the men. I'll be downstairs in five minutes."

He opened the desk drawer, took out his Mauser and stuck it in the belt holster on his right hip. He threw on his jacket and left the office.

THEY HUDDLED together amid the cornstalks. The rain had turned into snow, but it was not yet accumulating. Once it did, any movement they made would be easily spotted.

"Let's get out of here," said Norbert. "Gabriele's safe now, we can call the police and tell them where the group is and go home."

"I agree," said Pete. "There's nothing more we can do."

Sigismund and Hannelore looked disappointed.

"No." It was Gabriele.

"We *can* go. And yes, we should contact the police, but first I want to go back. There's some unfinished business I have with Ulrich."

"You're not going alone," said Christopher. It was funny, he thought, something about her made him not even try to dissuade her from going back. He thought he had a good idea what it was she wanted to finish. "I'm not leaving your side again."

Gabriele looked at him. "I'm going to kill him." Her voice sounded so bitter, but yet so calm and matter of fact. "I have to. I could never live with myself if I didn't."

"I know," Christopher said. "But I'm not leaving you. Not now. Not ever."

There were tears in her eyes. He touched her face tenderly. He could feel the swelling of the tissue on her cheeks and around her eyes.

"He did this to you." It was a statement, not a question.

"Yes," she said, then paused. "He raped me, too."

Christopher felt as though he had been hit in the stomach with a sledgehammer.

"I should have fought him off. I let him, because at first I thought it was a test to see if I was really going to go along with them. But it wasn't a test. He merely wanted to rape me. He didn't beat me until the next day, when he told me he knew I had called you." The tears were flowing more freely. She winced with pain as they seeped into the cuts on her face.

He opened his arms. "Gabriele." His voice was soft.

She sank into his arms and sobs welled up from deep inside her.

He held her, touching the back of her head carefully, afraid of irritating her wounds and hurting her further.

He said nothing, and in his silence she felt the strength of him. His love flowed into her and filled her.

"I hate to break this up," said Pete, "but there's a lot of activity over by the house. We've got to do something soon."

They broke apart, but not before looking deeply into each other's eyes. They both knew that words were no longer necessary. They would not need to resort to them again.

"You're right," said Gabriele, collecting herself.

She stepped back. "First, they have the capability of arming and programming the missiles, and they're planning to use them. Ulrich is quite fanatic. Colonel Thalberg, I'm sure, both from what I've seen and from what Christopher witnessed in England, is using them. Thalberg is working for American interests. The United States would never ally itself with people like Sievers unless they had a broader plan in mind. The others, I think, are duped. But Sievers may be working hand in hand with Thalberg and his intentions."

"Well, then the quicker the police can capture them the better," said Pete. "No matter what they're planning to do with the missiles, it can't be good. The only good thing would be not to have the missiles in Europe at all. But better that they are back on the American base than in the hands of these extremists."

"Shall we go to the police now, then?" Norbert asked. "Or are we going to wait for Gabriele to carry out her plan of personal revenge?" His voice had a note of sarcasm in it.

"We'll split up," said Sigismund. "I'll stay with Christopher and Gabriele. You three take the VW and go to the police."

"Good idea," said Pete.

"I want to stay," said Hannelore. "Look," she went on when it seemed Pete would object, "Sievers and the others are certainly going to look for Gabriele the moment they see she's gone and they've secured the missiles. I can help...."

"Shhhh!" It was Christopher. He had been looking toward the house when he thought he heard something.

"Someone's coming." They ducked down and spread out slightly, their weapons ready. It was only then that Christopher realized, with some amazement, how they had all been carrying their weapons as if doing so was second nature to them, as if this was an ordinary everyday occurrence. My God, he thought, what would I have said two weeks ago if someone had told me I'd be standing here like this tonight! He crept closer to Gabriele.

"It's Sievers," she whispered.

He leaned back toward the others and motioned with his head in the direction of the approaching footsteps.

They crouched lower.

Sievers and Helga could be seen walking along the edge of the cornfield, peering into the stalks, looking for a break where someone could have entered the field.

Gabriele was holding the HK-54 to her shoulder. She had made sure the clip was correctly inserted and that the safety catch was disengaged. She had never fired any kind of gun before in her life, but she felt absolutely confident that she would shoot straight and on target. Ulrich was in her sights and he was getting closer and closer. She would wait until he would look her right in the face and then she would fire. She wanted him to know, as his life was snuffed out, who his killer was.

He was approaching.

Closer.

Closer...

Now!

He saw her, and his highly tuned reflexes saved his life. At the very second he caught sight of her amid the corn, he fell facedown to the ground. Pure instinct.

The air was split with the burst of machine gunfire, illuminating the rim of the cornfield. When Ulrich fell to the earth, the bullets ripped into Helga's chest and neck. She fell heavily, a mass of blood covering her instantly and pouring over the frosty earth.

Ulrich slithered rapidly backward, slightly protected by the mound of earth next to the furrow in which he had fallen. He retreated awkwardly for several yards, then rose and threw himself diagonally into the corn.

Gabriele swung her automatic in the direction of the sound and fired off another salvo. Dead cornstalks were ripped in half. Christopher, at her side, raised his weapon, but saw nothing at which to aim.

"Spread out," hissed Sigismund urgently, and he ran off far to the right, attempting to swing around on Sievers from the side.

Sievers heard the sound and fired blindly to his left. He was answered by shots from two sides now as both Gabriele and Sigismund fired at him. And then, to his surprise, a third gun joined in from somewhere in between.

"Verdammte Scheisse," he hissed quietly. Three of them! He started crawling backward quickly. He had to get back to the house and to the others. He cursed the fact that he had no more grenades. Once he felt sure he had gone far enough he got to a crouching position, turned around and ran swiftly through the corn. When he arrived at the edge of the field, where there was a final open area between him and the house, he ran at top speed.

Christopher saw him running and stepped through the last row of corn. He aimed carefully and deliberately and fired several shots, but was sure he had missed. Sievers was too far away and was running too fast.

"Goddamn it!" shouted Gabriele. "Goddamn it! I had him in my sights!" She walked over to Helga's body and kicked it in frustration.

Hannelore bent over and took the weapons from the body. "Okay, now what?" she asked as the others approached.

"Let's get out of here," Pete suggested. "You had your chance, Gabriele, now it's too late. They'll be better prepared now that they know we're here."

She was staring down at Helga's body. She felt nothing. Not even loathing and contempt for the woman she had killed. Well, not exactly nothing. She was glad. Glad she was dead. But she knew she wouldn't rest until she could look down on Ulrich Sievers's body.

"No, I'll not leave now."

"Let's do what I first suggested," Sigismund said. "The rest of you go. I'll stay with them."

"All right. All right," said Pete. "I wish you'd come, but I see you're too headstrong. I almost want to stay myself, but someone's got to get to the police."

"Stay if you want," said Norbert. "I can go to the police myself."

"Okay. I'll stay, too. Go."

Norbert hastened off.

"Wait a minute—" Sigismund ran after him "—let's get the rest of the ammunition, we may need it." Pete went with him.

Several minutes later they could hear the car start up and move slowly away. Then Pete and Sigismund returned.

Sigismund handed them fresh clips for their machine guns.

"We left the crates where the van was parked. Let's go back. We can't stay here. This is where Sievers will start looking for us. It's time to work out a strategy. We'll blow this fucking place apart before they can do any damage."

CHAPTER NINETEEN

Washington, D.C.

THE PRESIDENT LEANED back in his leather swivel chair. "So there you have the situation, gentlemen."

There was silence in the Cabinet Room.

The Secretary of State was the first to break the silence. "Of course complying with their demands is out of the question."

"Absolutely." The President cleared his throat. "I was just on the telephone with the chancellor and he's got his crack antiterrorist force looking for them already. Remember their success in 1977 in Mogadishu, freeing that hijacked Lufthansa jet without losing a single hostage or commando.

"Anyway, we'll find them and then we'll apprehend them. What I want to learn from you gentlemen," he said, surveying the group around the table, "is exactly what the effect would be if one of those missiles was actually launched." He looked at Air Force General Collins.

The general looked down at the tabletop.

"Do you mean," the National Security Adviser broke in, "political effects or destructive effects?"

"We *know* what the political effects would be, damn it," the President said angrily. "This administration would be embarrassed!" You jackass! he thought as he glared at the NSA. Then he looked over at the general again. "General Collins?"

The general coughed, took a sip of water. "Well," he said, "that depends on the target. Each missile, when armed with a conventional warhead, is powerful enough to destroy a tank, or even an airfield if it hits a munitions supply—"

"General," the President interrupted, an exasperated expression on his face, "would you mind getting to the point? We know these particular missiles have nuclear warheads and the terrorists claim they have armed them."

"Well..." the general drawled, "each warhead has a relatively low destructive capability, compared with other nuclear warheads, such as those in the ICBMs...."

"General! You're digressing again." The President raised an eyebrow. The man was a fool, he thought. Too many years vegetating behind a desk.

"Well...let's put it this way. Each missile has the destructive force roughly equivalent to that of fifteen times the strength of the bomb dropped on Hiroshima."

"Thank you, General!" said the President. "Now that helps clarify the magnitude of the problem. But what is this you said about depending on its target?"

"Well...if, for example, they should choose to launch them at a missile base or a nuclear power plant, they would be far more destructive than if they struck a city. They could possibly set off other nuclear missiles if they hit a missile base. Or if they hit a power plant, they could cause a meltdown and you would have the massive nuclear catastrophe all the antinuke protesters have been worried about for these past several years."

"I see," said the President. He looked around the table. "Ozzie," he asked, "what are the chances of us locating and destroying the missiles once they are in flight?"

"I think we're all aware of the special qualities of the cruise missiles, which make them nearly impossible to detect with radar. The terrain-matching guidance system necessitates their low altitude and thus makes it possible for them to escape radar detection. However, they don't travel as fast as the ballistic missiles, which can go halfway around the world in twenty minutes. If we know what a cruise missile's target is, and if we know the time of its launching, then we have a chance. We could deduce its flight path and have every available jet airborne looking for it. I'd say that then we'd have a fifty-fifty chance of locating and destroying it."

Everyone looked at one another around the room.

"The only thing we can do now is wait," the President concluded. "Wait and see if the terrorists communicate with us again. And wait to see if our men in Europe or the German antiterrorist squad can locate these villains."

He paused and looked at his advisers. "Any questions or comments? If not, then, that will be all. You'll be notified when I need you again. Be ready."

CHAPTER TWENTY

Wetzen

THE HELICOPTER LANDED in the center of the roadway behind the barriers erected by the Federal Police. Holzauer stepped out and, automatically ducking and running in a slight crouch while holding on to his hat, hastened over to the senior police officer in charge. He saluted.

"Hauptmann Holzauer, Commando Unit," he introduced himself, shouting over the sound of the helicopter.

"Hauptmann Schlobohm, Federal Police." The salute was returned. "I'm glad you got here so quickly."

"Can you brief me?"

"Yes." Schlobohm motioned with his arm for Holzauer to follow him. They wound their way through dozens of police cars—lights flashing, radios crackling, men running and shouting. "Over here." He led him to the rear of what had once been the convoy.

Holzauer examined the two burned-out vehicles.

"There's another up front. All the men were killed. The gap here is where the two large trucks carrying the missiles were stationed—the TEL and the LCC. We think the terrorists had some casualties. There are areas in the grass by the roadside where there seems to be blood, but we don't know how many, just as we don't know how many took part in the raid or how many vehicles they had. Whatever they had, they have two more now. We're still analyzing the evidence; there are abundant tire tracks by the side of the road.''

They approached a man who was sitting in the back of a police car. He was wearing an American uniform. He appeared to be very shaken and on the verge of shock.

"This is the only survivor. Corporal," he called to him in English, "may we have a word with you?" He introduced the man to Holzauer.

"Do you know how many of them there were?"

"No. I only saw two...." His voice broke, his eyes looked from side to side, almost panic-stricken. "They're murderers. They killed Jerry in cold blood...." He stopped. Holzauer looked at Schlobohm.

"That's okay," said Schlobohm, "you don't need to go into that again. Captain Holzauer only needs a few questions answered."

He turned to Holzauer. "They left a letter with the corporal that restates the demands they read over the radio to the American Commandant. The media have already picked it up. It will no doubt be in all the newspapers tomorrow verbatim, although the government is denying everything, trying to suppress the release of the news as long as possible."

He showed the letter to Holzauer. It was in both German and English.

"There were more than two, weren't there?" Holzauer prompted the corporal.

"Yes. But I didn't see them. I heard all the shooting, but I didn't leave the cab until I was forced to. The two I saw were a man and a woman."

"Were any of them wounded?"

"No, but it seemed to me they were concerned about their partners. Perhaps some were wounded or killed. I don't know. It all happened so fast. There was an awful lot of shooting going on, and explosions. There must have been a lot of them.''

"The Americans will be here any moment," Schlobohm said as they left the corporal. "We got word a few minutes before you arrived. Perhaps they'll enlighten us somewhat about what we're up against."

Holzauer nodded. He walked back to the helicopter in which he had just arrived and radioed to the four other helicopters that were circling the area with his men. No one had spotted anything suspicious on the dark Lüneburger Heide. He ordered one of the helicopters to land on the road, and told the others to expect the arrival of the Americans any minute.

"We already have them on our radar screens." The crackling reply came to him from one of the pilots aloft. "Eight choppers. Four of them large. Probably troop transports."

Holzauer signed off, then walked forward in the direction that the destroyed convoy was facing. He looked at the derelict truck blocking the road. Some police troopers were also examining the area. "There might have been some flares along the road here," he said to the officers. "They obviously staged an accident with this old truck to force the convoy to stop."

Scheisse, he thought, why the hell didn't those idiot Americans have the foresight to have a larger security force? The German police or military would never have allowed such an important exercise to take place with real missiles without sufficient protection. It was almost as if the Americans were asking for trouble.

ULRICH RAN IN through the back door. "They've killed Helga!" he announced to Erich and Thalberg, who were in the hall. "Gabriele's here and she has others with her. Quick, we've got to go to the barn!"

Sievers ran upstairs to fetch the rest of the weapons from his personal supply. He stopped in astonishment when he saw the ruined door to his room.

He picked up a briefcase, took the two high-powered rifles and a machine gun and tucked them under his arm. He ran downstairs.

"Klaus," he shouted, "get the emergency shortwave set and take it to the barn. There's no time to lose."

Alex had just entered with wooden beams and a hammer to block up the kitchen door. "Forget that," Ulrich ordered, "we've got to secure the barn. We're being surrounded. Activate the mines at the entrance. I don't know how these people found us, but we're going to trap them here now."

Alex went to the cellar and opened the large metal circuit-breaker box attached to the wall. He threw the switch that activated a row of mines that crisscrossed the entrance to the dirt road. This was the only precaution they had originally thought would be necessary, since the farm itself had not been a source of any suspicious activity. Besides, he thought, as he ran back upstairs, the missiles themselves would be their strongest defense. No one who knew they had them would dare attempt to open an attack. But why were they under attack? Or had Ulrich suddenly become an alarmist? If they were under attack then the attackers obviously didn't know the power that they had at their command. Yet . . .

The others had all gone to the barn, to the TEL. One entire side of the structure, where the eaves came down and flattened out at normal ceiling height, contained cots, water and food supplies and a large array of weapons. In addition to automatics, hand guns, high-powered rifles and grenades, there were even mortars and bazookas. Most of the weapons had been purchased, illegally, from international arms dealers through German underground sources at inflated prices. Money, however, had not been a problem.

Klaus was setting up the radio unit in one corner while Sievers spoke with Thalberg about the launching of one of the missiles and the content of their next message to the outside world.

NORBERT HAD STARTED the car and begun backing along the road the way they had come. He had gone almost half a mile when he realized that now that the vehicles had all arrived at the farm there was no reason why he shouldn't use the road that Sievers and company had used. It was a better road and closer to the main road and civilization.

He stopped, changed gears and started bouncing along in first when the car stalled. Cursing softly he tried starting it again and quickly flooded the engine. He kept turning the key without success. Finally, trying to calm himself, he waited twenty minutes. It was the only way. His hand kept reaching for the ignition, but he forced it back. And waited.

Feeling somewhat calmer he cautiously tried it again. It started immediately. He sighed and eased forward and arrived back at the crossroads several minutes later.

He spun the wheel to the left and stepped on the gas. It was possible to go fast enough to shift into second, then third. He was debating which way to turn when he arrived at the *Bundesstrasse*, when he heard a sound ahead and above.

A helicopter!

He strained to look through the windshield. Although the snow flurries had let up again, it did nothing to improve vision, but still, he thought he could see the dark form of the helicopter ahead and slightly to his right. Yes. There! He saw a flashing red light.

Norbert switched the headlights of the Volkswagen from high beam to low and back again. Several times in rapid succession.

He was still flashing the lights when he hit the mine.

The explosion was deafening, but it was probable that he never heard it. There was a sudden vacuum and then the car blew apart. Flames leaped up, into the sky, illuminating the countryside.

"EXPLOSION BELOW," the copilot announced into the radio.

"Yes. I can see it," Holzauer answered from the second helicopter two miles distant. "Go in for a landing, units two and three," he ordered. "Four and five remain aloft and circle the area, report what you see." He replaced the microphone. "Okay, Ernst," he said to the pilot, "let's get over there and see what we have."

Holzauer's helicopter landed a few minutes later near the other two. Unit three radioed to the police at the hijacking site, giving their position and asking for the entire road to be blocked off and for several cars to be sent up to join them. Another police unit was ordered down from Lüneburg with instructions to cut off the approach from the north.

Holzauer and two of his men neared the burning car. The flames had receded, for the gasoline had mostly burned off. "Careful," he said, "looks like it hit a mine." He indicated a hole in the dirt road.

"There'll be more than one," said the man at his side.

There was no sign of the driver, but they could read the remnants of the *Atomkraft Nein Danke* stickers that were now blackened along the side of the remains of the car.

Several more commandos had come up to them.

"I think there's no question—" Holzauer pointed at the burning wreckage, "—that this was probably one of the terrorists' vehicles. Does anyone know where this road leads?"

No one did.

"Check with the police."

One of the men ran back to a helicopter to use the radio.

"Probably leads to a farm. We'll cordon off the entire area and see what we've netted." He turned to another of his men. "Corporal, get the mine-detecting equipment and disconnect any other explosive devices you can find."

"Yes, sir."

"Unit five calling, sir!" a voice from the nearest helicopter shouted to him.

Holzauer hastened over and grabbed the extended microphone. "Go ahead, unit five."

"We've spotted a farm. The buildings are partially concealed by trees. Must be about three kilometers from where you are. Two very large buildings—one of them is large enough to hide those launchers—and several smaller structures. We can only see one light and that's coming from behind the farmhouse. No other signs of life. You'd think that someone would hear us and come out to have a look."

"Good work. Circle the area, keep us informed the moment you see any movement whatsoever. But keep your distance."

"Yes, sir."

Holzauer switched the microphone to transmit again. "Holzauer to Schlobohm. Holzauer to Schlobohm."

"Schlobohm here," a voice crackled over the speaker, "I've been listening in on your conversations."

"Good. Send every available man up here. We've got to surround this place as fast as possible. I know this is it. Alert the Americans. Have them send the military."

"We're coming."

"WHAT'S THAT SOUND?" Alex asked.

"Helicopters." Ulrich's eyes narrowed. He looked over

to Colonel Thalberg. This was not part of the game plan. At least not yet.

Thalberg thought it must be Matecki coming to get him out, but it was too soon for that. But what else would explain it?

"I should have killed Gabriele right away," Ulrich said, "instead of playing cat and mouse with her. She's one of them. Probably was sent to infiltrate us in the first place."

They all looked at one another. Their plan had been so foolproof. How could it have gone awry so quickly?

"Unless they're just routinely checking the area, looking for clues to the hijacking. But somehow I don't think so. Gabriele is behind this. She's working with them. Why didn't I see it sooner?"

Thalberg said nothing. If Gabriele was working with someone, it was with Benton. Benton had been the thorn in the side of this operation for too long now. Who the hell were they? he wondered. Who were they working for?

They listened. The helicopters could be heard circling.

"They're not going away," Thalberg said finally. "It's not a routine check." He looked at Ulrich. "It's time to move up the timetable."

Sievers stared at him uncomprehendingly for a moment. He was thinking of Gabriele, and listening to the helicopters.

"Yes," he said, "you're right. It's time to show them we mean business."

The colonel nodded and walked toward the TEL. He surreptitiously moved his right hand to his left wrist, pulled out the stem of his wristwatch, twisted it and pushed it back in.

GENERAL FORMAN TURNED from the radio console to Captain Packer. "They've found them," he said softly.

"The German police. Such goddamned Teutonic efficiency."

Suddenly a low beeping sound came from his watch. Quickly he pushed a button silencing it, and looked at Packer.

Their eyes met in silent collusion.

COLONEL MATECKI WAS in the lead helicopter as it flew from the base to the hijacking site. They had only set down for a few minutes, surveying the damage, when Holzauer's message had come through. They had taken off immediately and headed for the farm.

Christ, he thought, this is going far too fast. Thalberg had better alter the timetable. He was thinking of Thalberg when his watch beeped, almost as if responding to his thoughts.

He turned it off.

It was Thalberg's signal that missile number one, the all-important first missile, was about to be fired, and that Matecki was to pick up Thalberg at the prearranged rendezvous.

Well, Sam, thought Matecki, you want out. I'll see what we can do. We just didn't count on Hauptmann Holzauer and his hotshot commando force.

CHRISTOPHER WAS COLD. His anorak was zipped up tightly, but still the icy wind penetrated. They were all soaking wet, and as the snow began letting up, the temperature began dropping.

The five of them had seen the figures rushing from the house, carrying objects in their hands and barricading themselves in the barn.

They had also heard the distant explosion and could see the sky to the south lit up from the ensuing fire. But they didn't realize it was Norbert's funeral pyre. Then the helicopters arrived. They watched in silence as two helicopters hovered over the farm, then began circling. Widening circles, then narrowing circles. Then widening again.

"It's the police," said Hannelore, straining to identify them. "We better signal before they get too far away."

She stepped out into the open and raised her machine gun to get their attention.

"Get back here!" shouted Sigismund, yanking her arm. "*Bist du verrückt?* Are you crazy? You fire a signal shot and they'll think you're firing at them. They'll blast us off the ground thinking we're the ones they're after!"

Hannelore stopped, and released her finger from the trigger. "You're right." She stepped swiftly back under cover.

The helicopters were out over the area on the far side of the compound.

"Come on," said Gabriele, "let's go. They're all in the barn, we'll surround it until the authorities come. If they try to leave we'll kill them." She paused. "I hope they try to leave."

Before anyone could raise an objection she had started off across the field. They followed after her.

"We've got to be quiet," said Sigismund unnecessarily. "You go around back," he said to Christopher. "Hannelore, you and Gabriele take the sides, and Pete and I will cover the front door."

They spread out. Hannelore went around the far side of the house and approached the side of the barn from the rear of the house. Christopher joined Gabriele alongside the outermost shed. They cautiously peered around the corner of the shed, watching for any movement from the barn. There was none.

They crouched low and ran to the rear of the barn and pressed themselves against the wall near the corner. Gabriele looked around the edge and surveyed the side of the building.

Pete and Sigismund had hidden themselves behind two of the trees in the yard directly across from the entrance to the barn.

The front doors swung open and two people carrying machine guns emerged and stood on either side. There was the roar of an engine as the TEL began rolling, slowly, almost sluggishly, out of the building.

As THE DOORS OPENED, Ulrich picked up the radio microphone and pressed the transmit button.

"To show the forces of American imperialism that we are serious," he said in his monotonous drone, "we have moved up the timetable. We will launch one of the missiles within ten minutes, unless we hear the voice of the President of the United States announce to us on this wavelength that he has decided to acquiesce to our demands.

"We fully expect that he will not do so, thus we have arranged this little demonstration at Munich's expense.

"If his reluctance continues, then we will have no recourse than to fire the other missiles. Their targets are the American base in Wiesbaden, NATO headquarters in Brussels and the nuclear power plant at Brokdorf. If our sincerity or expertise is doubted, than all we can say is 'watch the skies.'

"Ten minutes."

He turned the transmit switch to the off position and listened to the undefined static hissing over the speaker.

WHAT *ARE* THEY DOING? thought Sigismund as the vehicle passed by. He looked at the two guards at the doors. Should he open fire on them? Or attack the TEL? He looked over to the tree where Pete was concealed and saw the same puzzled expression on his face.

COLONEL OSTER HAD already picked up the red telephone
before Sievers's communication had ended.

"The President," he said urgently, "priority one! Red
Alert!"

The delay seemed interminable. His eyes were glued to the
second hand on the wall clock. "Oh, Christ," he moaned.

A full minute went by.

"Mr. President. Thank God! We've got to patch you into
their radio frequency immediately. They demand to hear
your voice. They want you to acquiesce to their demands at
once or they will launch the first missile in—" he looked
over his shoulder at the wall clock "—eight minutes."

"That's preposterous," the President said, the rage in his
voice scarcely affecting the familiar paternalistic sound of
it.

"They claim the target is Munich. The other missiles are
targeted for NATO headquarters, our base in Wiesbaden
and the nuclear power plant at Brokdorf. But they have not
set a deadline for the firing of subsequent missiles."

"Colonel Oster, I think they're bluffing. I think they
won't even be able to launch the missiles, much less arm or
program them."

"Will you speak to them? Maybe you can stall them."

"No. I will not speak to them. No one will hold this government hostage. Let them try what they can and the blame
will fall on their own heads."

There was a pause, and it seemed there was a whispered
consultation in the background.

"Has the whereabouts of these people and the missiles
been located yet? Do we know who is behind them? Is there
a Libyan connection?"

"We don't know anything about who is behind them, *yet*,
but we're pretty sure they're on a farm in north Germany
near Lüneburg. Quite close to where the missiles were hijacked. We have helicopters and men rushing there now."

"Good. Have them go in and wipe them out as soon as they arrive."

"Yes, sir."

There was a pause.

"Colonel Oster," the President finally said, "we'll keep this line open. Report every development to my aide, Mr. Tice, who I'll now put on the telephone. Keep up the good work."

Good work, thought Oster, Christ, the man is thick.

Oster had a distinctly bad feeling in the pit of his stomach. A very bad feeling.

"UNIT FIVE TO BASE. Unit five to base. There is movement at the barn. We're going over to have a look."

Matecki's eyes were fixed on the landscape below as he listened to the report on the open channel. Off to their port side they could see the two police helicopters circling. Behind them, he knew, the rest of his force were coming. The police were gathering at the entrance to the farm. There was a great deal of activity on the B-209 near the intersection with the dirt road.

He transmitted an urgent order on the German police frequency to pull back their two helicopter units while he went in. "This is U.S. government business," he announced.

The colonel saw the dark outline of the buildings, the oaks and beeches largely obscuring the details, but he could see some light filtering up through them from the barn.

He had heard the message from Sievers and knew that Thalberg would fire the first missile within minutes. He looked at his watch. Here we come, Sam, he said to himself, and pressed a button on the watch casing.

"There's the TEL." He pointed out the moving vehicle to the pilot. It had arrived in the space at the edge of the field just out from under the branches of the trees.

"Head around behind it and prepare to land in that adjacent field."

COLONEL OSTER COULDN'T TAKE his eyes from the clock. He sat transfixed.

Five minutes to go, he thought.

"Captain," he said to the officer at his side, "scramble the fighters. Get every available plane up and have them ready to shoot down a Tomahawk missile that may be flying on a southerly heading in the direction of Munich from the Lüneburg sector. Also radio all Air Force bases in the country. Full Red Alert."

"Yes, sir." The captain saluted and picked up the telephone.

Within seconds the base alarm sounded and pilots were scrambling to their aircraft.

"Mr. Tice," Oster said into the Washington line, "I'm sending up jets to keep a lookout for the missile in case it *is* launched. Please inform the President and request permission to shoot it down if possible."

"Hold on."

A few moments later Tice spoke again. "Permission granted."

"Thank you."

SIGISMUND KNEW they had to act fast.

The launcher behind the tractor was fully extended. He was positive they were about to fire the missile. There was no time for making plans. They could no longer wait for the military or the police. Outside help wouldn't arrive in time.

He looked at Pete and pointed toward the launcher. He motioned that he was going after it. Pete understood.

The two helicopters that had been circling the farm were leaving the area. That was odd. As the sound of the retreat-

ing choppers diminished the ensuing silence deepened fore-
bodingly.

Sigismund ran out from behind the tree in the direction
of the launcher. The two guards, Erich and Alex, snapped
their heads toward him. As he neared the cab Sigismund
raised his automatic.

But Erich, too, brought up his HK-54, and before Sigismund could fire, he pulled the trigger. Bits of dirt spit up
into the air around Sigismund.

Pete leaped out from behind the tree and opened fire. He
saw one of the men waver, then drop to a prone position.

Erich raised himself on his elbows and fired another barrage, this time at Pete. Alex jumped back inside the barn for
cover.

Pete staggered and fell against the trunk of the tree for
support. His breathing became labored and his chest emit-
ted a gurgling sound. He looked down and saw the blood on
his flak jacket, then he looked over toward Sigismund, who
was limping, dragging his left leg awkwardly. He must have
been hit. Everything seemed dreamlike to Pete. He felt as
though he were wrapped up in cotton wool; a veil seemed to
have come between him and reality. But *this* was reality. He
was thinking. He was acting.

Sigismund began firing at the side of the cab. The right-
hand side. Shooting out the tires, then the windows, trying
to get the driver. But he couldn't see him.

Erich rose to his feet and sent off another salvo at Sigismund.

Pete tried raising his gun, but his right arm wouldn't
work. He thought that was peculiar and he kept trying to
raise it and operate the gun. But there was blood pouring
down it. So much blood. His head began reeling. He was
losing too much blood. Far too much. He switched the gun
to his left hand. And he saw Sigismund arch his back and
fall to the side, little eruptions racing across his body. Pete

fired at the man by the barn. He held his finger firmly down on the trigger, and waved the barrel of the gun back and forth. He saw the man thrown backward into the door and slide lifelessly to the ground. A swath of blood spread down the door from where his back had struck it.

Pete stumbled forward three steps.

And then the ground reached up and pulled him down.

He coughed once, and died.

SIEVERS COULDN'T LEAVE the radio when the firing had started outside. But once the ten minutes had elapsed and neither the President nor anyone else had spoken, he grabbed his automatic and joined Alex at the door.

"The bastards are not even replying," he muttered. "Well, they'll soon learn how serious we are."

He looked out the door. The shooting outside had suddenly stopped. "Damn it," he said. "Why doesn't Thalberg fire the missile? It's time."

HANNELORE SLOWLY APPROACHED the corner of the barn. She flattened herself against the half-timbered wall.

Everything was suddenly so deathly quiet. Too quiet.

She carefully peered around the corner and saw ahead and to her right, just past the copse of trees, the crippled launcher. The tires were shot out, as were the windows on the near side. The erector, however, was in its fully extended position. A forty-five-degree angle, ominously pointing skyward.

Near the door of the barn a dark form was lying motionless. Another lay near the launcher. And a third was between the trees and her.

Oh, God, she thought, they're dead. But who's still in the barn? Where are Christopher and Gabriele?

Suddenly her eyes shot back to stare at the distant form. Something had caught her attention. Yes. She was sure of

it. The figure lying to the right of the launcher had moved.
Her peripheral vision had picked up the movement.
Whoever it was was creeping forward. Very slowly.

She watched silently.

CHRISTOPHER AND GABRIELE stood near the far corner of
the barn out of Hannelore's sight. The TEL was clearly visible to them only forty yards away. It was obvious that it
would no longer be capable of moving back to the barn, or
even under the trees. It was vulnerably stranded at the edge
of the field, in the open, in a perfect position for launching. The leafless trees hovered incongruously in stark
ghostly outline around the launcher.

There was a humming sound as the four stabilizing pods
lowered to the ground at the corners of the vehicle.

"They're going to launch a missile," Christopher whispered harshly to Gabriele. "We've got to stop them!"

"But how?" she said. "We can't risk hitting it. Won't we
chance setting it off?"

"I don't know. I know nothing about the triggering
mechanism. Maybe a chance shot from us will set it off. Or
maybe it can only be detonated when it's over its prepro-
grammed target. All I *do* know is that as long as we keep
anyone from getting to it, they can't fire it."

A rushing noise came from the field beyond the TEL.
They were both startled and stared past the truck. The sound
grew louder, a mechanical chopping sound.

"A helicopter!" Gabriele pointed.

They could see it settling toward the ground about thirty
yards away, on the far side of the launcher. Several lights on
the aircraft lit up the ground under it as it touched down.

They could clearly see the insignia of the United States
Army on the side of the fuselage.

"Good," said Gabriele, and she rose to her feet from
where she was squatting.

Christopher grabbed her shoulder and restrained her. "Wait a minute," he said.

COLONEL MATECKI HAD directed the pilot down as near to the TEL as he dared.

"Okay," he said, "don't cut the motor. We'll be taking off again almost immediately."

He cradled a new Armalite AR-18 in his arms as he slid open the door and lightly jumped to the ground.

THE MOMENT the firing had begun and the windows around him shattered like hailstones over him, Thalberg hit the floor. He was still lying there, the clutch pedal digging painfully into his ribs. His right arm was throbbing.

There was a lot of blood, and the pain was nearly unbearable, but he wasn't sure if he had actually been hit by a bullet or the glass, or both.

The firing had stopped, but he was too wary to chance jumping out and getting to the launcher. But he had to fire the missile now. Had to. The ten minutes had more than run out. He pressed the button to lower the stabilizing pods.

"Why the fuck doesn't Sievers get here!" he grumbled out loud. "At least he could tell me the coast is clear. He's probably scared shitless."

He peered up over the edge of the passenger door and looked through the hole where the window had been. He could see nothing moving.

"Christ, they're probably all dead."

He saw the helicopter landing. He leaned toward the left door and put his hand on the handle. As the helicopter settled on its pods he realized he had never thought the emblem of the United States Army would look so good. And he never even considered himself particularly patriotic.

He saw the man emerge from the chopper and move in a half crouch swiftly toward him. Matecki.

Thalberg raised the handle and, in a rolling motion, jumped out of the cab.

ALEX HAD STEPPED outside, swiveling his gun back and forth in a sweeping motion, but there was no movement or sound other than the helicopter.

He turned back to Ulrich. "A helicopter just landed. I can't see the markings, it's on the far side of the TEL." He paused.

"Thalberg showed me how to launch the missile. I'm going to do it now. Perhaps he was wounded and can't get out of the cab."

"I'll cover you," said Ulrich.

Alex jumped over Erich's body and started across the gravel toward the TEL. Ulrich stepped cautiously to the door, using it for protection.

"IT'S THE OTHER AMERICAN!" Christopher exclaimed when Colonel Matecki had crossed half the distance between the chopper and the TEL. "The officer who was with Colonel Thalberg at Greenham Common. The man who killed Colin Robbins and almost killed me."

"We've got to get them," said Gabriele. But just then she saw movement to their right. "What's this?" she whispered and sucked in her breath.

Alex approached the rear of the TEL. He stepped onto the control center platform and opened a metal panel.

They raised their guns.

COLONEL THALBERG LUNGED away from the cab, then took several rapid steps toward the launch control panel.

Sigismund saw the legs moving on the other side of the launcher. Without hesitation he raised himself on his elbows and fired between the wheels.

The colonel screamed and staggered as the bullets ripped into his legs.

He knew the shots came from the far side of the truck and that if he fell he would be dead by the time he hit the ground. The truck protected him.

Desperately he grabbed on to the side of the launcher. The shots still pumped into his legs, tearing at them, destroying his knees. He could no longer stand. Still he hung on.

Slowly and agonizingly he hauled his useless legs up so that he was lying on the launcher, protected now by the missiles themselves.

Alex wheeled toward the burst of shots, jumped down from the panel, ran a few steps around the trailer and opened fire.

Sigismund kept shooting at the launcher, even though he saw bits of earth popping up around him and knew that he himself was a target. And then his shoulders and neck exploded in tissue and blood. He was dying, but he kept his finger on the trigger as he slumped over on his side. The last vestiges of consciousness remaining in him took control of the weapon and his task. His entire body shook with a final spasm and then was still. Only then did his gun fall silent.

Alex raced around to Colonel Thalberg and got there just as Colonel Matecki, who had hesitated a moment when Thalberg was hit, arrived.

"Quick," Thalberg gasped, "the launcher!" His eyes were wide and frantic. "Alex! Launch the missile!"

Alex ran to the console and punched the buttons on the keyboard in the order Thalberg had shown him.

Suddenly there was a vibration as the launcher shook, and a burst of heat enveloped them.

"Get down," Matecki shouted over the roar and threw himself to the ground alongside the cab. Alex grabbed Thalberg's immobile form and leaped, with him over his shoulder, to the left as far as possible.

A bright light filled the area around the TEL and a huge cloud billowed over the three of them as the missile roared out of the launcher.

The projectile could be seen briefly above the launcher, a nuclear Daliesque still life seemingly hovering for a second, the smoke threatening to engulf it. Then suddenly it was gone, a mere pinpoint in the German sky, as it disappeared on its mission.

CHAPTER TWENTY-ONE

Wetzen

THE PILOTS of the two helicopters were just landing back at the road. They were the first to see the arrow of light piercing the sky.

But Dietrich Holzauer would have sworn that he felt a detectable rise in the temperature as the missile hurtled above them.

"The missile has been launched!"

To his consternation Holzauer realized he was screaming into the microphone. It was thoroughly out of character for him. Never had any of his men heard him raise his voice, much less lose total control of himself.

"Emergency!" Holzauer shouted, trying to lessen the anxiety in his voice and regain his composure. "The missile has been launched."

He looked toward the compound. A cloud was rising and dissipating. He spoke again into the microphone, asking for the position of the approaching American helicopters. One, he had noticed, had already landed, but there was no movement to be seen in the aftermath of the launching. Perhaps the terrorists had taken it out of action.

Munich, he thought, *Oh my God. Munich.*
Heike!

"YES, MR. TICE. You heard me correctly." Oster thought Tice was close to hysteria. Calm down. Quiet. He was astonished at how cool his own voice sounded to him. "Yes.

The terrorists have launched one of the missiles. Tell the President."

He paused and listened.

"I have thirty jets already aloft over Hessen. The pilots have orders to shoot the missile down if it's spotted. Unfortunately, it will be nearly impossible to detect its path by radar. Our only chance is to get a visual sighting of it.

"But there *is* that chance. They said its target was Munich. So we know at least *where* to look—if they told the truth."

The President grabbed the receiver impatiently from his aide's hand. "Let me know instantly if it's spotted!"

"Mr. President, should we alert Munich? Should we issue an order to evacuate the city?"

"Our base at Mutlangen has been alerted, hasn't it?"

"Yes. They're sending up fighters there, too, in case the missile gets that far."

"How much time do we have?"

"The flying time, I'd say, is about forty minutes. It's not a fast-moving missile by missile standards. It also depends on what kind of trajectory they programmed into it. They could feed enough data into it so that it would fly a deceptive circular route around Munich and actually approach the city from the south."

"Colonel Oster." The President's voice was calm. Amazing, Oster thought, how the man could remain so calm. "Colonel, I think it advisable that no attempt whatsoever be made to evacuate. There's not enough time. Furthermore, if we're fortunate enough to shoot down the missile, then we will avoid a general panic."

"As you wish, sir."

One of Oster's aides was trying to attract his attention. Oster turned to him. "Just a moment, Mr. President. I have some updated information coming in now."

"Colonel Oster, sir." The aide spoke rapidly and with efficient economy. "None of the squadrons have seen anything. Someone should have picked up at least some radar irregularities, but they all have negative readings."

Oster raised his eyebrows. "Alert all West German bases immediately. Perhaps they were bluffing. Perhaps their target is *not* Munich. See if anyone comes up with anything at all."

"Yes, sir."

Oster again spoke into the telephone. "Mr. President, there have been no sightings. But we'll find it."

"Keep the line open. I'm not leaving the Oval Office until you come up with a sighting."

"Very good, sir."

HANNELORE REACTED immediately.

Sigismund's gun had not quite fully ceased firing when she stepped out from the corner of the barn and ran across to the protection of the trunk of a large tree. As she ran she fired a swath across the area in front of the barn, sending Sievers back behind cover.

Once she was positioned behind the tree she pulled a grenade from her pocket and held it so that she could remove the pin at a second's notice. First, she would ascertain that Gabriele and Christopher were out of harm's way. Then she would toss the grenade into the barn.

SIEVERS DUCKED back in, but not before he marked which tree the woman had hidden behind. He moved to the rear of the barn and opened a small trapdoor low in the wall that led outside. He crawled through and, hugging the wall, moved up along the barn on the side that Hannelore had just vacated.

THE CLOUD HAD FULLY dissipated, and Colonel Matecki slowly got to his feet.

He looked over at Thalberg and Alex. The latter was dazed, but was beginning to stir. Thalberg had passed out. Perhaps he was dying. Probably, thought Matecki.

Matecki knew he had to get Thalberg out, alive or not, before they moved in and destroyed Sievers and the rest of them. The mission was accomplished. The missile was on its way to the Soviet SS-20 base in East Germany. The terrorists would be blamed and he would have the satisfaction of knowing that not only had they destroyed an important SS-20 base, thereby striking a blow at the Soviets, but even more significant for their immediate goals, the left-wing opposition in Germany would be forced to take the full responsibility. We can probably even demand that Bonn outlaw the Green Party, he thought, as well as crack down hard on the terrorists. And, of course, deployment will continue. There will be no detente. As long as I get Thalberg out of here.

He went over to Thalberg. He was still breathing. I've got to get him to the helicopter. He's the only link implicating us. Then Sievers will get his reward.

He lifted Thalberg onto his shoulder and started, in a trot, toward the helicopter.

CHRISTOPHER AND GABRIELE saw the figures moving away.

"We've got to stop them!" Christopher shouted, pointing at the two colonels.

Gabriele looked at him. "Christopher," she said.

"There's no time to talk, hurry, let's go!"

"Christopher." She touched the side of his face tenderly with her fingers. "You are a wonderful man. I've just begun to know you and I want to know so much more." She looked deeply into his dark eyes.

She kissed him quickly, raised her gun, and together they stepped out from the side of the barn.

"YES?" THE PRESIDENT SAID into the telephone.

"Mr. President, we've located the missile. Templehof Airport in Berlin has had a brief radar reading. It's southeast of them and heading on a southeasterly trajectory."

"Southeasterly! My God! What does that mean?"

"Precisely, Mr. President. As far as we can determine it seems to be on course for Görlitz. That's in East Germany near the Czechoslovakian-Polish border. These terrorists are fools. They botched up their course programming or perhaps they never reprogrammed the missile in the first place. So now their attempt to destroy Munich has become an attack on a Soviet base!"

"Are they mad? Are they actually trying to force an East-West confrontation? We've got to alert the Soviets! They will construe this as an act of war. Oh my God!"

There was a pause. The President struggled to compose himself. "Stay on the line. I'm going to get the Soviet premier on the hot line and you're going to have to be patched in, to give them whatever information you can so they can destroy the missile. Plot the probable course and let them know where and when to expect the attack."

"Yes, sir."

"Meanwhile, alert East Berlin, too. Warn them!"

SIEVERS ARRIVED within sight of the tree, but he could not see Hannelore. She was careful to remain fully out of sight. Now he became unsure as to which of the trees concealed her.

Hannelore saw Gabriele and Christopher leave the safety of the side of the barn and approach the rear of the TEL.

Now.

She pulled the pin on the grenade, counted to five, then leaned out and tossed it accurately through the open door. It bounced once right at the threshold, hopped into the air, then rolled several yards inside.

Klaus looked up from the radio console and started to gasp when he saw the grenade.

The explosion broke apart the night. The front of the building seemed to buckle outward, but it didn't collapse. Instantly flames began shooting up from the center of the barn and then there were several other explosions as ammunition fell victim to the flames.

Sievers sidestepped deftly and rapidly to his right, like a crab, away from the burning structure. But there was no place to hide within a reasonable distance. He turned quickly and without breaking stride raced in a wide arc behind the barn, keeping it between Hannelore and himself.

She had seen the movement and dropped to one knee at the left side of the tree. She fired at the fleeing figure, but then he was gone.

ALEX WAS JUST RISING to his feet and hazily watching Colonel Matecki carrying Colonel Thalberg to the helicopter when the grenade went off. He spun around.

Flames were shooting out of the barn. Suddenly a human form, outlined by the flames, hurtled toward him. Christopher.

Alex bent down to pick up his gun, but Christopher lashed out with his foot and kicked him viciously in the jaw. Alex's head snapped backward and he fell onto his back. Christopher raised his gun and Alex rolled desperately away, clutching out, trying to find his gun.

Gabriele fired one shot into his chest just as Christopher fired. Alex stopped moving. Then they raised their guns and fired at the fleeing Matecki and Thalberg. But the two had already arrived at the helicopter.

Matecki heard the shots piercing the fuselage and he moved faster. He heaved Thalberg off his shoulder and into the chopper.

"Let's go!" he shouted to the pilot.

The helicopter began lifting before Matecki had even grabbed onto it. He jumped and curled his fingers into the sliding door track at the edge of the floor and held on.

They were airborne.

He scrambled his feet onto the landing gear and pushed and pulled himself farther into the chopper.

Bullets were still striking all around him. He suddenly felt a burning pain in his foot and knew he had been hit. But then they were out of range. With difficulty he hauled himself over the edge and sprawled dizzily onto the floor, gasping for breath.

"FUCK IT!" Christopher was grinding his teeth in frustration as the helicopter lifted out of range. He and Gabriele had both emptied their clips.

They lowered the guns, discarded the empty clips and were attaching fresh ones when something caused them both to spin around.

Ulrich Sievers.

"Well, well." He smiled. "If it isn't Mr. Christopher Benton. The infamous Christopher Benton. And Gabriele. Really, Gabriele, I would have thought you had better taste. Have you explained to him what a real man tastes like?" His gun was pointed at Christopher.

She glared at him, shifting her weight slightly to her right, trying to put some distance between herself and Christopher, dividing Ulrich's attention. Gabriele knew that the loathing welling up in her endangered them. She was fully capable of lunging out at him, but it would only hasten the pressure of his finger on the trigger and by the time she could kill him Christopher would be dead.

"Why have you done this, Uli?" she asked. "I know you were never excessively intelligent, but this is simply stupid." She concentrated her energy on remaining cool and rational. It was her only chance to gain control of herself. It was *their* only chance. "Don't you realize you've been duped? Thalberg only used you as part of a broader plan. You'll be the villain and all you've worked for will have been in vain."

"Shut up," he returned. "Do you really think I believe all those things I've been 'working for' and saying at rallies? The fact that my act fooled even you only shows what a perfect cover it's been." He smiled sardonically. "You, my dear, were even part of the cover and you never knew it!"

Gabriele sucked in her breath. He swung the gun toward her.

It was the moment for Christopher to act. He leaped at him.

Sievers brought the gun back and jammed it against Christopher's chest.

"No!" Gabriele shouted.

Sievers pulled the trigger. Once.

Gabriele reacted swiftly and impulsively. She squeezed the trigger of her weapon and ran toward Sievers. Bullets spit into him, spinning him around.

He dropped the gun and fell to one knee. There was blood on his lips.

"You bastard," Gabriele said.

Suddenly she felt utterly and completely calm. She stood above him and through the nausea and heartbreak she felt engulfing her, there was another feeling, a stronger feeling, one that bordered on serenity. Acceptance flowed through her. Everything had come full circle now. She would lose Christopher and she had only just found him. Worldwide catastrophe hovered around her, but this was now the moment of her destiny. The moment of fruition. The dormant fear and anguish that lay just below the surface would come out later, and perhaps she would not survive the consequences of the pain she had accepted.

But so be it.

She turned the machine gun around and rammed the butt of it into Ulrich's teeth. There was a sickening cracking sound as he fell back onto his haunches. Immediately she pulled the hunting knife out of the sheath on his belt and stabbed with all her might into his groin.

"I want you to feel your death—" she stared into his eyes "—just as you made me feel death." She stabbed again. "Yes. You should see the fear oozing out of you." And again.

"Get it over with!" he moaned, his voice suddenly breaking into a shrill cry. "Please . . . get it over with!" His eyes were transfixed on hers.

He fell onto his back, trembling in terror. He tried to scream, his breath coming in gasps, but a primal fear of what she still might do to increase his torture transformed the scream into a pathetic whimper as it died stillborn on his lips.

She straightened up and kicked him in the face. Then in the horrible wound in his groin. There was blood and urine everywhere. And still she kicked.

And she knew she had become an animal.

He was half-sobbing, half-delirious with pain.

"Goodbye, Ulrich," she said, and leaned down and deftly ran the razor-sharp blade across his throat. "Remember," she said venomously, "this is your own knife."

Because she listened so intently to the gurgling in his throat and watched the spasms taking control of his body, she didn't notice Alex slowly rise to his knees, searching for the gun at Christopher's side.

"I KNOW, MR. CHAIRMAN. Yes. Yes. It *is* our fault. Our security was lax. But this is no time for recriminations."

The President ran his fingers through his hair, mussing it up. He was proud that despite his age he had such a full, young-looking head of hair. He paced back and forth as the Soviet leader raged, through his interpreter, over the telephone.

"Yes. The missile is in the southeast sector now. If you get enough fighters and firepower in the air you will have a good chance of shooting it down. Of course, if it does hit the base, we will consider ourselves responsible. Do you think I would avoid responsibility? I am calling you to warn you, to assist you. There is still time."

The Soviet premier said he would get back to the President, and ended the conversation abruptly.

Within minutes the entire Soviet command in the East German/Czechoslovakian/Polish zone was airborne with fully armed rockets ready to fire at the first sighting of the missile. They were well aware that the chances of finding it and locking onto it were slim. It had been precisely designed for avoiding this sort of defense. From the ground it was nearly impossible to get a radar scan on it, its altitude was too low. From the air it would be possible, but only if it passed within a relatively close distance to a jet. If the jet were equipped with enough rockets to send out an adequate pursuit barrage, then, just possibly, it could be destroyed. Still, there was the danger from the missile's nuclear warhead. The terrain-matching guidance system was geared to detonate it only when it arrived at the target. Whether or not it could be successfully shot down without detonation depended on how close it was to the target and if it had locked onto it before it met retaliatory fire.

COLONEL THALBERG WAS unconscious. Matecki was sure he wouldn't make it. He had lost too much blood.

Matecki's wound, although from only a single bullet, had apparently torn through the Achilles tendon on his left foot. The pain was mounting rapidly, and though it was cold in the open compartment in the rear of the helicopter, he could feel beads of sweat on his forehead. He was afraid he might be crippled.

"Get us back to Garlstedt as fast as possible," he ordered the pilot. "The colonel needs medical attention badly. So do I, for that matter." He grimaced. He looked again at Thalberg and the blood spreading over the floor of the helicopter.

Colonel Thalberg was dead.

In the distance the burning barn could still be seen.

He thought of the missile. And its target.

He knew that intelligence was even now monitoring all signals emanating from or directed to Moscow, accurately evaluating the Soviet response capability. In spite of the intense pain, he smiled.

GENERAL FORMAN PACED back and forth in the hall outside the war room. The missile was on its way. Soon they would know how accurate the guidance system was and how powerful its destructive capabilities. Even if it was destroyed before detonation, invaluable information would be collected. All he needed now was word from Colonel Matecki to move on Wetzen.

No witnesses. No prisoners.

He had to admit to himself he was nervous. But he always suffered such anxiety and worry during any mission. It was something the men on the line never realized—how much he truly suffered, how much he agonized over the success or failure of a mission.

When will Matecki call in? he wondered.

HANNELORE HAD RUN from tree to tree as she closed in on he launcher. No one took a shot at her but there was still no way of knowing how many of them were left. There were shots on the far side of the TEL.

The barn was now an inferno as the flames consumed it. The helicopter had taken off.

She crept to the front of the cab and looked around it. Gabriele was straightening up from a body lying on the ground, a knife in her hand.

Then Hannelore saw another man on the ground behind Gabriele rise up and reach for the gun.

HOLZAUER ORDERED his men to group into their pre-arranged squads.

"Move in at will and take the place," he said as they spread out along the road after all the mines had been located and deactivated. "Try to avoid any damage to the remaining missiles and the launcher. But don't let anyone escape. Remember they have no hostages. Still, try to take them alive."

The men moved stealthily out through the fields along both sides of the road.

CAPTAIN PACKER GAVE the general a nod and handed him the compact earphones he had been wearing.

"Matecki here. Everything is go." The sound of the helicopter's rotors could be heard in the background. "We're coming home. We need medical attention. Over."

"Good job," said Forman, "hurry home." He handed the set back to Packer and returned to the war room.

"Colonel Oster?"

Oster glanced at him from the telephone. He held up his hand in a waiting gesture and spoke softly into the telephone, then turned to Forman. "What is it?"

"I've just had word from our first reconnaissance chop
per on the scene. They've pinpointed the exact location o
the missile launcher and they're closing in on the enemy
from the south and west."

"Good."

"Send in the troops."

Forman stepped out and nodded to Packer.

The captain saluted, then snapped a few orders into the
microphone.

GABRIELE STARED at Ulrich's body. She was sure he was
dead, but his limbs were still jerking spasmodically. She felt
nothing—neither satisfaction nor horror.

There was a click behind her. She spun around, raising the
knife in her hand, and looked into Alex's face. He was
trying to get the gun into position, but she could see from
the glassy look in his eyes that the effort was almost too
much for him. But then the gun was pointing directly at her,
and she knew she had to move immediately or it would be
too late.

A short staccato burst of gunfire came from behind him.
and the glassy look spread from his eyes to his entire face as
he slipped over onto his side.

Hannelore rushed over from the TEL cab and set down
her gun. "Are you all right?"

Gabriele nodded. "I think we've got them all. But they
took too much with them."

She stepped over to Christopher and knelt beside him. He
was unconscious, but still breathing. Barely. There was a
single bullet wound in the center of his chest.

"The bullet may have missed his heart," Gabriele said as
Hannelore knelt down on the other side, "but he must be
hemorrhaging badly. I think he will die."

A choking sound escaped from her throat and she knew
she was about to cave in. About to give in to the horror and

he anguish and the sense of loss. *No. No.* She must keep herself in control now. Now more than ever. If there was any chance to save Christopher, then she needed all her strength right now.

"Come," she said, "help me carry him back to the house."

She lifted his shoulders while Hannelore took his feet and they trudged to the front of the house.

They set him down and Hannelore fired several rounds into the door, shattering the lock. The door swung inward and they stepped across the threshold with their burden.

They laid him down on the table in the empty conference room, the table on which the plan had evolved. Hannelore went back outside to see if anything could be done for Pete and Sigismund while Gabriele ripped Christopher's shirt away.

"Oh, Christopher," she moaned softly, surprised at the sound of her voice, "please, please don't die on me. I need you...."

She went to the kitchen and returned with some wet dish rags. She began to wipe the blood away from the wound. His breathing was labored. If only they could get him to a hospital right away. He needed blood badly. Maybe he could be saved.

Hannelore came back in. There were tears in her eyes, and Gabriele knew instinctively that they were a very rare experience for Hannelore.

"They're both dead," she said.

Gabriele straightened and put her arms around her. They held each other tightly for a moment. And then they wept.

After a few minutes, their sobs slowly subsiding, they separated and Gabriele went outside. The barn was destroyed, but she knew there was also a radio in the shed. Perhaps she could radio for medical help and relay the news that they had killed the hijackers.

Then she thought of Colonel Thalberg. No. One had got away. And the one who rescued him. Who was he? The American officer was part of it.

What would the authorities say? Would they believe her when she told them? The Americans, or at least some of them, were implicated. She reasoned that she must get in touch with the German police before the Americans arrived. No telling what the Yanks' role was. The police would be her only chance.

She sat at the radio console for a minute, examining the dials and switches. There was only static coming in over the speakers. She saw a microphone with a button labeled Transmit. She picked it up and pressed it.

"This is Gabriele Witte," she said. "Please help us. We have taken over the farm. We need medical attention."

She thought she'd heard an echo, then she realized it was her voice coming from the radio in one of the vehicles parked behind her.

She turned the dial and tried another band. "Please help us. We have taken over the farm. We need medical assistance." Over and over. Then another band. And the repetition. She gave the location of the farm.

Then she listened for a reply.

Nothing.

She tried another band and repeated her message. And she listened again.

SERGEI KOMAROV HAD only just taken off from the Soviet base at Jauernick. He could see the lights of Görlitz below.

It was a very astute action on the part of the base commander, he realized, to get all the MiGs aloft. If this errant American missile did score a direct hit, either at Jauernick or at Kolberg, damage would be held to a minimal level. True, most of the newly arrived SS-20s would be destroyed, but the majority of them had not yet been fitted with nuclear warheads. The Americans would suffer a great deal of embarrassment, for the people of the Third World, and even America's allies, would be made well aware of the warmongering nature of the imperialists.

There was a barely detectable blip on his radar screen, interrupting his thoughts. It registered from the northeast. Very clever! The missile had circled around the base and was now coming in from this unexpected quadrant.

He took his MiG-23 down to one thousand feet and banked in a wide curve. He knew his only hope was to rely on a visual sighting.

He radioed his position to base and to the others in his squadron. Two other MiGs were close enough to be able to join him. Perhaps if he failed then one of them would succeed in targeting in on the missile. If they could intercept the missile before it reached ground zero, he knew, the warhead would not detonate and a disaster would be averted.

There it was! He saw a faint speck of light in the distance several miles ahead at two o'clock. The speck was flying in an erratic zigzag pattern, both horizontally and vertically.

Komarov descended farther, preparing the wing rockets for launching. He released the safety and held his thumb a millimeter above the firing button as he closed in. Instantly he calculated probable velocity and course and without delay fired a salvo of heat-seeking air-to-air missiles.

The MiG-23 recoiled from the firing.

He watched the rockets streak off, made several minor adjustments, and fired another round. Then another. Until the supply was exhausted. He veered off and sought out a higher, safer altitude.

The speck of light had passed by and was closing fast on the base. Perhaps only a minute now, he calculated. Three of his rockets could be seen trailing after it in pursuit. They were gaining rapidly on it.

"Come on!" he said aloud.

His aim had been true, he knew, but would the rockets overtake the missile before it got to the base, or would they make contact too late? Seconds, he knew, would be critical.

The specks of light were no longer visible, but he followed after them.

Suddenly, there was a bright light up ahead near the ground. Too bright! It grew brighter, appearing to be turning into an expanding fireball, and he feared that the missile had won the race.

Komarov yanked back on the joystick and soared higher, expecting at any moment the concussion from a nuclear detonation. But the detonation didn't come.

He leveled off and saw the explosions as his other two rockets hit the target, destroying the last remnants, sending debris earthward. The missile's nuclear force aborted. And a joy swept over him unlike any he had ever known.

"MR. CHAIRMAN, I assure you we deeply regret this occurrence." The President's voice was resigned, frustrated, exasperated. The boy caught with his hand in the cookie jar. "We will make a public apology and beg the world's forgiveness. That is, I might add, far more than your government did after the shooting down of the Korean Airlines jet in September 1983."

"Mr. President." The Soviet premier's voice was cold and harsh. He spoke English for the first time to the President. "I fully expected your apology would not be a particularly gracious one. And your mentioning of the KAL episode is so inappropriate that I must assume you have not changed at all. You're forgetting that in our secret conversations after that affair, you uncharacteristically humbled yourself to acquiesce to our demands to abandon the monitor satellite. That was after *we* agreed *not* to reveal to the world the proof we had of the intelligence data being collected by Flight 007 in conjunction with that satellite."

He paused. "However, I shall recommend to the polit-buro that we accept your apology. Neither one of our nations can afford to let this unfortunate incident escalate into a full-scale nuclear confrontation. But we must insist that you capture the perpetrators of this infamous deed and send them to us. We will have a public trial and bring them to the peoples' justice."

"Yes. Of course. We will make whatever concessions you wish in this regard. I deplore this deed, truly."

"'Truly'? An odd word for you to choose... Do not forget, Mr. President, we want those people!" He paused again, then added, "Our ambassador in Washington will be in touch with you tomorrow. I expect him to be given a full progress report on the identities of the terrorists. I *truly* hope—as you might put it—that none of the terrorists is in the employ of your government.

"Enough. I know you will be accommodating. History will, in the end, be the judge. Good night."

"Good night." The President replaced the receiver in its cradle.

"Mr. Tice," he said, as he opened a cabinet and extracted a bottle of bourbon. "Assemble the staff. We've got much work to do. I'll have to address the nation within the next twenty-four hours and we've got to work out all the correct phrases. Have the congressional leadership meet me in the cabinet room tomorrow morning."

Tice left to do his bidding.

The President poured out a shot of bourbon and downed it.

HOLZAUER HIMSELF FOLLOWED the last of his men along the dirt road, watching them fan out through the fields. The helicopters were waiting on standby, in case they were needed.

There were footsteps behind him.

"Captain Holzauer!" It was one of the regular policemen. "Captain Schlobohm told me to fetch you. We've just had a radio communication from one of the terrorists. They're asking for medical help."

Holzauer followed the man back to the road. Schlobohm was standing next to a police car and talking into a microphone. He handed it to Holzauer.

"It's a woman. She says they've taken over the farm and they need medical aid for their wounded."

"Taken over the farm? That doesn't make sense."

"That's what I thought."

Holzauer spoke into the microphone. "This is Hauptmann Holzauer of the Commando Unit. Lay down your weapons and surrender. You cannot escape. Surrender to my men."

"*Hauptmann.*" Gabriele's voice was desperate. "Please help us, we have fought with and killed the hijackers, we need emergency medical help."

"You will get it, but first you must surrender."

"Surrender? We've done your work for you!"

Holzauer turned to Schlobohm and raised one eyebrow. "Sounds like they're trying some desperate ploy." He pressed the transmit switch. "I repeat, lay down your weapons and surrender. This is your final chance. You have launched a missile at a Soviet base in your bungled attempt to blackmail the government. We will not bargain with you."

He switched off, handed the microphone back to Schlobohm and returned to his men.

"A SOVIET BASE!" Gabriele was astonished. And frightened. My God, she said to herself as she ran back to the house.

"Hannelore," she shouted when she entered, "the missile was aimed at a Soviet base! The Americans plotted this whole thing, and they want these 'terrorists' to take the blame."

She stopped and looked at Christopher. His head was on a pillow and there was a blanket thrown over him. Hannelore must have found them while she was on the radio.

"They want us to surrender." She paused, but before she could continue, Hannelore spoke.

"As far as they're concerned, *we* are part of the terrorist group." Her voice was calm. "We're in a trap. There's no way out."

"Yes, there is. We must give ourselves up. Then we can tell our story. The truth. We can prove it!"

Hannelore didn't answer. Gabriele's mind was reeling. They had to think fast. Surely they would be believed.

But what proof did they really have?

She was not sure. Confusion and chaos faced her from every angle.

"They will kill us," Hannelore stated without emotion.

THE ARMY HELICOPTERS were only minutes from the farm.

General Forman's voice came over the radios in each of the aircraft, addressing the combat troops.

"We've just learned that these fanatics launched a missile at the Soviet missile base at Jauernick. Fortunately, it was shot down by a Soviet MiG. But all our diplomatic efforts are going to be in full force in the next few days in order to avoid a major confrontation. These people have brought us to the brink of a war that neither we nor the Soviets could survive. I'm sure I do not need to overempha-

size the importance of your mission in bringing these
criminals to justice.''

There was a brief pause. ''The President of the United
States has ordered that we are to take this terrorist strong-
hold and level it. There is no need to take prisoners who
might only be freed the next time another terrorist group
kidnaps a politician. Shoot to kill. Destroy their base. They
must not be permitted to launch another missile.''

Despite the somber mood the men were in, there were
several isolated cheers of approval.

CHRISTOPHER'S EYES flickered slightly and a sighing sound
came from his lips.

Hannelore had gone to the front door, and Gabriele was
alone with Christopher, looking at him, one hand lightly
resting on his shoulder. The bleeding had stopped, but there
was no way of knowing how much internal bleeding there
had been. His face was ashen.

''Christopher,'' she said softly, touching her fingertips to
his forehead.

His eyes fluttered again. She could see the movement of
his eyeballs beneath the closed lids.

''Christopher, try opening your eyes. Do it slowly. Very
slowly... Not fast. It's Gabriele. I am with you.''

The lids seemed to flicker. She was sure she could see
them move enough to see the whites of his eyes.

''Come on, Christopher. A little more. I need to look into
your eyes.''

They opened a bit farther.

She was afraid he was going to pass out again. ''Close
them and wait, then try again slowly.''

He did as she commanded. His hand also reached out to
her and she grabbed it, squeezing tightly.

He squeezed back and finally, almost as if the handhold
had given him leverage, he managed to open his eyes fully.

"Christopher." She felt the tears welling up in her. *"Mein Christopher..."*

For several minutes they looked into each other's eyes. He knew he was dying. There was nothing to say.

"We're going to get you to a hospital," she said after a while, forcing the bravado into her shaky voice.

He closed his eyes and seemed to shrug, then he opened them again. "Gabriele." He looked directly at her. "I know.... But..."

"Oh, Christopher." She felt her stomach churn. "No. You mustn't die on me. I need you! For the first time in my life, I need someone."

He managed a smile. "Gabriele."

She leaned down and kissed him, her tears moistening his cheek.

"Gabriele. You must...be happy. You've given...me...so much. You've taught me what...it is to love. It's the only time in my life...that I've experienced that. You...showed me a part of myself...that I never...knew existed.... And for that I'm so grateful."

He coughed. "If I do die now, then I die happy. You've given me that.... No one can ever take that away."

She thought her heart was being torn from her breast. She was so full, and soon she knew the inevitable emptiness would consume her.

"We stopped them, didn't we?" His eyes seemed to brighten. "They launched the missile, but we prevented them from launching the others."

"Yes." She nodded.

But she cursed herself for not having the strength to tell him the danger they still faced.

He tried to raise his head, but couldn't do so.

She leaned again to him and lightly touched her lips to his. "Christopher. You have opened me. *Ich liebe dich*...I love you."

His eyes glowed.

She looked into them and knew he loved her. It was almost as if the love was too much for him to bear, and his eyes closed.

She stood looking at him for a long time. Then she kissed his eyelids and left the room.

And she stepped into the void.

HOLZAUER'S MEN SPREAD out across the yard in front of the house. In the distance they could hear the American helicopters approaching from the northwest.

The entire area of the farm was still. A few flames still lapped skyward from the smoldering ruins of the barn, but there was no other movement.

The derelict TEL looked strangely awkward. It was difficult to imagine it as an instrument of destruction.

They moved in closer to the front of the house, using the trees for cover. The door was open and just as Holzauer was about to motion a few of his men to proceed around to the rear, a figure holding a machine gun stepped through the doorway.

At once, several of the commandos raced forward, spreading out and opening fire.

Hannelore ducked back into the building and fired a return salvo at the attackers.

Gabriele had just stepped into the hall and heard the shots. She ran past the open door, firing a round through it as she passed, and headed into the kitchen.

They could hear the crashing of bullets into the front of the house.

"Quick," Gabriele shouted to Hannelore, "they're not around back yet. We can get out that way. Once we're in the fields we might be able to go north before they have us completely trapped. There's the forest. I know how we can survive there and eventually escape!"

Hannelore followed her. She didn't need to ask about Christopher. The look on Gabriele's face told everything.

They could hear a roar, and suddenly the crescendo became deafening as helicopters arrived directly overhead.

Gabriele looked out the back door. Just past the garden, the shortest route to the cornfields was only about ten yards.

Ten yards.

She motioned toward the cornfield with her head. The noise from the helicopters was now too loud for talk.

Searchlights were illuminating the entire area around the house, then there was a sudden explosion. Gabriele's eyes went wide with fright. Rockets had been fired into the front of the house from one of the circling helicopters. Instantly the hall and the conference room burst into a mass of flames. More explosions rocked the upper stories of the house.

There was no more time to hesitate. Gabriele sprinted out of the door. Hannelore was right behind her.

A massive explosion sent a wave of scorching heat past them. Bits of debris landed nearby. Gabriele felt something hot hit her in the back, but she didn't falter.

Another explosion rocked the house, and as she leaped into the concealment of the field Gabriele turned and saw an incredible sight.

Helicopters. American helicopters. Four, five of them, she counted, hovering above the house. They were firing streams of rockets into the building. The building seemed almost to raise up off its foundation as explosion after explosion transformed it into an inferno.

She thought of Christopher. And of what might have been. And she buried him in her heart.

Hannelore was still out in the open. She had slowed down, and Gabriele thought at first that she was awed by the sight of the conflagration behind her. Then she realized that

Hannelore was wounded. There was a haunted look in her face as she limped toward where Gabriele crouched in the field.

"Come on!" Gabriele shouted. "Hurry! You can make it!"

Her eyes darted from Gabriele to the helicopter that descended above her.

Hannelore stopped and raised her gun. She held her ground and fired the entire clip into the underbelly of the fuselage.

"*No!*" Gabriele's shriek was lost in the cacophony. She turned and ran as fast as she could away from this scene of destruction. Northward.

A machine gun fired back at Hannelore from the helicopter. Bullets struck the ground to her left. And then, just as one of Hannelore's bullets hit the helicopter's loaded rocket launcher, she was hit. She fell to the ground and the helicopter exploded. Shards of metal and parts of bodies saturated the air around the back of the house. The rotor of the helicopter, still spinning, twirled up in slow motion and fell to earth several hundred yards away. The largest part of the fuselage, spinning wildly, crashed in flames on Hannelore.

HOLZAUER WAS FURIOUS.

He pulled his men back.

"*Damn it to hell!*" he said to one of his lieutenants. "We could have taken them alive! Why the hell did the Americans have to destroy the place and kill them all? They think they're fighting the Vietnam War?"

The lieutenant shrugged. "I suppose they didn't want any prisoners."

Holzauer glared at the burning building and at the helicopters now landing in the open field beside the house. Then he radioed to Schlobohm. "It looks like it's over," he said.

SHE RAN. And ran. Behind her everything was lost. Everything.

If she was lucky, they might not have spotted her, she thought. She might be able to escape.

She would be safe in the woods, and she could get herself to Denmark. She didn't worry about that. But was her life worth living now? Her story would never be believed, she knew. And possibly now there was no point even in relating it.

Her body instinctively reached out for survival. And she kept going. Away from the carnage. Away from the madness.

She would go north.

And she would never look back.

CHAPTER TWENTY-TWO

Washington, D.C.

8 January, 1900 hours

"AND SO, IN CONCLUSION, let me remind the foes of freedom that though we deeply regret and deplore this foul deed, we reassert our commitment to the world that we shall continue to fight for peace. The actions of extremists and terrorists everywhere must be crushed. We must remain ever vigilant.

"The chancellor of West Germany has assured me that there will be no further opposition of any kind to the policy of deploying missiles for the safety of Europe. Europe *must* remain free.

"The Bundestag has met in Extraordinary Session and outlawed the Green Party—the party that gave birth to and supported these terrorists. The party that came perilously close to electing one of their leaders, Ulrich Sievers, to office. Sievers was the chief German member in this terrorist group, second in command to Christopher Benton. Our intelligence services have discovered that Benton, using a friend in the laboratory where the missile guidance system was developed, furnished classified missile secrets to the terrorists.

"Unfortunately, by fighting to the death against the courageous combined efforts of the German Commando Anti-Terrorist Unit and the American military, these terrorists have deprived us of the satisfaction of handing them over, as I had promised, to the Soviets. They undoubtedly preferred their suicidal resistance to being brought to justice. But Christopher Benton along with his German collaborators will forever be judged by the freedom-loving peoples of the world as archenemies of peace.

"Our vigilance will never cease until we root out this cancer that seeks to destroy our society.

"No foe will ever sway us from this course."

The President stared solemnly into the camera. The spotlights dimmed and the picture on the monitor cut to the American flag waving from the top of the Iwo Jima Marines monument.

He rose and walked away from the desk as the television technicians began disconnecting the lights and cameras.

When he entered the Cabinet Room he was immediately surrounded by his aides. The Secretary of State shook his hand, as did the rest of the members of the cabinet. They all congratulated him heartily on his brilliant address.

The President approached two men at a distance from the rest of the occupants of the room. Colonel William Matecki, his foot in a cast, sat in a wheelchair. Brigadier General Thomas Forman stood behind him.

He grabbed their hands and shook them warmly. "Thank you, gentlemen. Thank you.

"Even though we were unable to accomplish the goal of crippling Görlitz, you have given us the double coup of wiping out the European opposition to this administration's policy, along with the significant advances we made in monitoring the Soviet retaliatory response to our Tomahawk threat. I'm deeply grateful and indebted to you.

"Thank you."

EPILOGUE

Copenhagen

23 February, 1730 hours

THE HAFEN CAFÉ was rapidly filling up. Most tables in the smoke-filled room were occupied by students conversing and drinking coffee after classes at the university.

The two Americans, one bearded, the other clean-shaven, both in suits, entered and stood in the doorway. They looked around for a moment while their eyes adjusted to the dim light.

They spotted her easily, sitting alone in the far corner, a cigarette in her hand, a red scarf thrown over her shoulders. Just as she had told them on the telephone. They wound through the room and stood at her table.

Gabriele looked at them critically, inhaled deeply on her cigarette and motioned them to sit down.

"Edward Leland, *Washington Post*," the clean-shaven one said, offering her his hand.

"Michael Goodman, *New York Times*," said the other. "You have a story for us?"

She shook their hands and nodded as they sat down.

Goodman asked if she minded if they used a tape recorder.

"Not at all," she replied.

And then she began talking.

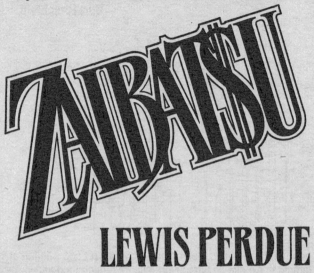

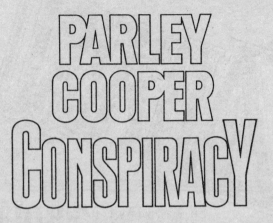

Dan Fortune is back—neck-deep in murder

MINNESOTA
Strip

Private investigator Dan Fortune is up against one of his gris-
liest cases ever! Hired to locate a missing boy who is determined to avenge the brutal murder of a Vietnamese refugee,
Fortune finds himself deep in a nasty network of white slav-
ery, narcotics, prostitution and . . . hired killers.

Chilling novels of international espionage, intrigue and suspense

		Quantity
STRATEGIES OF ZEUS—Gary Hart A frighteningly authentic tale of man's race toward destruction, written by former Democratic senator, Gary Hart.	$4.50	☐
ALPHA AND OMEGA—Bert Whittier The CIA's most deadly and destructive killing machine becomes active again....	$3.95	☐
AIRBURST—Steven L. Thompson Ex-stock car driver Max Moss races to avert America's most dreaded nuclear nightmare.	$3.95	☐
BURIAL IN MOSCOW—Fred Dickey Khrushchev lives! A Soviet legend returned from the dead sparks the most incredible operation in CIA history.	$3.95	☐

Total Amount	$ _____
Plus 75¢ Postage	.75
Payment enclosed	_____

Please send a check or money order payable to Worldwide Library.

In the U.S.A.	In Canada
Worldwide Library 901 Fuhrmann Blvd. Box 1325 Buffalo, NY 14269-1325	Worldwide Library P.O. Box 609 Fort Erie, Ontario L2A 5X3

Please Print

Name: _____

Address: _____

City: _____

State/Prov: _____

Zip/Postal Code: _____

🌐 **WORLDWIDE LIBRARY**   ESP-1

Take 2 books & a surprise gift FREE

SPECIAL LIMITED-TIME OFFER

Mail to: The Mystery Library
          901 Fuhrmann Blvd.
          P.O. Box 1867
          Buffalo, N.Y. 14269-1867

YES! Please send me 2 free books from the Mystery Library and my free surprise gift. Then send me 2 mystery books, first time in paperback, every month. Bill me only $3.50 per book. There is *no* extra charge for shipping and handling! There is no minimum number of books I must purchase. I can always return a shipment and cancel at any time. Even if I never buy another book from The Mystery Library, the 2 free books and the surprise gift are mine to keep forever.

414-BPY-FBA6

Name   (PLEASE PRINT)

Address   Apt. No.

City   State   Zip

This offer is limited to one order per household and not valid to present subscribers. Price and terms subject to change.   MYS-BPA3